SIRENA

A. LAUREANO

Sirena
Copyright © 2023 by A. Laureano

ISBN
978-1-961601-59-8 (Paperback)
978-1-961601-60-4 (eBook)
978-1-961601-58-1 (Hardcover)

Sirena

TABLE OF CONTENTS

PROLOGUE

My father sits frustrated in the living room on Thanksgiving Day. He hears the laughter of myself and Gramps outside on the porch on the big house of his great-great-grandfather. What frustrates him the most is the topic my Gramps always stirred up with pleasant stories of the mermaids. I remember him telling me to leave and go to my room. From my room I can feel the vibrations of the walls coming from the arguing of father telling Gramps to stop indulging me in mermaids, about a world that does not exist. Later, thanksgiving dinner felt less thankful especially with my father's expression being hard. I remember that expression because after that day we stopped visiting as much. I remember always asking if I can sleep over Gramps house, and he'll always say, "Someday." Which always meant never, I had to run away at night just to sleep over at Gramp's house.

ACKNOWLEDGEMENT

To my beloved family and friends,

CHAPTER 1

Growing up as a Hanks was difficult and once treasured all at the same time. Thinking back towards my happiest moments from my South Carolina childhood. I grew up living with my grandfather and a huge part of the Hanks family. Now that I think about it, there was pretty much nothing to do around my hometown besides fishing and canoeing. Other than that, there was that one movie theatre and a whole lot of churches. But those cheerful memories mostly surrounded my Gramps.

When I was young, it was the best being tucked in by Gramps, and being told remarkable fantasies of— *Mermaids known as the affectionate duchesses of the sea who protected the oceans as well as the mortals from the sirens who were known as the demons.* Nevertheless, my parents were opposed to these tales over time, in particular my father who grew tired of listening to them when he was a child himself.

I remember being only nine at that time, with my eyes wide opened after every story, I'd be awestruck as I ask, "Really, Gramps, did that really happen?!"

At the moment, Gramps was my idol and a man who knew so much about the sea. Not only because he was the greatest fisherman of all time, but because he always told me he would never lie to me which meant those tales had to be true.

But I was only a stupid kid who dwelled in mysteries of the sea, living with a family who didn't know me…of course I wanted them to be true. Especially when Gramps would say, "Of course, Josh. I would never lie to you. Now, I'm going to tell you a quick story before I tuck you in. Now just remember…this stays between the two of us. Your folks now…well, they don't like these kinds of stories." I agreed but I never understood why his own son, my father, had stopped wanting to listen to the adventures of Gramps. I practically begged him to proceed with my expression alone.

As he breathed heavily, he began to tell his story that took me beyond our home, "Okay, so you remember a few years ago, when your grandmother and I were vacationing in Cape Cod. Well, what you don't know is the part when we went diving looking for seashells. Oh, your beautiful Grandma used to love doing that for her shop on the pier. I saw this gorgeous shell that I really wanted to surprise your grandmother with; and just in the nick of time, when I was about to grab it…a mermaid! She came from nowhere and snatched it for herself. I wasn't surprised at all by the mermaid. I was surprised that she just stole my seashell," he said, chuckling, as his chubby belly bounced up and down. "Now go to sleep, so your father could say I'm doing a good job and invite you over more often."

"Okay, Gramps!" I said with the leftover smile from picturing Gramps belly giggling up and down.

As a kid, I loved visiting my grandfather. He'd always took me outdoors; camping, stargazing, fishing on his boat to catch beautiful lobsters and fish, and then we'd end the last night with a dinner at Mario's Pizzeria where I could order anything I wanted. My visits at Gramps were just as enjoyable, especially when my irritating cousin Cheryl wasn't around to barge in. Together we worked on refinishing the house, making sure that we added extra sturdy bones to the Hanks old-fashioned home. Then he'd always ended the night with a story.

"Gramps, why would sailors do that to her? Why did they hurt her?" The memories of my fairly 10-year-old self would cry out.

"I don't know, Champ. People do cruelest things sometimes when they're angry." As he would look deeply in my eyes, holding me to make me feel better as he would continue, "The mermaid fell taken with a human," said Gramps. "Even though, she was a sea-maid, and she couldn't come up to settle with him up in the dried-out atmosphere, it would have destroyed her even more to be without him. Therefore, she failed to forget him, and she didn't allow herself to survive without him. She couldn't even sleep for thinking about him led to unimaginable dreams.. All she desired was to remain with him."

"Wait, you're telling me she would've died in the air, what about the other mermaids you've seen before?" I asked.

"Well, it's more complicated than that champ, sea-maids can't live absent from their natural water for too long, some had tried but they had turned dried and brittle later fading into salty sand dust." Gramps said as if he had envisioned this happening before. "Anyways, back to the story… well, the man couldn't stop thinking about her either. The glimpse of the mermaid burned in his mind all day. And the mermaid felt just the same. When the tide was high, she would swim up into the cove, then up the stream, as close as she could to the church, to hear him singing in the choir."

I remember my father Alaric was this profoundly serious man growing up. Many of the Hanks wanted me to grow up the same way as them, which meant getting down to business and leaving behind the dreams. My father would continuously ask me with a stern face about my visits to Gramps. And there was never a time that I wouldn't jump up and speak about the dreams and stories that my Gramps told me. I loved every moment I spent with him; he was the only one who had made me feel like I could be my true self. Like when I planned out my future working as a marine biologist at Sullivan's Island's Marine Research Center. Gramps allowed me to dream big, but my father argued with him about keeping my feet on the ground.

I remember telling my mother that my father didn't have to worry so much. I didn't have high beliefs in such folklore, I only loved sharing such stories with Gramps because it was something he had shared with me, unlike his other grandchildren. But she told me I had to grow up and speak about real matters, even though that wasn't me.

She told me to wait in the car for them. I gave Gramps a huge hug and thanked him for the bedtime story. Then I sneakily waited at the front of the doorsteps to listen in.

"So, uh, what have you been telling Josh?" Mom sounded very upset.

"Nothing. Just one of my mermaid folklores!" Gramps never understood what the problem was.

My father jumped in, "Yea, but something Josh takes with him to his goddamn school and his friends…if he has any no thanks to you!"

Gramps couldn't believe it, his son used to love his stories when he was young, "But wait a minute, my Champ, is a very particular boy. He doesn't need those useless friends that just stare at video games all day. He's better than that!"

Then my mother jumped in, "May I speak, I did take a couple of psychology classes. Gramps, the reason we're here is that this is far more serious than you think, then a young boy believing or not believing in mermaids."

Father scuffs and says, "That's right, because Joshua thinks that this whole thing actually is real. And he needs to believe in more serious things. He DOES need friends, to build bigger social skills beyond just his grandfather!!"

Then in a psychologist tone my mom says, "Gramps, what was the last thing you and Joshua did…before you tucked him?"

Gramps chuckled and sarcastically said, "We took the boat out: looked out for some women: did some shots of brown liquor and hmm…peed into the ocean…I just told him one of my bedtime stories!"

I laughed at my Gramps answers. Yet, it wasn't funny to my parents and still with a therapist tone mom continued, "And what bedtime story was that?"

Gramps sounded defeated therefore he answered sarcastically, "Uh American Playboy. For goodness sakes, guys! I made a bedtime story up. Just like I did with you when you were young, Alaric! Come on!"

I watched my mom crossed her legs, "And did you guys see any mermaids?"

Gramps continued to chuckle looking at his watch, "This is ridiculous. I don't have time for this. I'm going fishing with my neighbor."

My father was dressed in one of his suits he wore to work, "Ridiculous or not, Gramps, for Joshua, this isn't some dream. It is real. And I want him to follow in my footsteps into the family business. That doesn't happen when you dream about mermaids."

My mom brushed my father's shoulder as she believed the same things, "You need to sit down with Joshua. Explain to him, that there are no such thing as mermaids."

Gramps sighed, "But he's just a kid. What's wrong with a few dreams?"

Tension grew and the worst words said, "Gramps! We mean it, you're not listening. We are concerned about this, if Joshua spending time with you is the best thing for him."

He came outside watching me on the doorstep, I told him how I overheard everything. I thought he was here to tell me there was no such thing as mermaids, instead he took a different take on things. "We've got to talk about the mermaid thing. Joshua, th-there is no…there's no reason why we have to tell your parents about the mermaids, they stopped believing a long time ago and sadly they think I'm crazy. You don't want people to think I'm crazy right?"

I looked at my Gramps, I really do believe everything, he wasn't crazy, people just didn't believe anymore. "Oh, you mean like a secret."

That's when my parents listened to my Gramps dishonestly following their rules, "Do you have any concept of how dangerous this is to a little boy? You were going to have our own son lie to us?? Come on, Joshua, we're going home. Gramps if you don't get your act together, so help me—"

Over the years, I still did my best to visit Gramps, but asked him to keep the mermaid's lore to a very minimum, it was enough I wasn't following my father's dream but if he found out I still spoke about mermaids he would never be supportive about me being a marine biologist working in the ocean. Our Gramps-grandson relationship change…most notably when I left South Carolina for college in New York, before my nineteenth birthday.

A few months ago on January 31, 2006, I turned 20 years old, while Gramps ended up in the emergency room due to a minor stroke. My parents didn't bother to stay that long, which created greater animosity between myself and them for a long while. For my birthday I rushed to my Gramps side, stood around Carolina the whole time; bathed him, dressed, and fed him each time until he actually got better, and until I had to go back to New York.

Over several nights, I've been trying to reach my parents and wish them a happy anniversary, but I haven't heard from them. Was our dispute that bad? At work, I saw two policemen approaching my cubicle. The pit of my stomach began to tighten, making me feel nauseous. As the one started speaking, I frozen listening to his words of my parents surprisingly being killed during a freak storm in the Atlantic Ocean heading to Kiawah

Island. My hand hovered near my mouth, stopping me from screaming. But my thoughts are scattered that functioning normally isn't possible.

I drove slowly crossing the river on an old-fashioned drawbridge as the gravel dust blew across, as I turned into the road and saw the place for what it was, not for what it was right at the present moment during the day of my parents' funeral, but for what it had been when I was a little boy. Everyone's favorite diner shop where everyone gathered after school or work for a famous burger. The ice cream man that had the towns children ordering just about every flavor of ice cream you could think of. The kissing bench down near the pier, which I still haven't written my name on like tradition after you kissed someone. I hadn't dated anyone at my hometown, and I was way too busy for women in New York. I wasn't old but I felt I was in the late phase of loneliness. I can see the huge chessboard in the square where all the elders usually gathered around and occasionally, we threw festivals. If I unleashed my memories, I could remember all the great times I had with my parents and grandparents at those festivals when I was a young boy. I see the abandoned movie theater is still standing, probably didn't make as much since everyone knew someone who would sneak them in for free. It was beautiful in the country, as it always had been. I loved the way the Spanish moss draped around the branches. I drove around slowly, looking for my next path, taking deep breathers. Now let's see, if I make a right outside the town I can revisit a rush of memories. However if I make a left I can drink helplessly at the bar then eat something, and sleep in at the inn.

My parents have died for only an hour, and I already felt it in the pit of my stomach that I wasn't going to be the same in New York. I began catching panic attacks, withdrawing from my second semester at NYU before I failed, and quitting my job as a marine biologist.

Late in the day, I paid my rent earlier than scheduled and left my roommate with a lingering question, if I would come back with any knowledge of my returning. My emotions hit me hard like huge waves crashing on the shore as I drove fast entering back to South Carolina.

Mile by mile, I have abandoned the rest of my life in the rear-although I figure some might argue have it had abandoned me first- as a result I was in the closing stage of starting all over again, which destined for me leaving

New York. And so forth, this Carolina– humid morning, I was pursuing a pavement ride out to the countryside.

I was approaching towards the town square of Sullivan's Island, South Carolina. A town I grew up in with my parents and Gramps when I was younger. I wasn't ready for visiting Gramps right now, so I went for the Palms inn.

I'm not clear if I was here to begin something or to bring something to an end, like my goodbyes.

* * *

Although Gramps had just woken up out a deep slumber in arriving at three in the morning, you wouldn't been able to tell by the way he'd shown me inside, with a mighty hug and a mug of bourbon. He always knew how to make me feel better, in spite of the fact that I showed up quite unexpectedly after first sleeping at the inn.

Or perhaps Gramps had been expecting me to come. Maybe he knew it would take time for me to step foot on my father's land. Especially now that I wouldn't get the solace that I needed from him or even from my mother. It has taken me all this time to seek their reassurance, I hoped one day I will live to see the day they were both be far from amazed; however, I would never see that day.

I ditch this morning's dark funeral clothing, ripping it apart as if I was allergic to it. In my childhood closet, I hauled open the long wooden floor tile that without a doubt was just like I left it five years ago. The scent of dust and cobwebs filled my nose.

I had on an old college T-shirt and a pair of denim jeans from my old drawer when I visited while going to school here. I stood facing the entire mirror in the corner and investigated my reflection. It's like nothing has changed, I wasn't as muscular as I hoped, however my heart in smithereens darkened.

The reflection ahead of myself was something of a time loop— I was wearing these raggedy clothing without my parents. Even more so that when I looked into the mirror, I see my father only with my mother's eyes.

I began to remember the aroma of my mom's famous shrimp and grits as far as the guest house. They were spot on delicious, she made them especially on days when she saw that I felt so sad. Or how about the memory of my father's studious voice whenever he taught me how to build boats. As much as I never desired that idea of following the Hanks pass down business of building boats, I have always desired how much effort and love he put into it.

The friendly sight of my comics, my old Pokémon collection, and my family's photographs still existed, thank goodness. Though looking at the pictures comforted the pang in my chest. Agony followed me like a shadow as I walked towards my father's dock.

I walked onto the beach front grabbing a shell, listening for the sounds of waves. It was calming compared to everything that was happening now. I remember a few calming memories. Holding my father and mother's hands when I was young, Gramps was with us and it was a good day as he said, *a seashell is your ocean of possibilities in your hands*. I placed the shell back realizing that my possibilities felt lost.

Sitting there on the dock, I splashed water around my feet. I submerged myself into the ocean to dunk the memories into nothingness. Was it achievable to backtrack and get a revise on life? Pretend that parents from Carolina never died, that a marine biologist student living in New York just bailed his reality and continued pretending that when Gramps would come back my parents would be right by his side with the shopping bags.

When I lifted my eyes, seeing the old boat resting on the grass brought me some memories, then I noticed something new, something I should've noticed earlier. The lighthouse on the opposite side of the guest house had finally had a working light. All my life it was never on, till now, guess Gramps decided to finally invest in one since my parent's accident. You can never be too careful, and you wouldn't want to be the lighthouse that failed to do its duty, like the one on Kiawah Island. The light was so vibrant, I found it strange it was on when it wasn't even foggy or close to sunset.

The house has been cleaned and straightened. I've cleaned it from top to bottom. The dining room table has been set for a nice dinner, complete with China, candles, and a floral centerpiece. It's 6 o'clock in the afternoon and my parents have just been buried. I couldn't go, I had to stick around, and help prepared things for the guest...at least that was the excuse I pushed in my head. Gramps left a message saying he would get more groceries. While there was time, I went back to the dock and looked out to sea. "I know this sounds pathetic, but losing you hit me to the core, I'm sorry I couldn't make it to the funeral. Goodbye father, goodbye mother, I love you both." I glumly ignored whatever was splashing in the ocean and the chiming I began to hear; it was probably a new trap my Gramps made for fish. As I turned around, I spotted guests all wearing the sorrow color of black as they entered the Hanks home, so I left the dock to join them.

Oh no, here comes the Foreman's. They secretly resented each other yet pretended to be happily married. Quite similar to my parents, only that my parents actually fought to save their marriage. As a wife to one of the descendants of the founder families, Mrs. Foreman didn't want to ruin her reputation around the town, by having people know of her husband's love affairs with younger women, especially a student to rise the crowds. But worst of all I hated her casserole, she made it for every occasion.

"Killed by the ocean?" One of the aunts were trying to whisper, cousins shrugged as they wondered what happened to my parents. Their fake smiles hid their human souls and fake tears ran down the sides of their eyes drenching every one's face…gosh, were they really only waiting to hear the will?

Nice to know we have at least one person who is actually being themselves, our bartender Damon, just sitting on the couch in his light grey tuxedo drinking his scotch while watching a baseball game.

Some cousins kept snickering as they made up stories and gossiped about their lives, my snobby cousin, and Carolina's bombshell, Cheryl, walked around behaving like her manipulative mean girl self. "I heard my dear auntie, Spencer Hanks, wasn't found because she caused the shipwreck…or do you think there's a chance dear o' Uncle Alaric, had chopped her up and threw her into the ocean, while he would escape?"

"Interesting story, Cheryl, but they found two bodies."

Her full lips said, "It's not like we saw the bodies, it was closed caskets, anyways I heard she told someone that she's been planning her deceitful escape, she was waiting for the perfect storm to jump off and leave her dishonest lifestyle!"

"And where did you hear such news? Sheesh, Cheryl catch a grip!"

Oh, on good days my dear Cousin Cheryl knew how to kill people with kindness and a dash of kittenish, but today we are all just getting what her famous quality as the town's gossiper and false news. If only I could stuff her in a coffin, maybe Carolina would have fewer cheating marriages and better news.

As she added redder lipstick and checked her tight black sheer dress for the third time, she continued, "Have you even seen Joshua at the funeral, I caught a glimpse of him here dressed up like he wasn't prepared for the heat! And where the hell was the old man?"

Keep it on Cheryl, it's not like I'm around the corner listening, I can take this heat. Besides rumors were like rum to her, and she sure was becoming more and more intoxicated the more she drank the rum. But she's right about one thing, where was Gramps?

In the dining hall, my old alma mater pal, Dustin, helped me set the plates and napkins on the table. Dustin blathered forever about his latest commitment to living in the moment. Earlier years of pining for his neighbor, and dating plenty of tarts, Dustin has finally met Mrs. Right. Evil tidings, it's my cousin Cheryl. Their relationship had progressed rather fast, they used to despise each other. But supposedly Dustin saw Cheryl's attitude as a defense mechanism and lonesomeness, poor Cheryl, I wonder why? Then suddenly he fell in love with her boss lady sort.

Who would've thought the high school football player was more of a lover boy instead of going after the pros.? I feel awful however I did hear Dustin's voice saying that my mom and father got titanic, so what the heck? I did my finest to keep my shield up and not allow the insults to trouble me. Besides whenever I tried to speak, Dustin kept talking over me, admiring the joys of living in the now and never planning for the future. What the fuck was he on? My parents were just buried!!

Later on, I heard the most annoying voice ever, it was Uncle O'Connor with his five year rather hard Irish accent that was most times difficult to catch up with. I prepared myself to be stuck in the negative vicinity and listened to the extreme. I remember a long time ago, possibly before his daughter Cheryl started behaving like a loony, he used to have a very hard face with laughter lines instead of angry ones.

"Nah, I knew for sure, deir son is not gonna last a day in New York City…Waat makes ye tink me nephew deserves anythin' from deir will. Obviously, ye man still a large trace of shame, dat I'm actually surprise our blud an' me broders runs in his." My uncle was an asshole and began boiling my rage, I needed to walk around the hallways to blow off steam.

Nobody ate in the dining room, they just picked whatever they wanted to eat and walked around gossiping. Thank goodness because if I had to sit at a table with them, I would know more about everyone's life, and it would make me feel in-control of my own family and neighbors' secrets. Something I didn't want to hold.

My uncle's eyes wandered to the chair, clearly, he didn't expect me to stand. "So, nah…" Uncle O'Connor took a long swig of his Guinness as I just sat across from him. His refusal to smile showed warmth that was hardly any fair at all.

I followed his lead, preparing myself for the issue that awaited that lingering halt. Uncle O'Connor placed his Guinness down and smoothed down his ginger mustache. "How long ye plannin' on stayin' dis time round, or ye too city for us?"

He said the words with a taunt, still Uncle O'Connor wasn't questioning the length of my visitation. He was ensuring if I stood around that I been taking care of Gramps.

He never respected my father nor Gramps, his stepfather. He hated the fact that when my grandma was young in her college years before Gramps propose to her, she lived in Ireland for five years, and in those five years had met a man and had a son. But one day a call from America, otherwise Gramps, send her back…leaving him with his father. At some point, she told Gramps that their son that they had together also had a five-year older brother in Ireland, she needed to pick him up after his father past and he was left with nobody.

After that, he grew up with so much reasonable heartache that he despised other things. He despised everything that his younger half-brother had, he felt like the world wrapped around his finger. He despised the fact that my father made the best boats in Carolina and expanded, he despised that my father got the girl, and to my Uncle I was the spawn of the devil and Gramps belonged in the looney bin. However, whatever he had he didn't notice, like the love from their mother and Gramps. Which is why he hardly helped him around and the house looked like crap when I got here!

As the moment unfolds, it becomes clear that I will not even let the fallout of a lighthearted joke slip past me uncommented upon.

"Or ye sweatin' already from de heat?" I could see his nauseating mouth filled with cornbread beginning to raise an irritating sneer, a smirk that was partially sardonic and mocking.

"I can take the heat; you guys are assholes!" My family's bull and hypocrisy were the primary reasons it became easy to leave for New York.

"Ye know somethin', as I can recall Alaric said, he wus frustrated in ye cos ye jist lef our home til de deadly city til jist settle. Yer father wus drinkin''ard cos as he said, ye were supposed til take in'is legacy t'at'onored our home an' dat he created from de groun' up. Nah accordin' til de will it's gonna someone who we don't even know!"

That's fucking bullshit, if he believed that, and I seriously doubt that he had the wrong. Anyways what does it matter? "It's my damn life. Can live it the way I want to. So, he was frustrated in me because I'll settle for being a marine biologist instead of a businessman, is that what you're saying? What a load of bullshit?"

I was angry he inspired a dark intensity in me, so I tried to knock him out, but the guys got to me first before he punched me in the face. After an awkward silence, I left the house with the annoying family I once loved, as Cheryl laughed hard…I just kept wondering…where was Gramps?

I attempted and flopped to notice the sentiment provoking that utterance. If it was grief or mistrust, I wasn't sure. The lighthouse kept flashing its light, so entranced I went to walk inside as it felt like it was warning me of one kind of crazy for another. I went inside the lighthouse and suddenly the lights inside turned on. I went upstairs to look out the window and saw something big splashing around, it was dark so I couldn't really tell what it was, so I ran downstairs just in case it could have been a trapped turtle but there remained nothing but scary black water.

CHAPTER 2

My father once told me love was like a beautiful burning glass molding people together to create something magnificent. My mother snickered, as it was the first time he had spoken to me about love, and it was actually reasonable. Walking away the Hanks house, I thought to myself about how badly I needed that burning beautiful, molded glass with someone.

Between the guesthouse and the dock, there was this attractive angelic-looking woman about my age, sitting on a bench near the water. She had stunning long teal hair with periwinkle eyes and long lovely legs. She must've been some type of Brazilian model because she was so uniquely attractive; not only was she in shape with a lovely bronze complexion but she reminded me of Gisele Bundchen. The salty air blew through her teal tangled hair. She stared into nothingness over the waves as she dug her bare feet into the sand. I caught her wearing my oversized Metallica t-shirt that was drying earlier on the clothesline, she looked cute in it— especially seeing she wasn't wearing anything underneath. I watched her waiting for the right moment to talk to her, but she didn't make it so easy.

It took me a while just attempting to, but I walked up to her and tried my firmest not to flush, "Hey, excuse me ma'am this is…this is private property, I'm sorry, do you need any help, miss?" While she bit her lip seductively, she smiled at me and said no. I tried talking to her without looking at her, though it was very difficult, "Were you here for the funeral?"

The two of us came eye to eye, surprised by her beautiful endearing expression she looked at me with a presence of suspicion in them. Her long hair all in kinks filled with soiled seafoam as well as dark-green seaweed from the ocean's cool waves. I was rude and I didn't even politely asked her for her name. I completely stopped, as if I should run into a wall. "Were you crying?" I said as the woman lay her head back between her legs with her feet in the cold wet sand before the shore.

She must've felt a compulsion to sit back, as she wept a bit, "Oh dear, a funeral…someone died? Today IS a horrible day, I'm running from a doomed marriage to someone I hate and haven't even chosen. Ha-ha oh gosh I'm crying over that, while you've lost someone. How selfish am I!"

I stood back, still conscious of her space, her voice was heaven inviting, but I already made her feel bad. Poor girl had her own troubles too. Again, I caught her staring into the ocean, she must've felt calm watching the waves.

"I'm so sorry for both frightening you, and for the distraught you're going through, you should always have a say. Sometimes it helps when two people just talk together, about their problems. At least that's what I hear. Can't hurt so bad, we don't really know each other."

As I shook her hand, we exchanged names. "Hi, my name is Joshua, Joshua Hanks."

"Hello, Joshua Hanks my name is Sirena."

I stared at her teary striking periwinkle eyes, I knew before that although she didn't know it, I saw the possibility of us as burning molded glass. She was as perfect as the ocean on a summer's day.

And so, from hour to hour, we continued the day making each other laugh, oh gosh she was truly amazing. I couldn't help but wrap this beautiful stranger in my arms when it got colder. Moments later, sitting comfortably by each other on the smooth sand, we disregarded the short-lived remorse hanging over us. Suddenly our bodies were making tender motions folded at the seashore. I couldn't stop staring at her, she was a dream. I woke up in the middle of the night on the beach, caught using the clothes off my body as my pillow while hugging the bottle of rum I sneaked away from the dinner, and having my annoyingly "precious" cousin Cheryl look at me with digust while still letting everyone know about my whereabouts just to mortify me.

While telling her to fuck off I stared menacingly at the crumble and carefully built sandcastle. I remember the beauty looking at it then at the shore as if she seemed content to disappear.

Was it all a dream? What was her name, S-S—Selena??? No.

I told Gramps about everything that night, he told me to be careful with the rum and to continue to sleep it off in my old room upstairs, the party was over, and he believed my nakedness had a lot to say. Of course, nosy Cheryl was still around and couldn't help herself, "Oh my poor cousin Joshie. To feel so dreadful about life nowadays, you'd take a hit from my father, and you'd drink yourself to hallucinations. Obviously, you had way too much rum, and for a city boy as yourself, way too much ocean."

She's just envious that she wasn't the one to meet such a gracious beauty.

I went to bed to my old room, but I couldn't stop thinking of that gorgeous splendor; her long teal hair, her periwinkle eyes, and her delicate voice. I hoped to see her again.

Following the sounds of the clanking, I walk to the kitchen. Gramps faced the stove wearing his lobster claws potholders, piling crab eggs benedicts onto a platter. Gramps only remembered the recipes my late grandmother taught him, all around, he still kept the fish collection embellished in the kitchen cupboards, arranged in diversity like they strode in an everlasting parade. I grinned.

"Morning Gramps. Breakfast smells surprisingly delicious! I really don't know what to say, you had gone through all this trouble, especially after last night's embarrassment." I really did feel awful, it was me and Gramps against the world, yet I made a mockery of him.

Gramps scuffed and jerked a browse over me, but his face remained serene. "Oh hush, put these frozen peas on your eye. Forget all that nonsense, it is not daily my only grandson makes an appearance for a spontaneous visit. So, you got socked and you came in your bathing suit, who cares! I've been naked around this town plenty."

"Why aren't you mad at me? I missed the funeral too Gramps." I felt so shameful.

"Oh, shit don't apologize kid, I didn't go either, I would have looked like an embarrassment to their name. Besides, I said my goodbyes right after everybody left." Wow, he felt just ashamed as I did, he just had a better way of showing it.

"I know but the whole family…the whole town was upset." I still couldn't shake the thoughts that were being said at last night's ceremonial dinner.

"Well, don't worry about them."

"I tried getting here as quick as possible, I loved my parents even through the mess!"

"Well stop apologizing, you missed only the ceremony! That doesn't mean anything compared to your love, we can always go see them whenever we want before fishing"

Staring at the Father's Day mug that said,*#1 Father.* I said, "He must be disappointed in us!"

"Well, Alaric's going to have to forgive, in order to enter whatever beautiful universe there is for him and be beside your lovely mother."

Thinking about my mother I became tearful. "I'm so sorry, if I let you down Gramps, just like I did with my own parents!" I began bawling out tears from last night.

"Hey, stop sobbing out all that nonsense, you have never let me down and you haven't done that with your parents either. Your father was just a prick, but he loved you. He just never got to know you like I did. Don't pay mine to the Hanks family they have problems of their own."

* * *

After a few weeks, I transferred to a college in South Carolina, moving back with Gramps. Living with Gramps would be helpful filling the hollow I have for my parents' memories. His stories has been crowding my heart with happiness and love, that has been missing for a while. I still enjoy all his stories. Strange as it seems though, lately I've been feeling that he may be hiding something from me; and usually he's honest.

Fueled by anxiety and the nice feeling of living with Gramps again, I've been sleeping or hanging around at the dock most days, until one night I found out Gramps was late with certain bills. I had to get my act together and take on some responsibility, so I decided to work as the marine biologist at, Sullivan's Island's Marine Research Center. Meanwhile, I worked at my father's company as well, until I could pay those bills and find someone who could take care of the Hanks business. Gramps thought it should stay in the Hanks legacy, just like when he taught my father how to build a boat, but all I had were asshole cousins and the one I knew most was half Hanks, which was Cheryl. On the other hand, my asshole uncle thought he should take in the company but knowing him, he would get bored of the wooden boats built by hand and begin using fiberglass. I was stressed wondering what to do! Doing both jobs can help in my favor; keeping the ocean clean and having my own ships if I need them. My mom's warm hand would've been placed on my back, pulling, or pushing me through these difficult times.

I was now finally moving everything into the guest house, unpacking all my stuff I had from New York. The knocking came soft and delicate, and so my door opened. Then she appeared. She strides from the rays of light, stealing my gasp. She is mystically devouring me in the midst of her eyes, passing her fingers through her tresses, meanwhile I can't completely figure out if I'm just a part of a very nearly overlooked dream.

But she hasn't got anything on! Around was nothing more beguiling than her nakedness, she appeared smooth, and her breasts seemed to be so warm. I suddenly felt a little shy and began spitting out words. "Oh my gosh, come in, come in, come in!" Josh catch a grip! Say that anymore times she'll think you're crazy…oh but each time I saw her she's so naked, why me? And I say that in a thank goodness, but I know I still have to be a gentlemen way. I opened the remainder of the board up windows, as I let the daylight stream down on her even beyond, trying my hardest to speak to her without looking at her. "This is my home for now. Oh my gosh, I really thought I dreamt it all from drinking the hard stuff…umm Sirena, why are you naked?" All regarding her is natural and I adore it!

I must've really drunk the hard stuff that night because I haven't remembered her name until now. But she was real and that's all that mattered. I had desired to lay my hands on her naked spine, to stroke the warm honey skin that looks so delicate and velvety. Then she had glimpsed up at me with those unforgettable eyes, and I'd felt a startled. Then I noticed that she had sensed me catching sight of her, that she was slightly bashful by the unwavering attention. After that one occasion with her I think I'll definitely break if she leaves for a second time. I need her, I wish she could do with me just as much.

Sirena later explained that while talking, I drank more of the rum than she did. Then she started chasing after me as I ran around the house, as well as the beach naked. She said I knew how to make a girl laugh on the worst day, but she still had to go home. She wasn't sure if she was ever coming back after she rejected her fiance. But what about the memories of us making love. She said, "Once you fell asleep on my lap, I sang to you. That's why you had those peaceful sensual dreams."

Leaving the guesthouse I told her to stay put and I would be back with provisions, but when I arrived after running back down the beach she was nowhere. However noise was coming from the garage, I had to hurry if I didn't want anyone to see a naked woman in the Hanks car garage. Footsteps echoed as I came into the garage door, I witnessed her unclothed struggling to keep secret in an old-fashioned vacant car my father and I never got to repair. Sirena rubbed her eyes and raised her head with a twitch at the sound of my whisper of her name.

"Sirena?" I said quietly.

She looked through the window of the car and smiled as she ran out towards me. I was standing on the bottom staircase balancing a platter on my hands. A weighty bag draped around my forearm. The tray shaken and I struggled to steady it with one hand. "I only supposed you may perhaps enjoy some breakfast. I gave you a bit of everything," mopping my forehead with a handkerchief. "My Gramps doesn't usually make that much for breakfast, hence I added more." Sirena's mouth began to water; however, she did not know anything that was on the tray. I explained to her, "A hot stack of Belgian waffles, country fried steak and over easy eggs, biscuits covered in creamy gravy, and hash browns." She started shoving food into her mouth and she enjoyed it, then I took out the stuff from the bag. "I don't know if these will fit you. My cousin Cheryl is always leaving something behind. I admit she has a particular extreme taste, compared to your pure beauty. Still, at least you won't be stuck wearing only my clothes. Which I'm still baffled as to why?" I certainly began pondering greater regarding that question.

"Thank you," she said and took the platter, she said it once again reducing her tone of voice as she collected the garments.

I shook and grinned, "I don't want to go assuming so many questions, but there's an unoccupied cot in the lighthouse if you're interested." I had a promising expression beyond my face.

"What are you thinking?"

I did not intend on telling her that for once in my life, I had images that been extraordinarily strong, they were nearly compelling. The notion of lying in bed with her sparked a flood of passions.

I was stirred by her aura each and every time I sought out to recognize the dimpled beam that adorned her face as her emblem— all the time warm, not at all inhospitable.

That smile. Good heavens, that flashed a dimpled smile. It's like a breath of fresh air.

Afterwards we became inseparable, knowing she was a newcomer and hadn't spent time in my small town before, I spent days after work showing her around my home. Everything seemed new or unrealistic to her. She loved the carnival, dancing, and going to the marine parks. Whenever the heavy rain came all the way, it clanked against the house and honeycombed the ocean. The thunder created boisterous blares that later were roughly flooded by the noise of the downpour. Each rainfall, I wanted her with me the most, I supposed it made me think about my parents and I just wanted to be with her. But she was never found.

We seemed to argue about the unusual things, such as her adding salt to everything she ate and drank, or why she had this fixation of swimming alone and naked into the depths, but still I felt as though I've known her for so long. My attention focused on her lips. We spent hours talking about our dreams and who we wanted to be, still looking into the future. I never felt so consume by any woman, no one ever cared like she did, so I couldn't resist her.

I leaned in and gave a peck on her cheek, enjoying the sea breeze and vanilla, womanly aroma of her. She stayed on her tippytoe to offer me a peck that would rest on my neck although I shifted in such a way our lips greeted; first softly, but later further enthusiastically and she realized her arms had in some way in a circle wrapped around my neck. I can feel her heart thrashing against my chest. What kept me waiting this long from kissing her gorgeous lips. I wondered if she asked the same. The smoothness of her lips stunned me.

I hated it when she disappeared for a lengthy time, it left me with memories of her everywhere. My name finally on the kissing bench next to hers, where would eat ice cream, as the wind would blow through her hair as her eyes sparkled with joy from every lick. Always smiling at me with those beguiling periwinkle eyes, as I spoke to her about how I wanted to take care of the oceans.

It's been a few days, and I still haven't seen or heard from Sirena. She doesn't leave any postcards and she never calls. I'm not even sure she has a phone, which would be weird around this decade. Gramps notices my unhappiness within my appearance and encourages me to a fishing day. He recommends it's the most excellent thing for a fractured heart or at best an aching one. We were on our way to Fire Island when he began telling a very new story. "Josh, for me, remember this champ! There's an entire cluster of mysterious and profound existence that lies within this world." Though I knew coming to this island he would eventually bring up mermaids, I didn't really care to hear. For at that moment, I only wondered where Sirena was or if she abandoned me as well. However, Gramps was just trying to heal my heart, so I tried my best to listen.

"Now champ, this story is true but it's also a sad one. Remember the times I told you about my life as a fisherman. I was working for a very insignificant company known as Ocean Tide. But the ocean was my passion…" Grandpa was known as a very modest fisherman who did his angling at Lake Orchid. He was a humble fisherman with a huge family to take care of. All the townspeople had disbelief of Lake Orchid for the reason that they knew the small lake had only fish that were small-scale or none at all. Nevertheless, he continuously had hope to keep trying.

"Then and there…finally, one day I found more than what I meant to catch. A beautiful mermaid stranded midway on the shore. I fail to recall how I might have injured her. Nevertheless, I carried her back into the ocean. I felt flabbergasted, but as I was leaving the area, I turned back to notice the mermaid had returned to the surface." He walked back over to her, and she held out her hands to him. In them was a beautiful and flawless pearl unlike any he had ever seen before. She handed him the pearl and spoke briefly with her gentle voice that would continue to dance around in his ears for the rest of his life. "I'm giving you this gift, because I trust that you are a friend and not a foe. Please don't fail to remember me," she said to him.

He wept and said, "I could never!" They shared together a brief moment of silence.

She then asked him, "Why were you at my home?" He chuckled and then went on to explain to her about his line of work, as well as how difficult it was to provide for his family day by day. "From that day forward, as an expression of her gratitude, the mermaid assisted me on my fishing voyages by capturing impressively large fish and shellfish that I would likely not be able to obtain on my own."

Gramps had finally turned out to be recognized for finding massive underwater creatures and made the formerly insignificant company of Ocean Tide develop into a colossal seafood chain. "The mermaid and I turned out to become great friends, but then I noticed at some point she vanished; I at no time saw her yet again. Even though she was only my best friend she was also the love of my life. Not just cause of the fish, but because she showed me a bond between two different species, we talked about everything, she made a pearl necklace for your grandmother…who by the way also appreciated her."

He looked up at me with watery eyes glistening in the light and said to me, "Maybe mermaids…maybe they don't live for so long." I could tell by his tone that he was holding back the tears. "Maybe they swim around the world in cycles each winter," he said with a chuckle so as to not sadden me. It was clear that her disappearance had shattered his heart like glass.

When Gramps recognized my face, he explained to me that he wasn't saying I was dating a mermaid it was just a story expressing his own understanding of being brokenhearted of a mysterious girl. Then he chuckled, "And it doesn't matter what species you're dating, or friendly with, individuals just run out on you. After that, we all experience lovesickness." I'm not exactly sure if this was the picture-perfect advice Gramps had ever given. Part of me thinks he just saw the young child Josh, however I tried to look at it as if it was helpful. Later, I got up and walked away to catch fish on the other side. Perhaps it was just the memory of my grandpa's story that was causing my imagination to run wild, because when I looked at the Fire Island shore, I could've sworn I saw a massive tangerine fin emerge out of the seawater. Throughout the night I thought about what I had glance at, but I kept telling myself it was just my mind playing tricks on me.

The following day we went back home and still no sign of Sirena. For the next week and a half, I did extra overtime forcing myself to think of anything else but her. I dreamt about her almost every night, and it was always the same kind of dream; we're swimming, diving, looking for seashells, and her beautiful lips brushing mine. The next two Sundays I went to Fire Island; it was calling me like last time. And startlingly I found her, she was exposed resting on the rocks as if she was sunbathing. She said she had been waiting for me since that morning. That's pretty long, I would've left a long time ago, I'm sort of not tolerant with waiting. "Sirena don't get me wrong. You're beautiful and all, but why are you always in the nude?" She smiled with her beautiful, plumped lips that I'd been longing to kiss, and she simply said, "I swim better that way." I laughed at such a response because I thought of a scuba diver like me, observing a beautiful naked lady swimming in the waters and why? Because she swam better that way. Come to think of it, maybe I should try it someday, "You know, I've been thinking about you for quite some time. I have so many questions for you. Like why are you here after disappearing on me, once again? You just keep disappearing and you never tell me where you're going, or if you're even safe. The hardest thing I can't seem to understand is how you never call me or at least send a post card! How did you even know that I would be here? What's up with you Sirena, do you even care about me like I care about you?"

CHAPTER 3

irena looked at me apologetically. "Of course, I do! Stop sounding like that! Your voice is different, and I don't like it. Listen, let's just forget all that rubbish right now but do tell me something. Is it true? Have you really been thinking of me?" She asked me as if she had never heard such a sweet thought like that in her life.

"Of course, I have. I even have dreams of you. The dreams are always alike, here on Fire Island. We're diving into the ocean, kissing at the moment that the waves make love with the rocks." I threw the *handsome gaze* at her tenderly, but unfortunately, I don't think it worked. Gramps taught me that gaze when I was a teenager; apparently it worked for him, and that's how he greeted my grandma.

However, Sirena seemed pretty distant today; she kept observing into the ocean as if a sea monster was going to hurdle right out and take hold of her. I supposed maybe she wanted to take a swim…foolish idea. As soon as I asked her if we could go swimming together to make part of my dreams come true, I was not sure what happened. Nevertheless, she looked at me with desperate great fear and it triggered her for a head start. Again, she then ran and leaped into the waters. Maybe she was being cute and playful with me with a cheating head start. I'm not quite sure.

No, not this time! I didn't even care that I didn't have my swimsuit. My only thought to myself was that, *I have to swim after her*. After she jumped in, I stormed into the ocean right behind her. Okay, what the heck? Maybe it was because I was swimming without my goggles, so the water created a bit of blurriness, however I held my flashlight securely. Still, as soon as I leaped into the water right after her, there was something different. It looked like as if Sirena's legs were no longer legs, more like a long tangerine-colored fin. However, I kept following her, though I was not even sure if she knew that I was. I was hesitant why I even kept on. It's not like I was able to breathe underwater like her, and with the confusion or hallucination, I just started choking to death. All of a sudden, about five strange-looking women also with tails came toward me. They looked oddly bizarre from their *tail half*, to be precise. They started seducing me, trying to take off my shirt. This must have been a dream because no woman in their right mind had seduced me in such a way and not to mention five women! I was like the nerdy Ross from *Friends*. I had five fish women to grace with my presence to, even though I was still drowning in this dream. But it wasn't seduction as I assumed, as they began charging at me. I struggled swimming away although they remained attacking me, and so looking to kill. One of them tried ripping me with her sharp nails, but I knocked her and briefly overcame her. Next thing I noticed, was that right away Sirena came along, hit them with her tail, then screeched and hissed at them. Perhaps it must have been some type of Brazilian accent for, *get the hell away from him*. Didn't realize Sirena would be such a jealous type in this dream.

But that's another question? Am I dreaming or dead from drowning? This was too unusual. Oh shit, this wasn't a dream at all! I actually did feel the water clogging up my throat. I really was drowning. *Bye, cruel world, bye, Gramps, and especially bye to the Brazilian women with tails.*

When, I soon opened my eyes. I began coughing up a storm or for this moment the sea. In the beginning, I felt a little lethargic later. I had started to sense her beautiful teal hair, nearly smacking me on my face, and then that's when I saw her lovely periwinkle eyes gazing into mine. I then turned toward her. I had perhaps thumped my head truly rigid from a rock or swallowed way too much seawater when I went after her because I was so disoriented that I, "I had this strange dream, and I could've sworn you had a—"

She grinned at me as she completed my sentence, "A fin?" That's the minute she flipped her fin out of the water. I leaped up from where I was lying and was completely shocked. Then she began to calm me down. "Josh, pay attention, you're entirely fine! You aren't hallucinating from swallowing an excessive amount of seawater, and you never thumped your head on a rock. You're physically and mentally stable! Now I request that you do me a significant courtesy and pretend like you by no means saw any of those events that occurred…regardless of what you saw! Or you and I, are finished!" Wait, what? I never knew we were even a thing. Wow! I had a mermaid girlfriend if that's what she meant in the first place. I did realize she talked sort of queer, like from a different realm.

"Sirena, how do you expect me to undo those thoughts? Do you know my life has been surrounded around mermaids!"

She looked at me sadly and a little bit upset, "Can I sing to you something that my mom used to sing to me? It's quite beautiful." I was so happy to know she was letting me in, I jumped up to the idea of listening to a mermaid sing. Then she began to sing with a beautiful harmony,

Allow the recollections of these events,
End to yet be past tense.
Let bygones be bygones just as fair,
Be unable to call to mind today, nevermore

* * *

I woke up to the overpowering smell of my room smelling musty, assaulting my nose. The guest house was soundless separately from my heavy breathing and the sound of cooking in the background. I sluggishly opened my eyes, peeking in struggle to polish the distorted images before me. I squinted all around, "Sirena is that you, how long have I been here?" I closed my eyes, seeking to recall what had just transpired. But then everything strikes me in a flash. The memory of everything begins to engage my thoughts.

I thought I made it. I finally leaped. After plummeting into the ocean, my lungs cannot take in the oxygen as I have swallowed the water. Anxiety and further panic, when smashing my head on a rock after cliff diving. I remember feeling Sirena's hands wrapped around me dragging me out from the shore and dropping me on my bed. The pain pushed through my frame.

Abruptly my defenses are simply paper, being drenched by means of the heavy plummeting salty tides. I really couldn't be mad with Sirena anymore especially right after realizing she took care of me. She ran to me with a bear hug for my spirit. It felt as if, before I was able to engage the air my body required, I had softened into her shape. I can feel her delicate chest along with the heart that beats within. On a whim, my fingers journey towards the back of my head, pressing the pulsating section. I touched the wound and winced at the aching. I attempted to stand up. After I finally finish off resting there pitifully, I wait on for the agony to carry away.

I was eager to finally reunite with Sirena just the way I intended to. That night came when our soul connection revealed from our eyes, in each of her pleasurable strokes, and my passion of that much-awaited caress. For that moment was the delightful release, the chance for joy to take center stage and dance. I couldn't get her off my thoughts so I told her, "I wondered if, um, if you would like to get some seafood? And pie." She blushed as she said she would like that very much, and she could not believe this was truly happening.

That night, I led Sirena to a small quaint table in a quiet seafood restaurant. A late hour for dinner, many of the tables are empty. I pull out her chair as she sits. Looking around nervously I sat across from her holding her hand. The only light is from a few well-placed candles. A waitress approaches and I order two salty dog cocktails for us, and I smile at Sirena knowing it was her favorite drink. Suddenly, the waitress with the huge smile looked at Sirena and responded lifting her right eyebrow and slowly said, *"suu..re,"* as she wrote down the orders. When she came back, I noticed how improper she was, she gave me both drinks and almost gave me Sirena's order of seafood as well. I felt quite embarrassed, I insisted it was for my date. Perhaps, she thought that Sirena wouldn't eat or drink like that, she did look like a model after all. After the rude waitress left, Sirena begins to look overly excited looking at her meal.

I was very amazed by how beautiful she looked. Sirena was incredibly uneasy. She began tensely stirring the cocktail with her finger. She appears to lose herself in the reflections and gazes keenly on the cocktail glass. The salty dog commences to churn. I could have sworn I saw an image in the cocktail. My gaze alters from Sirena's appearance to her salty dog, and I lean in seeking to catch a better glimpse. Nevertheless, the waitress stops by as she looks puzzled once again as she replenishes her cocktail glass, and the image that I supposed I noticed vanished. Sirena chuckles and starts to swallow her seafood. She picks her enormous lobsters up with her hands and continues to take monster bites, exterior and legs! Sirena endures to dine on her shellfish as if they were burgers and French fries, along with everybody all around the restaurant is gawking at her, I clarify to my fellow startled diners, "She's especially starved." She notices, blushes. A shy smile slips out. I loved watching her, like a voyeur looking into a secret world. I smiled warmly back as if to comfort her, though I was a bit shy of what to say on this date. She then gets up and says she needs to powder her nose. I gazed at her as she walked away, soaking it all in that I was on a date with someone lovely.

Suddenly, Cheryl sat across from me with a bitchy smile, "Hey Joshie!! So, you look pretty fancy to be eating here with the old man, do you think with cocktails you're going to get laid??" She said as she drank from Sirena's refilled salty dog.

"Heey! That's my girlfriends drink you're putting your disgusting red lipstick on!" Where was Sirena? It was annoying spending this time with my cousin.

"Girlfriend? Yeah right! You're such a funny sad liar, Joshie! So, does your she-friend know your darkest secret?"

Cheryl and I practically grew up together so she could be talking about anything in my life. She could even be talking about something that wasn't known as a secret, just something she believed was embarrassing to me. So do I ask her what she means, or do I tell her and her evil claws to stay away from me.

"You remember…about your parents?" Cheryl did have a slightly vindictive side.

I kept looking around her, hoping that my date will pop up anytime soon, but for now on I was still with my cousin, "What are you talking about, you sound ridiculous?"

"And you sound ignorant?" Her confidence began to sound very spiteful.

What the hell was she talking about, there's always something that's up with her. Why was she being secretive with me?

"It was when you were 16 years old, we were both walking from school on our way to Gramps. And we saw that your father…well, you know…" Cheryl began laughing hysterically, making fun of me. Being blissfully discreet, that's when I knew what she was talking about then, it was a memory I was trying to forget for a very long time.

My father was having an affair with a younger college student, and we locked eyes through the glass of his boat's window. He knew he was in deep shit when he saw that Cheryl saw as well. Since then, my father and my mother were on and off going to counseling, however I never made it better.

Since he was such a hard ass to me, let's just say Cheryl put it in my head that I had something against him, a reminder. Therefore, every time we got into an argument; if my grades slipped, if I came home late, I just mentioned him screwing a younger student.

I slapped my parents in their face when I started sleeping with the college professor and didn't care less that they saw me with her. It broke my mother's heart but then I realized it made my father feel superior in some sort of way, so I stopped.

Supposedly, that boat trip was a way for them to reconnect on their anniversary, if that was true, the reason for reconnecting was because I made things worse.

Since those days I used to have nightmares a lot. My mother is having arguments day after day with her husband. Me walking with Cheryl, slowly about to turn the corner, spotting the other woman. Getting beatdowns, time after time by my father from embarrassing him. These nightmares always felt real. My father is a big man, when he yells it feels like he's growling, and when he hits it feels like he wants to put an end to me.

"Cheryl can you just go back up to your date, just like I'm on mine?" This was only Cheryl's way of manipulating me to intimidate me from being in a relationship, I don't know there was something about my cousin that made me always feel like she liked me way too much, it was pretty creepy. She left and a few seconds later Sirena came back, but now that thought was stuck in my head throughout our date, just when the date was becoming eventful. I told her all my secrets, and though she didn't scorn me I had to finally ask her about her honesty, *where did she come from, why the nakedness, why the disappearance?*

Sirena looked pretty sad, maybe even upset and then she responded, "I was honest when I escaped my home because I was fleeing a betrothed marriage. My family think of me as someone who is grand to them, I have to live by their standards which is extremely strict and fleeing to enjoy any piece of life is betrayal to them. We have lots of security where I live, therefore I have to escape as soon as possible, even if that means getting here naked."

As we got home, we passionately made out staring into the sea, though soon after Sirena said she didn't want to create any chaos with her family. When Sirena left, she leaned forward and caressed my cheek, enduring nearly over a single, significant moment. At that moment, my body understood the call-in areas lower and welcoming. But she was leaving, once again. Sirena's lips ablaze on my cheek, so gentle and with the slightest touch of freshness. As she walked away from me far on the other side of the shore and suddenly disappeared. The rule was for me not to follow in case her strict family were keeping an eye on her. I remember her leaving with the words, *"Addio, amore"* after that I snapped inside, snapped like delicate crystal, and felt the slivers splitting at my innards. My thoughts began drifting as I stared into the sea, as my eyes began to close. That night I dreamt of haunting enticing singing luring me while the waves harshly rolled in, up until I finally saw the lighthouse guiding me where to swim.

I woke up thinking today something entirely new was ashore. There was a shift in the air of Sullivan's Island, and I can sense it. It was nice waking up to Sirena appearing right by my side, though we still haven't reach making love, I'm not regretting the day before it has even begun. Because I know my day would be cocooned by her. And for the single time in a long time, I feel fantastic to admit that.

At last, she rises from the bed, and before everything she stands at the heart of the room. Staring into the full-length antique mirror, she gazes at her reflection of her stark-naked body in front of her. She didn't realize that from my bed, I was watching her just standing there feeling up on her legs, then with a sudden, silent wail she clutches at her neck, plucking off her handmade pearl necklace, which bursts across the room. In a hysteria she pulls at herself, her clothes, her hair, I can't stop looking at her wondering why is she so upset? Does she have any clue that I'm even here, if so, am I the reason why she's so offended? She's so unhappy she tosses an antique hand mirror I gotten her against the wardrobe, smashing it.

She looked at me and began talking while sobbing, "I'm sorry, it's all my fault! I was mistaken. I supposed that I could smile and take pleasure in the few months passing by, imagine like it would all be okay. That I was safe, and I had an idea." She sobs touching her face gently and sadly says, "I wanted to start up my own shop…for therapeutic creams…. and a collection of beautiful handmade jewelry." She looks at me, swaying around wiping her tears away and hugging herself as she continues, "I wanted to transform who I was, form a living with someone new that I chose for myself. Shorn of history, short of the agony. Somebody more alive than I'll ever be. However, it's never that simple when the awful things remain by your side. They'll shadow me everywhere I go. I can't flee from them despite the fact that I want to. Nothing more I can do but to look forward for the righteous, so as far, I am inviting. As I sought it. I sought it out terribly."

Sirena shoves me away from holding her when I try calming her down. It began pouring suddenly and the clouds were darkening, when she said to herself, "Oh no, I got to go now!" She ran naked along the extremely long dock in back of my guesthouse. I only wore my briefs, a puzzled expression on my face, and icy lashes of rain across my skin. All I could do was watch with bewilderment, as I froze at top of the hill. Sirena looks tousled, her hair gone with the wind. I can tell she's wiping streaks of cries away from her face. More so, I see her angry, her furious! I begin running towards her to see she's shuddering with feelings she doesn't recognize…animosity, self-hatred, despair. For a moment, I'm wondering how I am going to bring my girlfriend back on earth, do I show her stars blazing when this rain passes, do I speak to her about the funny forecast and afternoon we just had.

Sirena doesn't see me a few feet away as she enter the floating dock and begins yelling out at the ocean. Her breathing snags in an infrequent weep, which she restrains. She slams against the windsock pole and clings there, naked and crying. Panting as she stared out at the chaotic black water. While she keeps repeating, "I don't want to go back! I found my life here!"

I begin to panic seeing how close she is, imagining the floating dock tossing her off. I got closer and cried out for her to come back and that everything was okay, however she dove into the water. And just as I plunged into the sea right after her, I see her legs melding into a powerful tail keeping her steady despite the salted tumultuous waves— unlike my wonky arms, legs, and huge surprise.

A trail of bubbles followed the swift downward slope. Sirena stood neutrally buoyant submerged in the ocean, staring into fear and shock flash across my face. My body suddenly stiffened, and I did what all mortals did when plunged beneath the waves at night— swim the wrong way.

Having fallen into a melodious domain, Sirena grabs me. Though I tried shaking her off and kept swimming into the darkness where the lovely harmony was being heard. Sirena spared a moment to grab me again this time with force. She provide a bit of oxygen for me while underwater with kissing me on the mouth and putting air in my lungs, later she smooth my hair, lay a hand on my face, vigorously screaming, *I have you, you're safe, now swim with me…*As I finally did the rest of the swimming above the ocean, I gasped for breath once the water broke, only to be splattered by ripping waves and a spray of foam.

How do I believe my Gramps stories, but never believe I would see it for myself? I've grown accustomed to people being born, growing old, and they die. I haven't seen the world of magic, no sorcery, no everlasting life. I thought individuals were believed to be who they say they were, and not be dishonest or conceal their genuine natures. This is why I think I was genuinely hurt? I should ignore what I saw, tell myself it isn't likely, and that I'm not a believer. I can't be. Although exactly how can I refuse what's right in front of me? Ever since that night we haven't spoken to each other. She tried so hard not to reveal herself; she desired a smile that was only meant for her, that when she finally uncovered her true self, I was thoughtless to take in her secret as she did with me. All I could ask from her is if we could talk in a few days. It was so low from me, but she accepted it. In three days, we spoke where we had our first chat.

I sat down initially but then stared at Sirena through my periphery vision. She turned and gazed at me seriously. My heart pounded excruciatingly, as I was attempting to swallow something wedged in my chest. Passionate periwinkle eyes, cool and soft. Looking at her everything explains her appearance, her teal hair and her eyes. She explained to me about how everything she told me during dinner was still the truth, however she only left out the fact that she is from the sea. She explained how much she really liked me, and she really liked to stay. I found her more intensely stunning and that was startling.

CHAPTER 4

Oddly, a few days later when Sirena came barging into the guesthouse huffing and puffing, appearing pretty in heat as she said, "I know. Although not enemies is one thing; becoming devoted lovers is another. Even supposing we can, it would start tremendous chaos!"

It was difficult to acknowledge, hard to bear; she had to escape from it. She shoved her seat away. "Forgive me," she whispered, standing irregularly to her feet.

"Sirena, what's the matter?" I rose as well, looking at her thoughtfully.

She wouldn't answer me because any response would be awfully treacherous. Without so much as a word, she scurried away from the table. I called after her, nevertheless the sound of her name forced her to run faster. She reached the Hanks house before I caught up, scarcely seeing a few dismayed faces as she traveled towards the beach.

Soft sand covered our feet delicately. Her small hands are tucked about my back, taking me in nearer. My hands were on her naked spine now, and her honey skin was all over so sweet and smooth as it appeared. Her hair had plummeted down her backside and above my hands like cozy, blooming tremendous satin. She was thoroughly motionless, barely taking a breath, but her daintiness was pushed opposed mine and I felt every arch, feeling her warmth.

"No," she uttered remarkably faintly. Her head tipped backwards gradually as she glanced upwards at me, and moonshine gleam dimly in her eyes. Facing my chest, her fingers straightened and spread, never trying to get rid of me. My own fingers were rousing, agilely penetrating the evenness of her spine, as one hand rode up toward her neck, at which time the other located her back. She felt very tenuous over mine, as rare, and my full framework was responding recklessly, my entire sensations then heightened it was nearly agonizing. My essence battered upon my chest, furthermore a bounce here, spontaneous yearning fixed deep down with a pulsating crave.

"No?" I whispered, recognizing that I wasn't processing fear now. Her eyes were huge, bent on my face, her lips slightly spaced and shuddering. I can sense our bodies trembling, sobbing for the lost periods we will no way get in return.

"I forbid you. Don't allow this to happen." Her tone was slightly further than a whisper.

My arms secured around her. "You knew this was going to happen, didn't you? That's why you disappeared on me."

The confession she had petrified her, abandoning her side in excruciating peril. "That's demented! How might I dare think- Leave me alone, Joshua!" I drew her head back then clean the tears with a rough touch, I trusted even my coarseness brought further comfort than my heart and soul can carry.

"You knew," I kept repeating, my tone strengthening furthermore going rugged. "You feel something, as well."

Sirena shaken her head, except this was a vulnerable gesture, not negative. This was the overcome sensation of lure she had ever experienced, for the most part because it seemed novel to her.

Being in my embrace feels marvelous. Her frame had been aware that the split second had it touched mine, also she couldn't shoot down the fierce pleasure swelling through her.

She heaved at wonder and directed a simple, stifling outcry. "Dare not."

Her eyes shut gently just when my lips caressed hers. The deal was relentless, and there was no return. She found herself approaching closer facing me, her arms rising to my shoulders, her lips breaching ferociously underneath the escalating force of mine. Once I kissed her is was delightful, soothing, and it flavored our cries.

Her bosom were compelled at my chest, sweltering me despite our clothes, our figures had been destined to be together. As if they were deeply drowning in heat waves, absolutely incapable of everything that happened.

That night I was interested and open to hear authentic beliefs, at my curious looks I looked at her, "Was that your home?"

She nodded, concerned gaze across her face, "What do you mean? Of course, the ocean's my home."

"I've been in the ocean before; it's never been so dark, secretive, seductive? Another thing, I never heard such a hymn in the ocean before, usually waters tends to muffle sounds." I stared at her with a perplexed expression and finally shook my head.

I had further dark and forbidding secrets lingering in every brain vessel like cobwebs catching dust in a lighthouse, but it was time to open up. "Joshua, you were getting yourself dangerously close to the sirens nest. Which could've gotten you killed! They would've lured you in, and *Sirened* you to breathe even in the deepest coldest waters. Later, they would've ripped you into shreds after all of them would have their chance to breed with you."

"OH FUCK I'm scared, but glad to know that I have a creepy siren lair around this beach." I said all freaked out and disturbed!

"Since, we're being truthfully honest, you have sort of already met them." She said with a facial expression that looked incredibly nervous.

"What are you talking about they been on land before?" If this was true, what if they were ever around my family.

She looked ashamed as she said, "Sirens don't particularly like the land, so no. Don't be upset, let's just say you saw my tail before while I was saving you from being lured by them near Fire Island. I had to erase your memory. You were so scared that you even looked at me like I was going to hurt you… are you mad?

"No…no, I'm not exactly mad; this does explain why you don't want to take baths with me, why you drink a lot of salty water and eat a lot of shellfish, and a better explanation of why you're always naked." I sort of lied, I was a little mad that I didn't know anything, obviously at some point I would meet them again.

Later I heard a new and truly angry voice call out for Sirena, "Sirena!" She yelled out, when Sirena followed the voice to the shore, I stuck my ear to listen and heard, "Sirena. Are you telling him about us?" What the fuck? Was she one of the sirens?

Sirena came back inside this time with a newcomer, who looked at me with fury.

"The sirens are my adoptive family, and they're just on the lookout for me. Their realm is modest unlike the mermaids. I have over five sisters; Seline, Sybil, Eirenna, Amara, Veronica, Myrtle, Valerian, Petra, the twins Kalidelia and Nerilena, and the oldest of our sisters Dianthus. But this one here is my true favorite sister Rosemarie. She came because she has something important to tell."

"That's a lot of sisters, umm…she looks scary, will she bite?"

"Josh! Don't be a jerk! And she makes it easy to choose, she's the only sister that truly understands me, she knows I'm different and she loves me just the way I am." She said holding her sisters' hands that I noticed were slightly webbed. Rosemarie smiled at Sirena and all I saw were sharp teeth. I was definitely scared.

* * *

Rosemarie spoke to Sirena, "I know why they're looking for you, I know why they don't want you to be with him, and it's not just cause he's a meal. Don't you know the tales?" She continued for a while, but I couldn't hear anything since she was hissing most of the time, and then Sirena looked at me sadly. I ran up to Rosemarie and demanded she explained to me what was up! She glared at me with a mischievous smile, instead how about I show you? She telepathically told me. She then waved her hands around and around, saying words that weren't familiar. Then as a magical orb of water appeared she telepathically said, it all started with the first Hanks and everything she said was revealed in the orb, the true story is buried in the lighthouse. There used to lie a deceased mermaid from decades ago.

Mrs. Elaine Carolyn Hanks found out about the affairs of Mr. J. Steven Hanks with the mermaid, so as they were a part of the founder families of Sullivan Island she decided not to take revenge with her own hands. She would have to think wise, for this town in South Carolina would think negative of her.

She told her sons; the ones treasured her and loved her of course. And as they took off on the fishing boat, let's just say as gossip goes, the lovely mermaid who is swimming about, waiting for the night to see her lover never thought that instead she'd be kidnapped by the own men she protects.

In the lighthouse she stood trapped, with shackles on her wrist, then Mrs. Hanks appeared and said she only wanted to speak with her, not to harm her.

She spoke to her about how she was happy that her husband finally found love, and she offered her a strange tea in which she helped the mermaid drink it. She pretended to think highly of the mermaid, afterwards she even un-cuffed her when the mermaid transformed.

This made the mermaid feel very welcome and even more hopeful of her love for a human. But later, a few more founder women from South Carolina came into the lighthouse, "Oh my dear, Elaine Carolyn, where did you find this one?"

"Sorry ladies, she's not a homeless, she's…oh I thought it was most important to tell you all my dear friends. However, we have a homewrecker, and not just any homewrecker, but one with scales…" Then she poured the water on her bare legs, and they transformed into a fin.

"Oh my gosh, Elaine Carolyn how could you, she's from the sea…"

"That's against the rules…"

"Ladies calm yourselves, it's also against God's rules, thou shall not commit adultery! We are good Christian woman, we take care of our men, and how do they repay us?"

"Elaine Carolyn we're speaking of your husband, you're making it seem like it's all our husbands."

"Well, hello ladies, I am a faithful Christian woman, and my husband had his fun, with this fish that has no religion, whatsoever. If it's happened to me, what makes you think it won't happen to another of us? What makes you think that her sisters aren't already meeting with your husbands? If they can calm the waves with their songs, they can probably enchant our husbands into becoming their new wives, while we're thrown aside."

Mrs. Hanks was really good at persuading all the women against Merfolk, and it all began with just one; one song, one kiss, one love. Mrs. Hanks didn't have to do anything; all she did was put a sedative inside the tea earlier to calm down the mermaid and to stop her from using any powers. Other than that, she didn't catch the mermaid and she surely didn't kill it either. She was back to being cuffed in a coffin stuffed behind a wall, she wasn't fed again, she couldn't scream as one of the wives sewing her mouths and eyes, and she was never wet again.

The women in the end were mysteriously committing suicide. However, Mrs. Elaine C. Hanks knew it was the mermaid's vengeful ghostly essence picking at them one after another, leaving her in the lurch. After months of listening to the mermaid's whispery grim song, she became deranged and finally without control she kept walking into the ocean where a group of sirens finished her off.

Gramps said he remembered his family finding a decayed woman's body in the lighthouse, and a decayed woman deep in the ocean. His father told him the story of who they were, and that she was the great-great grandmother of Gramps. Everyone back then believed there was a mass murderer 150 years ago in the late 1800s. Gramps father was also a police officer, so when he accidentally spilled water on a part of the lighthouse body and fish scales appeared, he realized the story was true.

Sirena told Joshua that as a Hanks he was a descendent of one of Sullivan's Island's, South Carolina founder families with a devastating secret. With his great-great-great-great grandparents as the first humans of South Carolina who betrayed the merfolk treaty, that once occurred. The sirens began to imagine that Joshua and Gramps had something to do with the oldest siren sister Dianthus disappearance.

I was becoming riled up listening to all of this, why was she looking at me as if she believed I would do such a horrible thing. Why should all the Hanks be held under the knife because of the oldest Hanks generation? This had me wondering and wanting answers of my own. "Sirena, you had your chance to speak, and you still don't trust me. Now, I have my own question, which never occurred to me I would ask. My father could swim a boat through anything, so it was curious as to how they died from a storm. Hearing that story of the past, makes me wonder if your fostered siren family had anything to do with my parents' death…Well, is it?!"

I was completely irate so I wasn't surprised when Sirena said, no Hanks can change, and ran away crying before jumping into the ocean. Rosemarie looked at me and said, "Look I don't know you, but you are a Hanks, so does it make me uneasy to know that you and your grandfather know about us, yes! Even more so when my sister is missing! I think you can understand that, so if you hear anything use this conch and call out my name."

It's been some time, and the very last time I saw Sirena, she called me a pitiful fake and perhaps wished to knock me in the face.

I have demonstrated moreover that I would do everything in this world to keep her safe, yet still the mistrust spread through both sides of our relationship like wildfire. She understood my heart and soul, although possibly I was mistaken. My heart continued pounding for her, although opposed to a chest that felt hollow. Sirena swam for a long time reflecting, encircling vessels of sharks, gliding among mysterious waves. That same evening, I was unable to sleep, therefore I took the time to reflect on myself.

Normally taking a stroll helps me to feel tired, thus I reflected all over the shoreside opposite sides of the lighthouse that nighttime. However, it was the greatest fault. Once I left the house, I overheard something in the sand dune bushes. I supposed it was just a coyote or a salt-water marsh hen wandering near, therefore I resumed walking. Just then I heard tones, genuine and gorgeous chanting lulling me as of the coast, where three beautiful women were ready and waiting for me. The stars gleam down on us with no mists in the heavens.

I did not acquire a great deal of time to yell, far less time to breathe when the sea engulfed me whole. I did not fight back for this was something not merely incidental. The briny water overflowed my mouth, so far someway I was able to still take breaths as the sirens lured me to their nest. One of the sirens cast a charm that created a snorkel bubble giving me continuous supply of oxygen. Finally, we met with the person who looked like a ruler of all sirens, Queen Dionysus. I know she wants answers for her missing daughter, but they are speaking in tongues as well as, I don't even have any answers. I could tell we were in an abandoned underwater jail cell, as the pressure of my chest was tight.

After an hour of listening to sirens screeching at each other, Queen Dionysus came down to where I was caged. She finally opened up to me and spoke in English. With anger she desperately begged me for her daughter back, telling me that Dianthus was her first baby and just like any of her daughters she cannot bear to think of losing them especially to a fisher. I kept yelling at her I did not know where she was, nor did I even know how she looked. She put her hand over my head to give me a vision of her daughters' appearance, then she said she was going to send me back and that I had a week to find out if there was any news of Dianthus being captured or worse. She sent her daughters to take me back to my home, and now I had a task to look for a missing siren, meanwhile Sirena wasn't around to save me in any way.

Ah, how good it feels to be back home! After washing up, I sat across my television making a list of potential ideal places where Dianthus could be. The door rings. I jumped. I'm nervous to open the door because I'm scared it's those wretched siren sisters again. Then the bell rings yet again. However, I begin to hear paces on the doorstep in back of me. She's gazing at me, looking down. My stomach begins somersaulting, my guts weaving in knots.

"Sirena," I say, half in surprise and half just to say her name once again. She's wearing an appearance as she's awaiting rage from myself, anger that just doesn't exist. Everything I possess for her is more than love itself, I only want to protect her. She won't accept it at the moment; she feels greatly mislaid remorse. There was a moment, I attempted to speak my voice waned into jumbled mutters, I meant to tell her that I love her just I didn't imagine she'll trust me; and I'm terrified it will seem meaningless. She's disheartened in me, she doesn't realize I never abandoned hope she'd come back. So, I draw nearer enough to touch, her eyes are the constant periwinkle, still that outstandingly charming woman from the shore. But then her hand rises, soundlessly while she touches my face.

CHAPTER 5

irena came back from the ocean and explained that her eldest sister, Dianthus, was overly protective of her and had planned to kidnap Sirena. She ended up separating herself from the sirens nest and swam too close to the surface for a couple of days spying on them. Rosemarie told Sirena, that she tried to stop Dianthus mad behavior. Which led to the last night that she saw her, they went out swimming in the ocean, searching for food as Rosemarie tried to talk some sense to her. However, Dianthus wanted Sirena back in the ocean just like the rest of the family, so she didn't care what Rosemarie had to say and ended up in a brawl. Rosemarie admitted it was stupid for both of them, because they must've shown their fins above water even at night. As soon as she left, she heard Dianthus cry. She tried to get back as soon as she could, but the only thing left was a harpoon gun.

I began wondering about the harpoon gun, which must've been a diver and I knew many of them in town. I told Sirena we might have to begin with narrowing down the divers, find out if we hear anything. The next day, Rosemarie realizes she should turn on the Hanks land next to my guesthouse, that the three of them together would be better, specifically since Rosemarie and Dianthus shared DNA and a deeper connection. The Queen didn't approve much of the idea of having a human ally, nevertheless she understood Rosemarie's potent connection with Dianthus. Beyond understanding that by doing this, she was bringing dignity to the realm.

Baffled and wobbly on her feet, Rosemarie turned her back from the sea and resumed trudging past me and towards Sirena until her legs failed her, this was definitely her first time on land. Walking towards Hanks Custom Boats, Rosemarie began examining each wooden boat around the wharf for all traces that may guide her to their sister. After I let my employees know, everything was okay and to go back to work, Rosemarie looked strangely at the Hannibal boat, she climbed aboard, and Sirena followed after.

Rosemarie reached for Sirena's hand and as she touched the base of the boat at the same time, they looked as if they were seeing something together. Sirena said she was seeing Rosemarie's vision. "Rose has many talents more than any siren, right now she can see what Dianthus saw that night. She got into a brawl with Rose, she swam away into a territory that was too close to the shore. Dianthus turned when she saw a diver all suited up with a harpoon gun. She tried to swim in the direction of the diver in order not to get struck, since she's the eldest, that makes her the fastest swimmer. But he was timid which helped him pull the trigger faster and hit her deep in her fin. Along with it shot three harpoons and was attached with rope. He was alone and was easily capable of swimming back to the boat, she tried to *Sirened* the diver, but she was held upside down and the harpoons dug into her fin making her scream. Because of the severity of a siren's anatomy such as sharp fangs, claws, venomous pelvic fin spines, and their barb stinger. Okay, I see that he went on the boat and used the rope to pull her in. She bled all over his ship, the diver removed his suit, but she didn't see who it was since she fainted."

I informed the sisters of the difficult news, which was that I knew whose boat belonged to the diver, it was Uncle O'Connor's. Which meant Dianthus had to be somewhere around his home, I quickly looked at Rosemarie's fierce eyes, and pleaded that she'd would not hurt me and said, "Trust me Rosemarie, I hate the bastard myself, he's a gigantic prick! I know he does horrible things, anything to get under my skin. But honestly, I never thought he would go this far. He doesn't even believe in my Gramps stories about merfolk!"

Sirena helped me to stop her sister Rosemarie from hurting me, so she said, "Help, get our sister and I won't rip you to shreds! However, I can't say much about your uncle. We need medicines. I feel her pain." I was confused by what she meant; however, I knew a great place to grab some medicine, we were lacking supplies anyways at the research center.

Getting to the Sullivan's Island Aquarium, the undersea women waited for me as collected the aid we needed, as far as the vision shown. The ladies observed the marine animals that was held in captivity. They watched the shark dive show, that included the trained instructor and the participants put in a cage— in the midst of encircling sharks. But the sharks sensed their appearance and came to be hostile. They began hammering around and crushing the cage. They could recognize Rosemarie was a hunter. Which led to her feeling enraged, hissing at the sharks, as her scalpel-like teeth began to show. Just in the nick of time, I rushed in their direction of them, quick enough to get the ladies away.

I'm becoming more and more concerned regarding the sister's wellbeing, what is more is if she was even living and breathing. As the sisters stood at my house creating what looked like an, enchanted meditation bond to locate Dianthus. I kept searching for any further clues, during the course of the first two days all I could do was shake my head as if telling them, "Sorry ladies, nothing yet." The sisters agreed with me that even with the indications they had by far, they required to know the most recent. Though, Sirena shed many tears believing it might be too late. Unlike Rosemarie, she seemed very firmed for the both of them. In life, I've known that at hand there are so many beings who've come across moments when terrible fortune comes. And hence some pause to find out what on earth the universe has in the making for them, just how they'll be able to make something decent come from something slightly unpleasant. Before Rosemarie, I had never seen it in action before, I never seen someone understand when it was the time to cry and when it was the time to manage. On my parent's funeral day, my family didn't cope well, everyone was either crying or acting like assholes. I sat around crying, arguing, and ashamed of myself. Though, I guess with Sirena I managed my finest to create something magnificent flourish as of the ashes of what I loved so very much.

Later on, that noon, I couldn't doze off. As a result, I chose to take off and rummage around for Dianthus, even as the ladies were trying to slumber off a little of the tension. I felt like the greatest path to hear about certain noise was from our bar. As I pass by the remote lighthouse. My beliefs lingers keen on the mysterious imaginations amongst flashes. As the view sneaks away, a burst of wind leads me back to my pursuit. My uncle was indeed an asshole. I pretended to hang out at the bar called *Poe's Tavern*, just for my delight. When sailors returned home, this was the main spot they came to, especially after reuniting with their family. They lounged all along the tavern booth, as well as the seats. I sat on a bar stool in the center ordering a pint, scraping away the cocktail napkin in front of me. I needed to grab interest from either the townspeople who might've heard gossip from my uncle, or my uncle himself. I was paying attention to all the chatter and rumors spreading like a disease. The men from the bar were as fed up, just as housewives, and telltales only fascinated on a share of tragedy. The townsfolk went there when they needed to be found. On the other hand, my uncle sat alone abandoned at the booth table, bearded as if he was overly busy these days, and I faked like I didn't notice him. Uncle O'Connor drank a lot, but this day he drank more than usual, he had a few Guinness pints in front of him possibly out of his anguish and remorse. But then, he called-out for me just like I anticipated, though it sent my pulse ahead some notches.

"Nephew, over'ere, ah, I'm so glad til see ye. Dis is gunna soun' aff your nut, maybe I'm aff your nut, but you're roi. Feck me for sayin' dat, anyways. I'ave til tell ye somethin', but dis stays between us, roi?" But, of course, this was going to stay between us, as well as my hidden iPhone recorder and the sisters at home. That goes without saying. I began to question a bit how much of this conversation was aimed at being straightforward, given that he wasn't quite sober. Though, there is the fact that when the booze is talking, it amplifies your thoughts including your truths. Even if it's your secrets…let's just hope I'm the only one he amplified his thoughts too.

"Uncle, I don't know whatever you're trying to speak about. If you could perhaps hurry through and decide on a topic, that would be wonderful. Umm, this is like our extremely sociable single time of catching up, so can you just spit it out?" I stayed anticipating that sitting down in the opposite of him right now, felt like a waste of my time. I wasn't just as sure any longer if he was paying the slightest bit of attention to me. I set out to leave behind hope about unearthing any details of a capture, and for me that was gold. I may not have a true relationship with my uncle, but I've seen what those sirens can do. I rather hear that it was someone who stole his boat…anything else, than feed him to the sharks so for a moment it felt like everything was okay, just a drunk uncle, up until he finally resumed.

"But den again, maybe it's best til keep quiet, but I jist can't leave ye in th' dark especially whaen it may'ave til deal wi' me brah'der. So, I'm gonna tell ye de truth, an' ye cud do whaat ye want wi' it, maybe it'll'elp both av us. I foin a feckin cod doll, I'm not sure whaat she is, she jist screams…'ave'er'eld captive." Oh no, it was him! And that's the thing that rushed through my head. He enjoyed calling mermaids and sirens, cod dolls, when he made fun of me or Gramps. I in fact, felt the name was somewhat sweet. However right now, he was talking as if *cod dolls* weren't simply absurd rumors. What's more, he's creating such specifics as a normal abductor, in addition he considers they have something to do with my parents' death. What if he begins a larger conflict?

I look intently at him with an exceptionally concerned face. "Okay, Uncle O'Connor I think you may have had too much Guinness to drink. You don't believe in ocean stories. Besides, we all know is just Gramps and it's for entertainment." I pretend to doubt everything. As if, I by no means believed in Gramps tales. This here and now, was becoming to near too the truth, I was now wishing that he have been overly plastered and daydreamed everything. The creepiest thought slithered in my mind for a moment, if my uncle became a captor, what if he also became sick, such as a beast-like. What if he started to…I don't even want to say it in my head, but almost all abductions end this way…what if he craved her and began touching her. I would hope that my own prick of an uncle wouldn't do such a thing. For now, I stood calm, rhythmically exhaling echoes from within. I breathed slowly in, and then breathed slowly out. I hoped that my deceptions was convincing enough.

"I'ad til git away from me house, she screams loudly until I put a gag on'er mouth!'aha!" I hesitated for a short time, pondering the specific key words he used. The beyond specifics he gave me, the further sexual perversion I assumed. I began taking extra mouthfuls of the Guinness he bought me, struggling to feel fairly calmer than I was. I'm baffled however, was Dianthus attempting to make use of her siren songs opposed to him, if so, exactly how come it didn't work. Currently, I know the sisters and I are seeking for a siren who isn't going to be creating any sounds, all for the reason that she's gagged.

"Sure, she does…" I replied with a smirk on my appearance along with brows reaching the skies. I kept my incredulous expression after listening to his extra shocking secrets. Keeping the "I still don't believe you" appearance. Even though I had, and I remained utterly appalled by the thoughts. I watched my uncle and though he was telling the truth, he behaved like a lunatic. As he drank chuckling about the siren that I faked to not know about, his hair danced with the fans breeze hitting him.

"I'm not feckin lyin'. Ah, so it's onest for your Gramps til tell ye the stories, but whaen I say, I'm a liar. Question, ye tink dat within each av us thar's a demon? I 'ave til say it, I saw dat damn tin' swimmin' an' I bloody murder than been seen as a coward." Even though there's plenty I still can't grasp as of my uncle's accent, everything I understand by means of his reactions, is that he can't comprehend if he's done something in the wrong. Confirming to me he still has a bit of a moral conscience. Not that I'm going to introduce him to the sisters, but I guess I can say I feel something for the unfortunate asshole.

"And how come nobody else knows in this town, everybody knows each other's fucking secrets? Wouldn't you be notice having a fish large in your boat?" I already knew most of the answer to this, however I needed to hear it from him while still looking in disbelief. The sun-bathe was steadily retreating from the sky as sundown approached. My curiosity felt like it was turning into shades of dread along with fear. I wondered if Dianthus sensed her sister around on land, if so, if she tried making plans to escape. It did look like my uncle escaped from an island after a few weeks, his mustache changed into an almost full-grown beard. So, it was obvious that he kept a good eye on her. My lush imagination turned keen on overdrive with possibilities. How did every single element actually appeared, in existence?

"I went feckin fishin' in de feckin afternoon, it wus'ardly anyone round de docks. I didn't plan til go into de water. All of a sudden, I see dis big fin splashin' round, an' it wus naw shark or a whale. Called me feckin attenshun so I grabbed me gear, an' jist in case I'ad me'arpoon, an' I swam til check. An' whaat I foun' wus scary an' feckin amazing at de seem time. I tink she wus gonna til feckin kill me, I tart they were supposed til be gran', so I shot'er." Well, my uncle didn't know what he actually was dealing with. He must've been genuinely terrified. Although, I wonder how much he ever grasped from Gramps constant conversations as a child, because that could've saved both him and Dianthus, he wouldn't have been in his boat that size at that time especially by himself.

"Yeah, yeah, yeah. Well, those are the stories grandpa says, they are good stories they are meant to be only stories! I really think now you are getting things into your head with these drinks as well. Does this have anything to do with your divorce?" It was harsh bringing up his divorce, Cheryl was still upset about it, but I really had to be seen as someone who didn't believe anything he was saying. Even if it meant hurting him and making him feel crazy. Besides he wasn't the sweetest thoughtful uncle, especially at my parent's funeral.

"Do ye know I came til ye for feckin advice? Ye proobably don't believe me cos ye don't know de tip of de iceberg. I captured'er, she wus vicious spiky everywhere an' I tink she might be poisonous, I may be dense til ye but I'ave feckin brains ye know, I'm actually doin' studies on. Well, I'm delivering parts of'er an' givin' it til de research labs." Oh fuck! I believed touching her would've remained the most unpleasant grotesque news to hear, as it would create a greater monster beyond him than he normally is. Similar to an old-fashioned grim edition of *Beauty and the Beast*. Nevertheless, he was dissecting her, which is what I did not imagine by any means. I never thought of him being smart enough to try to dissect, hence I in no way supposed he would think of such things. Just how foolish am I? Anybody who captures something exceptional would choose to show off or sell it one way or another.

Experiments meant he was also getting ready to show it off to the world. I hope they don't know if they even know how to analyze her, but still if they could connect the dots in any way that would be dangerous to all the sea-folk. I kept listening, pretending I was very skeptical. But I thought to myself of the kind of experiments scientists would do on a siren. Analyze her voice box in order to captivate singing voices and lure as well, analyze her gills slits and webbed hands and scales in order to understand transformation, discover if her siren tears can heal or make ocean gemstones like in many myths, analyze her stinger by seeping her poison, and who knows probably check if her fertility is compatible with humans to produce hybrids. I felt bad thinking of a trapped girl in a water well who had no choice for herself.

"Let me cut you off there, supposedly you are doing experiments. Do you know how crazy you sound? But you know what, just for the sake of it since…you and I hate each other's guts…please continue because you're actually making my day." He had to seem like a ridiculous twisted soul loon, along with essentially believing it.

"Feck ye nephew, ye're de wan who first believed in dis cr'ahp! If I figure oyt a way til evolve us cos of whaat I captured, you're gonna kiss me arse. I don't really want til explain every detail cos I still can't believe it meself! Ye feckin preck! I'm only tellin' ye, in case dees cod dolls are responsible of de death of me brah'der an' your ma. Cos if so, den I tink I'm takin' feckin justice an' deir fishtail demons cud kiss me arse." I have got without a doubt that sea-folk might carry genes that us, as humans can benefit from. Imagine living on land as well as being able to breathe in the deep sea, or illnesses that you can't ever catch. Though this was still inhumane, and this was turning out to become a toxic path spiraling downwards.

"I think it's true that my parents died from a boat accident, not because of the fish woman. I'm sorry if I made you feel any way Uncle O'Connor, please let me listen…but stop with the drinking it's making me feel concerned."

"Concerned, concerned! I am in a de roi mind; so, I'm feelin' submissive til brutality an' infuriashun. She screamed so much in a weord angelic way, I'ad til gag'er especially if I didn't want til git caught. De town wus pretty much empty cos everyone wus at de parade. It wus easy til put me boat away, at de seem time put'er in de back of my trunk. But I'ad til leave nets on'er, cos she cud put up a scrap dat bitch! Yeah, she wus a fighter'til we got home." While speaking to him, everything I could see was a man that had darkness inside him. A darkness that intimidated me as I listened. His tone of voice slithered up my arm, as if I were listening to it from a horror film.

"I learned a few things dat first noight, she speaks any language. She spoke til me in English…pretty much…she is a tough cookie wi' a mouth. Den on top of dat, later on she got so dried up she started sproutin' legs, I didn't want dat. If dat'appened, den she'll run knowin' dat I wouldn't be able til make any…um…ah roi, analysis! But I maintained de bitch, nah I tink she's pretty much so weak. I'ad ter leave de house dees past few days, 'tis'er singin' dat I'ad til fend a way til take care of." Oh, my goodness, we had to find her shortly. The siren wasn't the same as maintaining a goldfish, she needed salty ocean water, and he didn't realize the way he held her captive was a disgrace. He wasn't only dehydrating her, from time to time, but he was providing fresh water to a saltwater mammal. Aside from the fact that my uncle revealed nourishing her through a cupful of blended canned fish using a straw, so she wouldn't bite him.

"Uncle O'Connor, you sure you don't have a girl, a *human* girl captured in your house? And does your daughter, Cheryl, know anything about this?" My eyes darted from side to side, as he continued. Up to now, I'm predicting because every person was loud-mouthed and intoxicated, they haven't overheard a word.

"Do ye tink I'm dense? Why wud I kidnap a girl? I'ave me own daughter ye know.'ell feckin naw, I won't tell'er dis. I know me precious daughter, she tells everythin' til everyone, an' I know me daughter…she's not really s-straight…in de noggin I mean. She'll probably get aff wit' de wagon." It was hilarious to know, that even Uncle O'Connor understood his daughter was a gossip diffuser and a sexaholic. In any case, I appreciate I wasn't the only one who noticed such things.

"Well, Uncle O'Connor that was a lot, that you told me…I'm not sure I'm much of a believer…I love listening to Gramps stories, but this one… is like top one! Perhaps you could say like the thriller versions of what he tells me. All I can suggest to you uncle, is to shave that beard because it's really scruffy, and lay off the rum please! Well, I gutta go now, I have a date. It was actually really fun talking to you, that was a really delightful story. Love you Uncle O'Connor it's nice to know that you actually have a creative side." I began walking away after giving him a nice pat on the back, leaving him to believe I never believed in such things. But I also couldn't allow him to think I had bad thoughts towards him, or that I had any plans against him, which I did. He given me all the necessary information, perhaps not the exact location of the well, but I now know the condition of the siren that Rosemarie even feels. I ordered a few more Guinness for my uncle, and left him to continue his sorrows, hoping he would end up absolutely drunk on the other side of Carolina.

CHAPTER 6

ver the last few days, so much has happened. Time and again, Gramps had been asking me about my whereabouts at college, work, and home. All I kept doing was brushing him off. The only time I haven't brushed him off, was when I asked him questions about Uncle O'Connor's land. But he never mentioned anything about a well and kept looking at me strangely. After Poe's Tavern, I sat near the lighthouse, Gramps was so concerned and frustrated with me and kept asking questions like, where I've been. I must've been a little tipsy and tired at the time because I literally said to him, "Trying to find a siren." I just walked away from him and went back into my guest house. That night, I told the sisters everything, though for now I left some details out, hoping they wouldn't ever find out about my uncle's project with their sister. They were heartbroken, even Rosemarie. No individual deserves that.

The next day, after giving up searching around my uncle's land, Rosemarie felt something coming from the woods. Therefore, we threaded through the forests with slow accuracy and mercy, weaving, and treading, by a whisker cracking any branches. Rosemarie, holding Sirena's hand, sang a siren song that wouldn't harm me but instead lead a trace towards Dianthus. We all knew she wouldn't make a sound, but the song was Rose's compass and we had to follow.

As we walked deeper in, we finally found the water well, right in the middle of the forests. Of all the times that I used to come over my uncle's property, I never acknowledged that in the vicinity was a water well. It was out of sight, with a mixture of twigs and leaves burying it similar to camouflages. Then we overheard muffling happening from the inside of the water well.

In a water well, a paralyzed Dianthus stood trapped in a prison formed of a tower of cobbled stones. Nearly close to the brink of death, in my uncle's woods. Her long, chocolate-brown hair hung lifelessly around her waist, her skin was drying up and any longer it would come to be blackened in addition to shriveled away. There, she looked malnourished, hurt by the harpoon, and by the look of the well from afar it was more than obvious that my uncle was examining her and taking samples. I truly hoped that he would be across Carolina because the sisters looked outraged.

Dianthus's fin had become irritable and flaky the longer she remained in the well water in her siren form. She needed to be in the salty ocean. Like Rosemarie, she was feeble only worse. They both needed some nutrients as soon as possible. For now, I was prepared with cups for all the sisters, especially Dianthus, with fresh herring and cod fish smoothies, her favorite like Rosemarie mentioned.

In Dianthus's human form she looked possibly in her mid-30s. She was staggering, struggling to flee from me in the loop of cobbled stones, covered in grime, sewage, and what seemed to be blood. As I stared in shock and apprehension. The sisters as well as Dianthus were sobbing, although not some normal cries. They were tears of terror, sorrow, agony, and potentially death. She was gushing black blood all over. I gazed at her in fear, as she attempted to shriek out, "You...don't...touch...me!" It wasn't unusual...her fear of my kind. She only displayed strange menacing actions against me because of the relentless cruelty. In spite of this, I volunteered to get in the well with her, in order to assist her. Dianthus turned out to be tremendously vicious towards me, trying to bite and sting me as her loathing for humans significantly intensified, as I tried moving in closer to her to check her wounds.

The sisters above tried to calm her hissing at me, Rosemarie must've said something effective because she finally stopped moving though still looked at me in a skeptical way. Dianthus health was deteriorating as her gill slits showed her breathing becoming more exhausting and she began coughing. Worried, I yelled up to the sisters that she was sick, and her wounds were infected. She was thin enough to carry her bony arms clasps about my neck, and her fin wasn't as heavy as it should be, therefore as I placed Dianthus in the old tin bath-and-pulley the sisters were easily able to pick her up.

Before anything, I needed the tin bath filled with water to clean off any evidence that Dianthus left, which included any of her body waste. I had to hurry for Dianthus's sake, and so we wouldn't get caught. But the evidence had to disappear now! Just in case, my uncle wanted to come down to check if he was going mad. Cleaning off the bloodied fingernails in the cobbled stones, shoveling her defecation, along with picking up each flaky fallen scale around the well deeply saddened me. But in the end, it had to be done and the well almost looked brand new. Simply one issue that was intolerable to me…though the well seemed tidy Rosemarie felt that my uncle needed to feel genuinely insane. Because after all he did see a fin, and he did see a siren. So, there was only one way she felt that he could forget this happened, as I was cleaning up, she put a drop of obliviousness potion in each of his Guinness, enough to forget a month.

From there on we went to my Research Center which was gratefully empty. Dianthus hesitantly granted me to analyze her currently human legs that had a few slices open with a 2-inch gash that were partially covered in faded scales. However, once she was isolated with me, she was so terrified that she began singing a siren song, radiating a mesmerizing sound that practically compels me. Though I was still *Sirened* I saw Sirena trying to suspend her singing, while Rosemarie just stood before me while laughing and slapping me in the face. I couldn't move, as if I was paralyzed however, I heard Sirena say, "You are very sick and wounded. He can help with your human legs, look at your scales they are gray and dry, and sister you're scarcely breathing." When Dianthus coughed a handful times, she cease the paralyzing siren song, Rosemarie was getting ready to go back in the ocean.

Sirena wondered why and Rosemarie said, "The Hanks may be able to sew up the gashes, but in order for those slices to heal correctly she needs one of my creams. And you know the only ingredients I use is from the ocean. Besides, I haven't been on land as long as you have Sirena, my skin is starting to feel itchy I need to get into the ocean to relieve it for a while. Once I gather all the ingredients I will come back and make my cream." Sirena's adoptive sisters' kinship were very overprotective in their ways, although we haven't agreed on certain terms. Rosemarie calling me, "Hank" proved furthermore how much she loathes me.

"I promise that I can heal your sister, I have bandages, plenty of fluids, and antibiotics here—" But Rosemarie just glared at me and interrupted me.

"You don't realize we are from the ocean, right? Come on, get it through your thick skull, not everything you do is correct! My sister is in pain, that is unbearable, and I feel it! And you will not understand why! We are connected by the ocean. By our mother, therefore our sisters feel the same pain! Do you expect that I will just wait months for your medicine to work, when I can use my creams to heal her in an instant?" Rosemarie's bluntness and hard-hearted attitude wasn't pushing away, I just kept feeling I needed to prove to her that I was worthy.

"But you might not even understand what's wrong with her, I can tell from the EEG's and the scans, I can research what's wrong through her blood and other samples." Rosemarie, as well as Sirena looked confused and quite shocked. As if they both believed I wanted to experiment on Dianthus. I admit it crossed my mind, I did feel like I had to understand my girlfriend and her family more. But perhaps their trust was more important right now.

"You can't! Are you that stupid? To collect examples from her, it's leaving breadcrumbs for anyone who finds them. You are such a Hanks! You may have helped found my sister, but I cannot trust you! Especially now with her life!"

"Rosemarie that's very unfair, you literally just saw me clean up earlier after her shit! I mean it, I promise you I'm only trying to help! And please stop calling me by my last name, I know why you're doing it." Calling me Hanks was like her way of calling me a lineage future murderer.

"I'll call you whatever I want! And, like I said, you don't understand us! Your pictures will only show her human form, but she uses her fin. She's not a dolphin or a fish, that you held captive and treated. We are different from you and other sea mammals. And so is my sister Sirena, even if she doesn't get it through her own head. I'm going to the ocean now, gathering ingredients and coming back!"

I quit my talking back to her, but I whispered to myself, "Please, take your time and hopefully get lost somewhere."

Dianthus's ailment had deteriorated further, so she granted me to finally look at her. Her entire frame was immediately coated in darkened peeling skin still in her human form, in addition to she was exceptionally dried. To calm her down as I looked at her, I told her how entranced her song was to me, and how I could still hear the echo of it in my head. Dianthus looked astonished to hear me speak to her as she was even an individual, individual who mattered, not simply a withering treacherous sea-creature who remained overly stubborn to die any faster. While my gaze fell on her, I felt a warmth that was practically too daunting to trust, and though my tone was uneasy soothing and delicate as well.

As a result, Rosemarie swiftly said her farewell, and at last vanished. From the cameras, I was able to see a few miles around the perimeter even in the ocean. Sirena and I watched the harbor's cameras, to make sure she was safe. From what I saw, I felt a bit sorry for Rosemarie. She began hauling herself along the pier and ultimately plummeted into the salt water. As soon as she appeared, she stripped her clothes off sooner than her shifting began. Then my heart raced, as I noticed that it seemed like she was crying in anguish as her change arose. It wasn't exactly the way Sirena transformed; her razor-sharp teeth appeared like shark teeth and her fingers changed into weblike hands with talons. Sirena didn't have any of that nor pelvic fins and the stinger. When she was done, she finally swam away swiftly.

Sirena said everything was great, and normal. So, I went back to my patient, however maybe Rosemarie was correct. Her traumatization didn't do me any justice when I wanted to give her IV fluids for her dehydration. Being treated as a lab experiment and suffering as a result of being prodded with needles, scales being yanked, poison being drawn, and undernourished to keep her from whipping and lashing around. Feeling miserable for Dianthus, I thought about how she was thrust into a realm of menacing darkness from the deep. She was compelled to bend at the wills of her captor, setting forth to encounter her identity as rather troubled. With the purpose of existing in a world where she was merely a silhouette, a cruel man's pearl.

While we hung around for Rosemarie, I closed my eyes for a brief time. I immediately recalled the moment of standing within the water well, just as if I were still deeply rooted inside. Struggling to get my head round every one of the gathered pieces of DNA evidence. Blood and feces splattered along the flooring. Partial fingernails embedded in the cobbled stones walls. Bearing in mind, the blood dousing my top. Urine and feces caking my fingers, my neckline. More than the appalling blood that engulfed my mind and suffocated the atmosphere of a foul-smelling rust sickness.

* * *

After grinding the ingredients into a porridge, Rosemarie realized that Dianthus wouldn't even consume. Rosemarie cranked her head towards the side, in the hunt for her back-up plan. She thrust her hand in her seaweed barnacle encrusted bag and hauled out a large precious wentletrap seashell. Then grinded sea salt, fish scales, pinch of sea sponge, sliver of salt meadow cordgrass and stuffed it in the seashells massive hole. As well as laid it to her sister's lips as Dianthus at last gave it a puff. Smoke fluttered her lips.

I gave her the stink eye. How in the hell was smoking any of this stuff going to work? As she remained burning, somehow Dianthus began breathing and her skin became hydrated again and moist.

I retrieved her barnacle encrusted purse from the other room, and stride back to Rosemarie.

I placed it on the counter and partly opened it, "Right now, what's this meant for?"

Rosemarie rolled her eyes as she snatched her purse back, rubbing fingers together. "Now that she is hydrated, she is able to breathe better, I can heal her wounds. Now, just sit!"

I did, although I vowed if she told me to *stay*, I was going to freak.

"So, what are you creating this time?" I began scratching my head, it started feeling beyond intimidated being about two sirens that really didn't enjoy having my company.

Rose said out loud, "A ointment! Now, let me think and leave me be!" I did, she seem like the witch of her family, and I didn't want to know what she could do with my food or hair gel. She began whispering the same ingredients she used for the seashell pipe, but then whispered, "Let's see, a few drops of sacred water from the waterfall, half a sea bass, two seahorses, seaweed, Coastal Sweet-pepperbush, and a sliver of Devilwood, along with a pint of octopus ink." There was something else that she chanted, although because it sounded like Italian, I didn't understand it, then unexpectedly the concoction turned into a lime ointment. She gently rubbed it on her sister's gashes and bruises, talking to her with very much love, in a tone that calmed and revealed amazing emotive affection. The side I haven't seen much in Rosemarie.

Clutching her sister's hand in hers, Rosemarie said she'd be better and gave me the *okay* to give Dianthus IV fluids, now that her skin was able to accept it. Part of getting better would be going back into the ocean. But after deleting the video tape from Rosemarie's transformation, I needed everyone to leave around my home.

* * *

Though Dianthus's gashes and bruises were gone within seconds, and her skin was moist allowing her to breathe, she couldn't swim yet. The muscular tissue in her legs that were constantly permitting her to plunge in the ocean, were now asking her so shockingly intensely not to. To locate a welcoming and cozy venue as Dianthus weren't ready to transform. She claims her head feeling like a whirlpool, and her head intends so greatly for mermaids to calm the waves. Everything regarding her, as of the muscular aches to the emotional friction towards exhaustion, the fatigue was irresistible —therefore, showing Dianthus my empathy for such matters I asked the sisters to rest in safety at my guesthouse to restore her strength. Rosemarie looked at me as she usually did, iffy, until I explained, "It'll be your sanctuary for now, don't worry about me…I'll be in my old room in my Gramps house. I'll visit occasionally. I think it would be best for Dianthus to dip her legs into the ocean when nobody is around, so her health can sort of regenerate faster." Dianthus looked at me as if she was impressed, but Rosemarie looked at me as if she were shocked, she hadn't thought about that first.

* * *

Rosemarie analyzed me for a while as I tucked Sirena to sleep. I decided to just come straight out with it, as well as longed I wouldn't get myself into any problems. I sauntered to her and asked if she could clear the waters amongst myself and her mother, for my peace of mind.

"Are you sure you don't need to ask me something else?" Rosemarie questioned sarcastically, as if I disturbed her with way too much already.

I answered, no, I just didn't want the Queen ordering her sirens to kidnap me or worse, because I would now be passing her scheduled date.

55

Besides, I wanted to gain the trust of Sirena's family. Their mother needed to know that I would do anything for her, even if it included taking care of her sister from dying. Then she glimpsed at me gradually, very nearly as if she were reading my thoughts.

She suddenly laughed, "I understand, what you're feeling? Yeah, between us, my mother can be a psycho bitch! I'll take care of it, in fact I was on my way to go hunting for everyone, so I'll stop by to persuade, mother." I couldn't tell if she was drunk exactly, or if it was natural for her to be a plain asshole to me. That night, Rosemarie came back from speaking with her mother and she came back with three things. Two great news and a giant fish. The first news was that the Queen had accepted her daughters to stay longer on land for as long as Dianthus got better, the second news was something that she said she would say later which felt sort of nerve wracking, and lastly was a giant fish as somewhat of a piece offering gift for myself.

CHAPTER 7

ach time, my Gramps seemed slightly more confused and annoyed the longer I chose to sleep in my childhood room, in his house. So, it seemed only natural he'd become very curious and even more frustrated of the deceiving performances, especially with the fish that I brought for dinner that Rosemarie gave to me as a gift. The fish was a magnificent huge, coral pink, extremely fresh, and it wasn't just an ordinary pink snapper. It was a lovely Opakapaka which is native in the Hawaiian waters, so obviously I didn't go around the town and caught it myself, and I mean fresh as it was still wrapped neatly in seaweed and smelled lovely of the ocean…not ice cubes. Besides, it was mainly caught during the winter months, so a *special diver* in all probability had her connections. He asked so many questions wondering how I got it and where? Seeing the ridiculously huge fresh fish that was not from these waters made him even more curious. He still cooked the fish, it's not every time we get a fish like that unless you live in the area and catch yourself. A smelled the delicious scent of Asian-styled roasted fish with soy sauce and scallions. One of my favorites, but it would have to wait…I had to check up on the sisters.

I opened the kitchen's back entrance then rushed into the gust and felt it softly slip back. I took a deep breath of the cold sea air, as the moonbeams came up. I raced by the kitchen window that is foggy with the night's breath. Although a large amount of South Carolina was coated in dusk, the seaside clouds gradually began to splash around the twilight sky, changing silver with the mirror image of the moon. A minute later,

I reached the guestroom and opened the doorway, only to expect an appealing surprise.

My hands trembled on the guestrooom's handle, and the shivering didn't originate from the chill, but instead full of interest seeing the two siren sisters stronger than before and together. As of that initial glance, from the first instant, it was greater than a room— further even than the extremely stunning room I had yet seen. Three women wearing Cheryl's last year trending beach shear or lace outfits without any bras, therefore I've stared at their breast for a while. I stood at the entrance actually sizing them, for instance Rosemarie and slender breast, Dianthus with the huge breast, and then Sirena with her perfectly plumped medium sized breast. All three had tall hourglass dancing around to a song coming from the radio. The way they danced looked like they were swimming in the ocean. The music and laughter is probably why they continued dancing.

For that moment, I wished I had a camera to film them and keep this dance secured for my thoughts. I adored seeing Sirena sprang in her dance, as if it remained the one way her body genuinely understood how to communicate, within the waves of air. Her sensualness surged through into the highly vivid portrait of a charming spirit. I gaze at them, Sirena specifically, twirl to the harmony inside my guestroom. Soon after, without warning, the feelings shifted.

All at once, they stopped leaping and twirling all across the surface of the guesthouse. And by instinct, the siren sisters unexpectedly soared, then stood within an attack stance while hissing violently in the direction of me. Being far away and impassive, I felt like a stranger to them. As Sirena turned her eyes from me to her sisters, she looked anxious. I stand still and soundlessly because those are the ways the sirens hunt by means of movements and sound. But it wasn't me they were looking at. At the back of me, the thick gasping breath forces me to glance around swiftly and look behind.

Gramps! My heartbeat hastened to an anxious rhythm in my chest. He saw the ladies and to him they were a sight of wonder, even in their defense. He just pushed me aside and walked in, "Josh, you have beautiful ladies here, and you didn't think of introducing me? Especially, as I cooked this lovely fish! Anyone hungry?"

Gramps stepped forward. As the sisters steps back, I see Sirena look cheery before she hesitantly comes-forward. "You all have uniquely beautiful eyes. I've only seen that once before; her eyes were like the colors of the sunset." Gramps chuckled with cheerful teary eyes, as he ordered me around to get plates and utensils.

Sirena face was bursting with expression, "I remember listening to your storytelling before, I heard about that, *friend* of yours, she never left your side," she said. "She definitely loved you very much…sometimes the sea just takes…" In all honesty, I didn't understand whether she was trying to say something else.

Sirena given every appearance of being overjoyed to encounter Gramps. As it looked like she wanted to take out an old thorn of his heart. However, the sisters were outraged and confused about how open she was to another human.

"Who is this mortal, are you trying to reveal to him who we are?" Rosemarie whispered as loudly as she dared. At this point, I felt like I understood from her perspective, Sirena was coming out extremely intense and it was confusing to the others.

Walking closer to Gramps, Sirena reacted energetically. After hugging him, she said very cheerfully, "Well, this is sweet funny Gramps! He tells many wonderful stories of the ocean. And…"

Dianthus hissed as she walked around looking from me to Gramps then to Sirena. "Wait, you met him before…you let him see you in your true self?"

"Kind of?" Sirena shrugged.

"Oh, you're so sweet dear, but you don't have to vouch for me…" As a gentleman, Gramps gives her a peck on her lovely hand. Then begins chuckling after she reciprocated the act behaving as if she knew what this gesture meant and walked with full confidence to her sisters. Soon after he said, "She never met me face-to-face, I just know more about the sea than others. I already know the truth behind you ladies. Like how you two are sirens and she's a mermaid. I'm surprised to hear you are family because your realms have wars against each other. You…sirens are definitely a force to be reckoned with, and I know I should be pissing my pants, but you ladies are exotically spine chillingly beautiful. Like warriors I wouldn't want to fuck with." That actually made the sirens blush.

"I won't say anything about this, I'm just feeling fortunate to meet you. I almost believed my friend when I was young was a dream. The only thing that told me it wasn't, was the truth about my ancestors. I'm sorry for what they did, by the way. To you three, your realm, and the ocean. I promise myself and my grandson would never do anything to harm it." And just like that, the sirens were sweet on him. He spoke to them more and admitted how long he had known about them. He even apologized for the Hanks old history.

The sisters felt appreciated by his apology but still wanted to find out how did Sirena know the old man, even he was curious. She said that sometimes by Fire Island, she would listen to his mermaid stories whenever he took Josh fishing. She loved listening to them, and it helped her fall even more in love with Josh listening to his reactions.

"What?" Dianthus asked.

"Nothing," Sirena wrenches her gaze from Josh.

"I told you; you're being stupid!" Dianthus yells.

"You thought me inside the water well was bad, imagine when I go home, and mom asks where are you? Imagine what she would do to me. Exactly should I say? *Mother there is a handsome human that Sirena is in love with.*"

Sirena just scowls.

CHAPTER 8

The next day, Rosemarie pulled me aside and we walked around the beach. "Let me ask you something," she said. "And it's going to sound confrontational but please know that I don't really mean for it to be."

"Okay…what?"

"Do I know everything about you, Josh?" With a glare she asked.

The question took me by surprise. It also made me think of all the drama she'd been giving me and suddenly she was trying to connect with me. "Rosemarie, of course not, there's still many things you have to know. Same with you." I spoke the honest truth.

As we continued walking, I shared to Rosemarie, "Do you understand the bravery it took for me to pursue her, to grant her everything that was in my heart? She let me in and beamed at me. I poured my soul out to her. I told her I loved her, always had. That I wanted her…*Wanted.*" I spat the word out. Rosemarie turned away from me as if I were nothing, I was completely vile to her.

Later that day I spent it with Sirena, there was a terrific exchange of sunlight, stroking the fences, which were decorated with a velvety yellow, making the garden very lively. Sirena and I ate some butter pecan ice cream with Gramps peach cobbler, while consuming hours speaking about our dreams— mine which was taking care of the oceans, hers which was becoming an owner of the best apothecary shop.

I questioned, "Your family is still opposed to you staying here?"

"We can wisely say, it's an empowering monarchy matter. And that my mother's not too pleased with me. They gave a hell of a combat working to maintain me in their realm." Sirena stated sounding ashamed.

"I'm really sorry," I said. "That must be difficult."

I crossed my arms as I saw her look like she wanted to roll her eyes at me, "No way, I have no problem with that. A great deal have emerged that have been festering in me, anyway. She wanted me to take the crown. Living with them has been a given. I'd be a brilliant Queen like my mother, only stronger because of my mermaid abilities. Even the Queen expected it."

"I understand but it's still not fair, you don't even care for your royal status." I demanded.

That night we looked at the starry night at the lighthouse. Sirena said, "I would rather you keep close to me. Nevertheless, it's just life that is standing in our way and sandwiched between. I want to put an end to everything for a while and just gaze into your eyes as well sharing a moment of affection." It stood silent still, as if I heard the burning flames from the stars itself. I didn't want to speak. "Would you wish to say farewell to me tomorrow morning, as opposed to tonight?" Sirena questioned, sticking out her hand after turning on the radio so we could dance.

"What kind of question is that? I am never going to say goodbye, never for good," I cried out to her. This dance wasn't going to be my last…I hoped not.

"Don't make this harsher than it is, I'm leaving tomorrow morning," she said, dismayed as she spoke resting her head on my shoulder.

"You're not leaving, I won't let you go." I wept out as I twirled her without looking at her and pulled her back in.

"Well then, I don't love you anymore!" She shoved me away and was about to leave.

The few words that swung up in the air amongst a sincere deep love. I knew that she'd spoken to them. I'd watched her lips move, although I couldn't entirely bind my mind around the full weight of their meaning. I wrapped my arms around her before she went downstairs and I whispered, "Don't lie to me babe."

"Joshua dear, if you love me, don't make this worse for me." And she left for the guesthouse where the others waited.

But I had no intention of offering the love of my life, a true and final farewell. Rosemarie made some tea for everybody and said that it was another thanks. After I drank mine, suddenly I felt weary and fell asleep; awakening to discover it was still daylight. Fuck! that bitch drugged me, then I sprang to my feet in a horrendous panic. Only a glimpse of my watch comforted me. It was still in the early hours in the day. She glanced up at me and slightly grinned. My heart surged at Sirena's mystifying sweetness.

CHAPTER 9

The ladies were ready to dive and plunge into the sea, but I recalled how hesitant Sirena was to jump back into her old lifestyle. I saw a tear fall aside as they finally did, she didn't even look back. To look back, would she just leave her weak to the knees and keep her on the dock as an anchor. If only she looked back, I'd beg her once more not to leave and remind her why she couldn't leave. That the things she learned and loved on land wasn't going to be found in her ocean's realm. That being on land meant she had more than living with her ADOPTIVE MOTHER. But she didn't look back, and I didn't have any moment to persuade her to stay.

The different colored fins did one more unison flip into the tide. Then all I felt was heartache from the huge wave that covered her for sure.

I found myself waving goodbye, standing at the dock. The town at the rear of me still slumbered in warmth. The sea lengthened from aquamarine to dark cyan, before me serene in the still air.

It's nearly dark. I can't imagine how long I've been out here waiting for her to just pop up. The blackness covers the ocean and reaches the beach. Alone I hid in the dark. My chest is hollow and empty, as if she is ripping out my heart on purpose. I wish I knew she was at least ripping half of it to keep the other half with her.

Dawn breaks unwelcome and hazy against the bay windows of my bedroom. I groan and pull the quilt over my head, until I hear my grandfather's voice calling out my name. It's been a while since I went outside the guesthouse, it's 3 PM, which means that for the first time that Sirena left me, I have been glued to my bed for the last two days. I am not ready for this. The bay window doesn't look like an outgoing and cheerful day, all I see is gray outside. It looks cold, but I know it isn't. The wind whispers throughout the dune grass just beyond the front of my door. I wonder what the sea looks like this evening. For the first time since Sirena's leave, I decided to check.

But it takes a while because my room is full of all things of Sirena's. There is nothing that is on my desk, on my wall, or in my closet that has nothing to do with her. A bunch of seashells she collected, jewelry she'd created, ocean paintings, a bunch of ocean remedies, especially the plush seahorse that we won during our carnival date. I felt sad looking at everything, yet empty when I thought about throwing it all away.

I opened the glass sliding door to a warm breeze. And my bare feet sink into the cool sand. I stop a few feet from the wet sand and plop down, joining my knees to my chest and screaming out her name while tears streamed down my face.

My grandfather finally came and put his hand on my shoulder, and just stood there in silence for a few seconds until he decided to lift me up and walked me to the house.

Time unfortunately doesn't make it easy to stay on course.

After a few months at my Gramps, I gazed at the withering sun plunge below from the balcony of our house. I desired to settle here after dark, more than ever having worked strenuous hours all day, and grant my thoughts roam.

Gramps was right, I had to chase after my heart. So, I thrust past my loudmouth cousin, Cheryl, and made my way down the stairs leading to the pristine sand, grabbed my snorkel mask and fins then plunged into the ocean. The sea-folk are always attracted to their own kind- which helps them find each other miles and miles across the oceans. Of course, not being one of them meant I had to remember the location of the nest by memory, from the time I was held captive. Nevertheless, I wasn't even sure if they put a glamour on it.

CHAPTER 10

eep in the sea, I can feel the temperature of the water drop. Without a second layer of skin, it was like a winter chill. Those once golden rays from above are only blue in this water; and the deeper I swim the less light can penetrate. The rocks are now silhouettes in the dim. This part of the sea is darker, and I welcome being cloaked by its enfolding gloom.

Below me, a bunch of eels slinks through the depths, its body on the slightly blacker than the water surrounding it. When I tried my hardest, I can see old shipwrecks and sunken little boats, leading me like a sweet candy scent from a witch's home. I told myself, this was as good a place to start as any.

I feel the pull of a current, and for a moment, I consider letting it take me, but then I remember my quest. I swim faster as a shark tries darting for me. I noticed I was getting close when I saw something from the distance swimming towards an underwater cavern.

Her scales were emerald, green, and her brown hair barely reached her breast, which looked covered with brown seaweed. She didn't see me, and I wasn't even sure what species she was. Something just told me to follow her, she could have been stranded for all I know, but where I was sung to me.

It was a long way ahead as I swam closer. But the closer I swam, I realized that soon many more sea-folks swam up above towards the ocean. When I looked up to see where they were swimming, I realized there was a ship tearing through the sea. And the closer I sneakily got; I saw the sirens swim above water. From where I stood hidden, between a bright green algae large fissure underwater, they must've been singing because all I could hear was a humming, some sort of tune that was being sung above the ocean. It was obviously their deadly siren songs. For me, this was an agonizing wait, as a bunch of humans became prey. Some time passes, and the women have finished drowning the sailors and the Tritones watch around while leading them back to their realm.

I stood at a hole shaken. Staring at the light from the flames above, engulfing the ripped boat as it sank slowly. I wasn't sure what to do, should I risk checking if anyone was still alive, and even if they were would I even have a chance to help them get away from here or should I continue looking for her?

Because I don't have any supplies and nothing more but a harpoon gun to begin saving people, I decided to go for the girl!

However, I was not as comfortable as I was when I entered the water earlier. Entering the same passage, I swam past the invisibility glamour I remembered and swam within the nooks and crannies!

The sirens nest looked grander than before. Over the past few months that they've been here, it seems that they've been redecorating the sunken ships. They had humongous grand pieces of architecture that loomed above the deep ocean floor.

A piercing green and brown algae covered each statue, as its cold old marbled clean light color became a mystery, feeling rather unwelcoming as I swam by. On account of the corals, the windows seemed almost nonexistent as light traveled through them barely. Windows that gave the residents blinded eyes of the palace, that prevented them from seeing much outside. The siren realm cast a dark long shadow onto the palace. Green and red algae including seagrass decorated the palace's other entrance.

It was easy swimming for the fact that there was a forest of kelp all around the columns and skeleton's decorating each corner.

I was able to move further and further into the palace, I was completely invisible until the instant I saw Sirena's teal hair, Queen Dionysus caught me.

The siren Queen said, "If I would've known you were coming to my kingdom, I would have put the air bubble over since it looks like you need to preserve your oxygen when you go back from where you came from."

I looked in panic when I checked at how much oxygen I had. I have been further below than 10 feet in the ocean, and I wasn't sure if the full snorkeling mask would be able to take care of me. My plan was only halfway thought out, and perhaps less.

Her scary eyes suddenly strikes me when she grabs me, and remarkably the mask works better than earlier. It's as if I can breathe underwater.

"I see you making eyes at my daughter, and I can only imagine what you're planning." Queen Dionysus creepily smiles at me. When her guardsman comes over to check if everything is alright with her, she yells asking if she called for them, once they said no, she called them idiots and said she was being escorted by me to the arena.

The arena? I asked myself.

There was blood spread in various hues throughout the ocean, as many worthy triton fighters have died trying to make it to the highest tier of the tournament. The Queen went ahead and explained it to me, "Don't worry, it's worthiness and fruitfulness that these Tritones are proving to our soon to be Queen." She looked at me with a smile, she knew who I was looking for and she knew that it was their future Queen.

Sirena looked fierce to be reckoned with like her mother, she even wore her hair tight in a bun like the Queen. She remained upright along with her shoulders back along with her chin in the air, the way she been lectured by a horde of governesses and the realms nannies. She sat back on that throne banging the bolt in annoyance. Showing that she had no intention of caring, she kept shifting herself about, struggle against her stretched breaks for a gasp, and continued calling her servants for a huge amount of delectable, as if she was just watching a film. Sirena, despite the fact it was stressful, grinned. She was a princess in spite of everything, and appearances were essential.

Given her realms tradition of arranged marriages for power. She knew the likelihoods of getting married for love were faint to nothing, but then I wished the dream wouldn't perish in her.

So, Sirena became Queen Dionysus's daughter— a royal daughter not born of royal blood. And from what I remembered Sirena told me, that the issue wasn't being called nontoxic blood, which was offensive because every siren should be born venomous. I remember her telling me that being a mermaid makes the siren pod almost invincible. Also, the fact that when since she was blessed to live in the siren realm, there were stories of Sirena's destiny spreading throughout the oceans.

Now, the excellent qualities of Princess Sirena had reached the ears of many Tritones spread all over the oceans. There were Tritones that just came back front their hunt; whoever had the best kills stood around. There were Tritones who battled each other afterwards. Then there was Sirena who continued waving her hand at her kingdom and signaling which Tritones could pass through. She did it as if she could care less, especially with the way she shoved more sushi in her mouth.

I looked down, to see the fiercest Triton warriors from across the ocean. They were almost fearsome, fuck that! They were absolutely brutally daunting, especially since they were skilled in battle, unrelenting in combat and known for their savagery ways especially if they thought that was their way of entertaining the Princess. The Queen continued on, "When most of their worthlessness, join the others in death after the tournament, it will represent a significant rise in their realms across oceans." She loved the way I stared at Sirena with a broken heart feeling defeated and she just wanted to remind me of that.

"However, when the last two do happen to triumph here, they will fight at the tournament with fiery ambition in front of Sirena. So, whatever happens, we believe the Gods have smiled upon them. Today is the day our lives actually start to mean something."

I stared down at Sirena from my view, she simply had no emotions. She wasn't happy, yet she couldn't cry. The appall Sirena was in a miserable perplexity at the realm she was raised in.

I was dreading the swim back home. Having to swim without the love of my life and having to swim without a magic bubble. Queen Dionysus must've read my mind when she offered to swim me back home. When we've entered the rear of the house I waited for her to get dry and transform, but she insisted she stayed in the water. Suddenly, I heard a wave of people passing on the boardwalk and I imagined them close to seeing her fin. I suddenly laid on top of her and hoped that the best-case scenario was that they believed I was hugging someone on the ocean surface. Worst-case scenario they thought I was a fat cheater, and I was into older women. However, she have been violated and was outraged. For the first moments, she misunderstood why her cheek was plastered to my chest. And there was definite awkwardness right before she swat me. Awkwardly, before she swam away, she kissed me on the lips, and I disappeared.

CHAPTER 11

After finding myself on the beach, I took a shower getting ready for class. The weeks were great, waking up then going to work or school. Everything was great. However, Gramps kept looking at me weird and he kept saying a name— Si…Selena…ugh I don't remember. Each day, I wake up wishing to be freed from the same nightmares I had each night. A nightmare of being drowned in the dark ocean, and a thing…a female is swimming to me always reaching out. Closer and closer each nightmare, but I never get the chance to reach for her hand. During class I turned to a blank page, and I set the tip of my pencil poised for my command and began redrawing the same image from my dream. I did this every day after my nightmare, each picture was the same, but each one later became more defined.

Closing my eyes, I suddenly redraw everything on a face from beautiful and familiar eyes, cheekbones, and lips. Everything that I've finally seen the night before. How was she? Why does her face look so familiar? The same night, I went through the same process but soon after my nightmare, because something awfully specific came to mind, so I drew it. I began chuckling, I couldn't have, I just finished drawing a…mermaid.

The next day I sketched her again while I was at work. It was a busy day, but I wanted to draw her once again. I was familiar with the hollow of her cheeks, while they dimpled when she smiled, and her eyes that said so much, though for some reason I feel like I know they aren't brown or blue.

As I shaded the rims of her eyes with my colored pencils, I stared into it and the hue spoke out to me as it should be close to purple. Not purple, not pink; but periwinkle. I remember in the dream her hair being teal. I longed to climb into the final drawing and ask her who she was. She was beautiful. If only she was real. "Sirena," I repeated, testing the sound of her name on my lips something refreshing. Like a shard of my heart fastened back.

Suddenly after a few months, poof my skin prickled with memories from our first meeting at the beach to the last night I seen her in her castle. I began remembering things I haven't for a while. A shiver went through me. The sensation when she gripped my hand— I could still feel it. And then, the brush of her breast to my chest, the press of her hips to my pants. Just thinking about it created immense resentment doubting how could I allow that malevolent siren Queen bitch wiped my memories. I should have pushed her away as soon as she went in for that *never return* kiss.

"Gramps, I remember…how could I forget her? Every time you said her name, it all seemed like a blur." I began sobbing hard on his shoulder. No memory during the past month. Before there was nothing. There was no inkling that I knew her, that I recalled her. I tightened my jaw while my color sapped from my face. I felt as if I allowed this to occur and I suffered as if I had ripped out my own heart.

At the beach, I spoke to Gramps about everything. I began thinking about how Sirena and I met for the first time. The two of us endured fractured smiles, all the same we found a way to heal. I knew beyond a shadow of a doubt that I would remain close to her, and I knew for a fact that her heart could not belong to anyone else. For her, I'll swim for miles and miles, just to live together with her in the Siren realm. It's remarkable— I can never get sick and tired of her!

I don't give a damn, if I am bound to spending day by day searching for her in the sea, if I have to. And I will forever be in love with her!

Despite that, I did dive far deep into the sea and swam extraordinary distances into the deep sea for her. I hoped to meet her half-way into her own world, further beneath the fringes of obscurity. I was eager to work ruthlessly on the way to keeping us strong, but she had Tritones fighting for her the last time I saw her. Who knows if now she was already married to one?

"You know champ, we ought to go down to the island and fish. How about it?" Gramps had been a trooper but lately he's also been extremely demanding to get me down to Fire Island. He said that his insightful instincts was telling him that it was the precise trail. Let's see, I just regained every memory of her, including the ones on that island, all I can imagine is how more excruciating it would feel being there without her. Sarcastically, I blurted out with an agonizing tone, "Yay, a reminder of the one woman who understood me, treasured me, and just like that leaving me without a trace while I had amnesia!" Feeling flustered; I felt just as though I were stifling. I'd would give anything to return that slip of the tongue, but it was after the event now.

This was one of those times when Gramps couldn't distinguish my sarcasm, when I really just wanted to scream NO. Gramps abruptly look intently at me then chuckles boisterously while shouting out, "I'm glad to see you still have plenty of spunk left in there, just like your grandfather. Now, hurry up and take a shower and get dressed. And wear a fresh shirt that doesn't smell like you drowned your self-pity in. We can't be late."

I looked at him and said, "I beg your pardon? Late for what?" However, he didn't give me any response, he was ignoring me while he loaded the boat with our fishing rods and tackle carriers. And more food than usual... that was odd.

On our way to Fire Island, I imagine that I might have realized my grandfather was up to something. Possibly, I gazed in the other direction of the ocean, for so long not wanting to admit where the destination was. As he rode the boat, I sneaked around and searched the ice box. It's usually just sandwiches and brandy. Only this time there was a huge bowl of home-made clam chowder and a horde of the finest sushi from Carolina's spot, *Skull Creek Boathouse*. And at first, I wasn't convinced why, but then it struck me, and adrenaline soared within my chest. This little fishing trip must have something more to do with Sirena.

We arrived at Fire Island, and it felt like the early times: like the memories of the cove where Sirena and I used to meet each other when we didn't want to get caught by her malicious sisters, there was that sapphire-blue sparkling ocean and the sandy seashore. As soon as we got there, I couldn't bear the sadness of hopefulness any longer, so I said, "Gramps, you're wasting your time! This was very nice of you and all... but...but Sirena, she's not comi—" I was coming to the end of my sentence, but something was swimming approaching the beach from the direction where the cove stood at. I told Gramps to step away from the shore and come closer to me next to the trees. From my experience, it could've been a gruesome unfriendly man-eating siren. Still, he wouldn't listen to me as if he knew for sure that it was Sirena, as if he had prearrranged this all along. I had expected too much from this trip; that perhaps after such a long wait, Sirena might finally persuade herself to meet me. But she didn't, and it wasn't her.

My heart felt that somehow this was irrational, and so it plummeted to the earthiness of the deep sea. Red wavy hair swayed in the blue currents; it was Rosemarie. "Gramps, get away from her!" My grandfather, as persistent as I, just merely disregarded me and on the go started chatting with the siren for some purpose. I was anxious she would try to siren him, what if she supported the entire misplaced memories. That would clarify why Sirena hasn't attempted to see me.

Nevertheless, she said, "Calm down Josh, I requested your kind grandfather to bring you over here. I apologize if I frighten you; especially after everything that occurred with you." She looked sincere, either my memories aren't all back and I don't remember her showing this much compassion, or she truly feels terrible. "I want you to know I had nothing to do with my mother's wrongdoings. But I'm here for Sirena more than an assurance. I slipped over here from the European waters to send you a message."

I was pretty bewildered and still speculating if this was some kind of hoax. "What message?" In the pit of my stomach, I had a funny sensation.

"Now listen, every time someone awakes from a memory loss song, it can lead to fatal causes later." What the heck, what does she mean by fatal, am I dying? "No, you're not dying but you will want to." What the hell does she mean I would want to? "Your memories come back, pay you a visit, until it distorts your memories. You'll become afraid of the world, even Gramps and Sirena. To you, they'll look like the dead shadowing you around."

"What the fuck did your mother do to me? Where is Sirena, she should be here at least one more time before I look at her as a zombie."

"Oh my gosh, Josh RELAX! If I didn't have the answer, would I really have double-crossed my mother? Bonehead, I have your medicine. And Sirena isn't here for three reasons; one to distract mother, two to continue saying no to a bunch of Tritones, and three the most important…if she was anywhere nearby it would only heighten the situation, the clock will tick faster." Oh, so Sirena isn't married still, "If that's the only part you got from that, then you must be a bigger dumbass then I believed…or you truly love my sister. Uhm, anyways here's the ingredients. You'll make it for the tea you'll drink twice a day for a week. It has lavender, Rosemarie, thyme, roman chamomile, water lily, seagrass, sea salt, and grinded pearl dust. I have to leave now, especially if I want to catch a ride with the marlins. One more thing, we'll be back in a month, I promise you, SHE'LL return."

CHAPTER 12

y heart pounded as I looked into my guesthouse and found wet footsteps. There's only one person who would walk around the whole place barefooted and wet. It looked like she walked around the house twice, she was looking for me. I ran in each direction of my room and then suddenly heard a splashing noise. It was her, so I ran out of my guesthouse screaming "Wait, wait, don't leave!" Still in my underwear I had dived in after her. We held each other so tightly and kissed each other more. I had to rush her inside my guest room just in case anybody was watching from the oceans. She told me everything about the trips, all the different clans she met, the funny stories about the annoying Triton's that she turned down, and then she added how she snuck out from the pod for good and wanted to live with me.

The following day it smelled of daylight, ocean, and beach and after taking her out to eat fluffy banana pancakes, we sat at the lighthouse and then I did something I've been wanting to do for such a long time. "Sirena, if I gave you something would you promise to never lose it while you swim?"

"Of course, Josh, then I take care of the things that you gave me, what is it?" I got on my knee, and since she didn't understand what I was doing she stuck out her foot thinking I was going to give her a shoe.

"You're so cute no I need your left hand, would you marry me?" I took out my old grandmother's old ring, that Gramps gave to me for this very moment. Inspired by the ocean, Gramps bought my grandmother a beautiful oval cut diamond ring. Underside diamond-embellished waves along with shells making it the perfect alluring oceanic vintage ring for Sirena. And she shrieked yes, before aweing at the ring.

* * *

Every person is gazing at us; I was promising her a forever. I promised her that no one would be gaping at her, but then again it wasn't sincere. Only, since I was unable to lie compellingly even to myself, I turned her chin to just look at me.

As I drove my new yacht in the ocean thinking about the future, I glanced to the right— in his tiny aluminum boat, Uncle O'Connor had turned his entire chest towards my focus. His eyes jaded curiously keen on mine, then I cringed towards the back, unsure as to why he didn't drop his gaze that looked pretty nerve-wracking.

This was without doubt the reason to at last drive out the wooden motor yacht I have been working on for such a lengthy time.

Later I recalled that I was driving from the second floor of the yacht and that these windows stood intriguingly tinted and that he almost certainly had no clue if I was even the driver, not to mention the fact that I for one noticed him watching. I attempted to seek solace aside from the reality that he wasn't actually gaping at me, simply just the brand-new yacht.

Simply for the reason that the past few months, my uncle had been making me feel unpleasant, I hastened to flee away from his surrounding area, I yanked on the throttle to speed up with no hesitation.

Engines roaring close to a low growling jaguar, the yacht jerked ahead awfully fast that my chest banged into the steering wheel and my hair felt the gust passing through each strand of hair.

At this moment, given that I was far away as of the town and in the vicinity of the open sea I began thinking to myself. I could only imagine how my friends and relatives were going to react to my new everything. My new job, my teal-hair fiancée, as well as the new yacht and house.

"The guys are absolutely going to believe I'm living life recklessly," I mumbled beneath my gasp.

It was a gorgeous warm day out— a classic sunny day of the week in South Carolina— but as Sirena explained it to me, everything felt like she was being ordered to be in the center of attention for everyone on land to see, she felt she was pulling interest to the lavish family heirloom ring on her left hand. Rather sea-folk weren't familiar with…a pearl ring after the tournament was the normal. Remaining on land, Sirena realized she wasn't the upcoming siren Queen any longer. However, it made her worry if her family exiled her enough to the point that they wouldn't turn up at her own wedding.

Her exile was starting to put a bitter toll on the early days of our betrothal. Every other weekend, I tried taking Sirena on a hidden island. We spent time there so she could take a longer dip without getting caught by any sirens. They were still in search for me and Sirena. They head us a warning to never come back home; Sirena is exiled from the Siren realm and I'm waiting for death. But for some reason I don't worry, and I don't fear. I accept our love, and all I feel is that the fin-folk should accept it as true. We have plans to consummate our marriage, hoping that Rosemarie is right that they won't be a bother to us on land.

After I went to my place, I noticed Sirena resting in the hammock. Nevertheless, she wasn't doing it, as if she was relaxing and reading a paperback. She was laying in it far more as if she was momentarily considering her troubles— perhaps ideas like future husband, wedding, banishment, land, and the rest. It distracted me; I really couldn't bring it all together in my mind if I in reality made the wisest decision. I remember her mentioning having a nightmare about being attacked as soon as she took a swim, while wearing the ring.

Despite the fact, she was enjoying the concept of dressing up in numerous white dresses along with trying out several cakes. Although this marriage would result in her dwelling primarily with me on land. Could she settle within a mundane, reasonable, and dry concept like land dwelling, even if it meant a love life together with me.

Unlike my fiancée, the moment I began imagining Sirena and our future I remained engaged in a thrilled whirl of "could-be".

Seeing her expression staring beyond the ripples leaves my heart feeling massively intense, the beginning of a stinging tearstained face was puffy and swollen in my eyes, and I was thankful Sirena didn't notice me. If she caught my cries, it would merely make her react all the more untrue.

"Hello?" Rosemarie called out to me, and I groaned in a slight bitter tone.

"Oh, hiya, Rosemarie! How are you…please don't kill me!" I was freaked out as she got out of the water and began transforming. This was so sudden I quickly begged her not to hurt me. She was the one I hoped to never see again, since she would rip anyone's throat out in a heartbeat.

"No worries, I just want to see my sister— The tribe probably banished her, however I haven't." So far, it seems that amongst the sirens, only Rosemarie was the most vulnerable with me, whenever it was about her sisters, especially Sirena. Let alone sirens weren't allowed to show their emotions.

I faltered for a moment, "I know she'll be more than happy to see you…To be honest, I think I probably messed up."

Rosemarie sighed. "No, no…I just can sense how much she needs me— wanting to plunge into the ocean, however she's frightened to transform. Simply going along with her instincts."

"Can you always tell anywhere your realm and others are?"

"Somewhere close to the realm in Italy. Probably, searching for the highest rank of long-distance relatives to conquer our realms crown."

"Any indication that they possibly will…"

"The Queen banished her; any connection would also lead to banishment. Her family isn't coming to that wedding, face it Joshua but she's betrothing a Hanks. Sorry, but it's the truth…However, I've always been a rebel, I'll be there…for her!"

Now I felt even lower, "Okay, Rosemarie, and that sounds wonderful. I just hoped for her."

"Well, I'm going to Sirena, um nice talking to you."

I smirked at the slight spirit in her speech. Yet going to the wedding was merely Rosemarie's ticket to getting banished from her family of sirens, I was gratified she'd acted upon Sirena's emotions. Having Rosemarie around would be a piece of Sirena's heart— a tremendous get together, however dire, to which position she was deciding in the long run.

In the guesthouse I overhead some of the conversation through the ajar window. Cuddling Rosemarie, Sirena chuckled while saying, "Rose, my lovely sister, consider yourself heartily thanked!"

I smiled inside my thoughts. The understanding that burst forth amongst myself and Rosemarie still to some extent filled my mind with wonder. It stood as validation to me, nevertheless, that things doesn't need to be so. That possibly humans and the sea-folk might harmonize all right, perhaps even coexist.

Although it was too soon for many of the sea-folks to play a part in that concept.

Rosemarie stared deep inside her sister's appearance; she sensed that Sirena was dealing with so much right now. I overheard her telling Sirena that she was a bit worried about her beloved sister becoming betrothed to a land-dweller within a few days.

I sauntered across the coastline, recalling the evening I proposed…I remember the look on Sirena's face, at first filled with excitement and love, suddenly it dimmed when her tribe heard of her banishment. Suddenly, she stared at the ring as though it was the start of something amiss.

* * *

I passed my fingers through my hair, a panicky fiddle. Abruptly, Sirena shouts, "Stop being so antsy, Josh. You came here for us remember!"

"Easier said. Firstly, I'm a Hanks descendant." He said looking around the corners for any guards. "Secondly, I'm the one aiming to take the Queens daughter from her. Thirdly, the one I'm most in fear of…since I'm in the Queens realm if anyone wants to kill me, you won't be able to save me this time."

The turbulence of the waves flushing through the caverns entrance hauntingly swished behind her. We settled there as Queen Dionysus glided through the palace hallways towards us with composure.

"Take it easy, Josh," Sirena uttered, attending to the burst of speed of my pulse.

Queen Dionysus came forward keeping her stern face, but you can sense she was pondering what was the occasion. She thought she didn't have to worry about me anymore, however here I was.

"YOU! What's the reason for this?"

I didn't want to ruin the mood; therefore, I didn't mention the mind erasing. The time came when I approached the Queen and asked for her blessing to marry Sirena. She'd simply shot me down, swam past me and didn't peek back. I had stood there speechless, although I felt like I saw this coming.

So, I swam rudely ahead of her. This time with a smirk on my face because the Queen was definitely a royal bitch! "I have tried doing this the pleasant way, however—" I paused just to enjoy looking at her obscure skeptical face, "Well, we have some good news."

She starts lifting her brow, glaring at the both of us for a short moment, before whipping her sharp fin near me, which startled me for a moment.

"Compose yourself, mother," Sirena spoke shortly after seeing the venomous fin approaching. "I'm alright."

I frowned, then she shrugged as she knew it was in complaint to the phrase, "alright." I would've used anything like superb or magnificent.

"You eloped, how dare you?" The Queen burst out.

Nonetheless, the matter was undoubtedly destined for Sirena, the Queen was gawking at me now, while her stinger pursued reeling in closer to my neck.

Lingering silence. Soon after, shifting my attention for me to speak. I stared ahead at Sirena, unnerved. It felt impossible to make words out.

Watching Sirena's smile gave me some courage and I swam to her, while Queen Dionysus stared me down. I said loudly, "Queen Dionysus, I'm your daughters' fiancé." I began beaming into Sirena's cherished eyes. "I love her beyond all within the world, beyond my very soul, moreover— through some phenomenon— she loves me, too."

The stillness continued significantly slower. Suddenly, I remember being wrapped in Sirena's bosoms. She swam me out of the palace, like a flash of lightning, while attacking any siren after us. It wasn't close to the outcome I was envisioning, including Sirena's own banishment!

CHAPTER 13

"The guys and I are going on the yacht, you don't need to worry about me, and trust me I will be missing you every second."

Sirena began saying nervously, "I still don't know what it's called…I don't have to go."

"You're going to your bachelorette party, besides Rosemarie will be there…unfortunately Cheryl is hosting it."

It was peaceful for some time, only the thump in my heart nailing, the split tempo of our sensual panting, as the hiss of our lips moving as one. Most often it were easy to overlook the fact I was smooching a mermaid. Our gazes locked in a moment of heat; her periwinkle eyes were so intense I almost imagined I could see to the very bottom of her soul. She had the utmost divine soul, beyond beauteous beside her thoughts or unrivaled appearance or her magnificent frame. Staring back at me as though she could see my soul, as well, and seemingly liked what she saw.

I turned Sirena's face again. I lay my palms over her face then leaned in, placing the softest kiss on her lips. I drew her lips into mine continuously.

"Now go," she whispered soon after.

She spoke the words, as the fingers of her silky petite hand clenched keen into my bronze hair, her left hand pulled tougher against the hairs. I caressed her face one last time, reassuring her she was okay.

* * *

"Sirena…"

"Hush now!" Her breath rises to my face as she compelled her lips to mine to end my concerns.

With the cozy softness hard-pressed opposed to my torso I kissed her back; even so, but she read my thoughts and saw I wasn't as engaged as before.

Consistently worrisome. It would've been different if I hadn't behaved so overly concerned about her.

I replayed the conversations between her and Rosemarie continuously in my head. "Are you certain? No room for doubt? The day is still young to have second thoughts."

"Why are you trying to forsake me?"

I smirked as I looked down feeling slightly uncomfortable. "No, never, I will never forsake you. I just needed to make sure. Wouldn't want you to do something you'll be disappointed about."

"Have you forgotten the love we fought for…because I remember I have given up my realm and family for us, any chance you'd forgot?" Sirena looked at me with a serious face.

I halted, was I ever going to stop making a total ass out of myself?

"Perhaps not the wedding, however later on— regretfully surrendering your history…like your loved ones and kingdom."

Sirena sighed. To state, she'll simply miss her sisters, while in her eye's exile was unforgiveable.

"But what about Dianthus?"

"If she appreciates me like a true sister, she wouldn't destroy our love." She confessed as she nodded passionately.

She then looked at me seriously again, "Every woman's dream is to find true love, even the ones who live under the sea. We talked about this constantly, this is what I want! If I'm going to marry; I'm going to marry for love, not because I'm told to for riches or a contract. I know there'll be difficulties, but I want you for an eternity."

With the remaining time I said, "Remember the other day when Gramps ask us if we were…pregnant?"

"He almost threw some newborn bash," she laughed confusingly. "Why does a newborn need a party?"

I smiled.

"What, Joshua?"

"I felt something…and it's called a baby shower. Being with a mortal, you'll never have the chance of motherhood."

She understood what I was saying, "All right, I shall do the same thing my mom did for me and adopt."

I chuckled, then my tone was lively. "You are exactly what I need, my other half. The one who sees clearer when I see things dimly—"

Sirena kissed my cheeks and looked deep into my eyes as she said, "take note, we are already the perfect, always and forever."

"I apologize that I had worries and I didn't tell you…but please trusts me when I say, that faded." She held me close on the dock. "But I see now, I'm just as sure about us as you were since the beginning, I've been waiting for this day."

Quickly a vessel with a band of my friends from university, work and still others in the hometown parked themselves at the dock. They were even now overflowing with liquor and exhilaration, getting ready to celebrate my shifts as of being a single man to a married man. The guys were jumping onto the dock and transferring onto my new yacht. They loved it…I rolled my eyes with laughter as I saw Gramps holding his party hat, running down the hill, making sure he didn't lose his place on the bachelor yacht.

"You all have fun, especially you!" Sirena said. I bowed down and gave her one last boyfriend kiss.

As I looked at the lighthouse, I saw Cheryl with a group of girls screaming, "It's time to party bitches!!" Oh gosh, this was cringy, I hope Sirena and Rosemarie could handle it. Then she looked at me and cackled, "Don't worry Joshie, if she still loves you, she'll meet you at the altar!! Just kiddin' she'll be wearing white, love you, Joshie!!"

Then I remembered Rosemarie saying she had other plans for Sirena, it included sneaking away from Cheryl after the girls got wasted. Then Sirena and Rosemarie were going to dive into the other side of the oceans, far away from the sirens…just enough for dancing with the waves, hunting, and singing with the whales. Something more like them. I truly loved that idea; I wanted Sirena to enjoy her last night as just Sirena. By nightfall tomorrow, she would be Sirena Hanks, it had a nice ring to it.

After the party that night, I headed upstairs to the lighthouse to rest up, it is going to be a very long day tomorrow.

CHAPTER 14

I woke up in the lighthouse's cold cot.

I enjoyed the feeling of the sun through the windowsills, and the lights reflecting off me like peach and mango irises of the sky. In my dream, Sirena and I were strolling under the sun, then bathing in the deep full of bliss. I was overjoyed to see her.

Eager to start my day, I got dressed and headed down to Gramps kitchen first. As he welcomed me with Gramps delicious old-fashioned shrimp and grits, as if she was here herself. I nearly cried, while eating my breakfast, he prepared two extra plates with extra shrimps for the ladies in the guesthouse— who were probably unaware of what to do. It was the first time I was actually sure about having, Cheryl across from me, eating a bowl of my favorite shrimp and grits as well. He didn't want to give me any of the specifics, but he came back with a huge grin looking so delighted. "They love it, now Josh lets go we need to get ready with the groomsmen." It seemed almost pleasant recognizing my family and friends who took the full day off for the wedding, unfortunately I can't say much for Sirena's "extended family."

Worrying of her nerves I give my bride a call, "Good morning my darling." My morning voice was rough, like the stubble of my beard. I asked her if she was alright, I can hear her nerves even through the phone. Suddenly I changed the topic to when I first saw her beautiful transformation, "You appeared to me. Mysterious and stunning, decorated simply in moonshine gleaming from the ocean." And that phone helped continue our important day.

Driving to the *Charleston Harbor Resort& Marina* we passed the colonial-style homes with gardens of peonies and roses. Spring had always been my favorite time of the year; it was perfect for a wedding.

On the way to walking into the hotel, I glimpsed back in the distance, reaching what was approaching around the sunset hours. A wedding on the beach.

Along with the efforts of having to get through amongst both land and oceans pursuits. I became flooded from both activities and the imaginations regarding this day— from all appearance, who was going to be there, as well as what Sirena and I would each be contemplating and feeling the entire time. For months, we told our guests it was a mermaid themed wedding.

I feel sick to my stomach knowing I won't get to see Sirena until everyone looks down at the aisle, in search of the bride. My biggest worries was what if she didn't arrive and hoped to make an amends with her family instead?

The wedding took place in the hotel's gazebo, between the shore and the beach. Our only concern was that it might unexpectedly downpour, although that was the good sense for our rooftop. Nevertheless, as for Rosemarie she would have to swiftly tiptoe into the sea. Yet, besides the scented midst of the ocean and the orchids, the weather conditions appeared ideal for this wedding.

I listened to Cheryl yelling at the other bridesmaids making sure everything was perfect and that I didn't sneak a peek into the ladies' dressing room; I supposed I just became increasingly curious to see how lovely my Sirena appeared. Every now and then, I continued to float by just to hear that my soon-to-be wife was trying her hardest to blend in, mirroring the ladies as they acted interested about Cheryl's date being a total…super hottie-patootie! Oh, my goodness, I often wondered how awful she already dented Sirena's mind when it came to human communication skills.

It was after I was already suited up, when Rosemarie floated over to the men's rooms in a light coral gown with her red wavy hair twisted into a braid that was twisted into a flower crown. With a hint of coral-colored flowers and pearls flowing throughout. If my soon-to-be family and still frenemy, was that beautiful I can imagine how stunning Sirena looked. At that moment in time, making things all the greater tense between the two of us. As she assured me before, I had personally insulted her with my vow I was promising now, and that to her had the air of me capturing Sirena in a fishnet. Even though she had remarkable sorcery and in spite of everything she still had her siren clan, she would be grateful to give up the whole thing to make the most of life with her own kindred soul to love for all time.

Though here Rosemarie appeared, secretly clinging along to all she genuinely desired in life but never would dare to admit. "Joshua, please promise me you will take care of my sister." I promised her. "Also, promise me Joshua that my sister will only live a life of bliss. She deserves everything and more." Then rather than letting a tear drop, she bolted back to the woman's dressing room. Startled, my jaw shockingly fell wide open. I stumbled about in my mind; I had never been Rosemarie's light in her life above land.

I looked at the beautification of the beach outside of the window. I wished my parents were here to see the transformation of myself and to play a part of my wedding. Like how my bride's favorite-colored orchids are teal, and they would decorate the day. Or how, Finn the photographer was acting like a barnacle as he took pictures of almost every second of me getting ready, I wonder how the bride must have felt, perhaps just as violated as I felt or worse…perhaps we won't use these pictures for our anniversaries to come.

Gramps finally appeared to me and the groomsmen, and a hysterical chuckle erupted through my lips as he passed around some bourbon and a cigar, along with the rest of the men. The cigars were supposed to be set alight during the reception. Following Gramps wonderful speech to soothe the nervous tension and remind me of my purpose, he left the room to prepare to walk Sirena down the aisle. He began breathing nervously, "Alright boys, wish me luck, I'm about to go walk one of the most beautiful ladies of Carolina."

Waiting under the alter; the same as the funeral, I can hear my cousin Cheryl's whispers boisterously and obvious, "This is most certainly, not exactly how I would picture getting married, there's far too much beach and it stinks like fish, unfortunate girl…marrying my cousin Joshie." She muttered to the other bridesmaids alongside her, Ava, and Harper. Behaving as expected, her entourage snickered and agreed with her despite having their own opinions.

However, I wasn't going to let my cousin spoil this day for me, besides I heard further joyous vibes between our guests. If only they had known the meaning behind the beach. It was not something we just picked from a newspaper clipping. This was a symbol of our love hailed in the midst of both homes, land, and sea. With a beacon of hope that any of Sirena's adoptive family would appear at the oceanfront ceremony.

There…I remained in my tux awaiting eagerly under the gazebo. I snickered slightly, as that moment replicated an hour spent in a tiny boat waiting for the catch of the day. Suddenly she showed herself. So stunning, so graceful. I knew she would look beautiful in any wedding gown, but she was more than ravishing. Sirena had on a gorgeous eggshell-white lace mermaid-style dress with flowing layers of soft tulle like the undulating waves of the ocean. With a strapless, sweetheart neckline along with the beloved stretched strand of pearls, gorgeously included along the back of her gown. A gown perfectly fit for a mermaid. It embraces her in all the proper places, by making her voluptuous hourglass figure overwhelm me. I can see the elegant frames of her neckline. And instead of the long veil I overheard Cheryl begging her to wear it; she wore a wreath Rosemarie made for her full of exquisite unique seashells, pearls, and petite flowers.

She is carrying a small, beautiful bouquet of soft teal and coral fuchsia orchids mingled in white calla lilies. Flowers that represented her and the ocean. I feel such a serene sensation wash over me.

From a distance, I can see Sirena gripping my Gramps, as he whispered in her ears. She paced down slowly. So many movies she watched to understand our ritual of weddings. And she probably realized that seeing it was completely different from actually doing it. The photographers snapping pictures as she walked slowly down the aisle and the unknown people around smiling at her.

I can tell she was pleased yet still very eager to keep composure, by taking intense gulps. I told myself, *one step at a time my love, as long as we meet that's all that matters.*

Finally, Gramps whispers something else in her ear and she begins laughing. I'm not sure what he told her, but I know it made her feel so much more relieved.

As soon as she completely ceased distracted about the surroundings, whispers, as well as her beginning to take no notice of her bare feet, she at last gazed at me. In a moment, her cheeks grow into a pinkish perfection; the more or less pinkish that bring corals to the imagination.

She finally reaches my side, and I take her hand, kissing her knuckles one last time before she becomes my wife.

I did not know what to feel as I looked at her, as I took her hand into mine and slipped the ring on her finger. I loved her, and there was the chance, now, finally, for a fresh start. "You are now husband and wife," the priest said. "You share the same soul, the same blood."

Same soul, same blood.

We were both crying by the time we were finished. After we swapped vows, we managed to say our, *I dos.* The words that would make us, *same soul, same blood* were said at sundown when Sirena and I unexpectedly heard delicate siren melodies far off. Sirena smiled at me and then at Rosemarie, as she said to me "They've given us they're blessing!" As she sprang on me and held me snugly, kissing me very willingly.

As she stepped down, I turned to face Sirena. Her face was radiant with love, the way mermaids have been. I leaned over and kissed her once again. She closed her eyes and as my lips slowly pressed against hers, her warm mouth.

The wedding and reception was everything- that we... well, that I could possibly ever desire it to be. I believe Sirena would've thought of something *deeper than getting your feet wet,* consisting of many rituals I'm still anew to.

CHAPTER 15

As we danced, for a split second, I'd almost forgotten we weren't alone. "Mrs. Sirena Hanks!" We hear my cousin's bothering voice disrupting us.

Disregarding Cheryl: Sirena presses her lips firmly against mine, as if she's been traumatized by my cousin and was hoping this kiss saved her.

"Oh my god cousin, now that we're family, follow me on Twitter love" Cheryl insisted, as she strutted to her giddily with wide open arms. "You'll have a glamorous honeymoon and that's a fault of mine!"

I grabbed Sirena mumbling, "Get away, Cheryl" as I grabbed her back to the dance floor. My cousin carried enormous pride in every project she accomplished, though she always neglects to point out who idea it was in the first place.

I froze after I heard, "OH Joshie! Just *fyi*, I went ahead and bought myself a ticket…I mean if it wasn't for me breathing you wouldn't be stepping foot on this here gravel." Then I raised my face from Sirena's eyes and scowled with annoyance at my cousin.

Shortly, Cheryl danced with the bride and Rosemarie for some pictures. She made herself stand out with butt slapping moves the ladies were perplexed over, beforehand snapping at the photographer, "Make yourself scarce now!"

After the reception, as well as a few drinks too many, my bride and I were ready to leave for our honeymoon. As we said our goodbyes Sirena troublingly looked around, there was someone missing…she needed to say farewell to her sister. It was getting close to our departure, up until we found her making out with Cheryl at the gazebo.

I hesitated, when I turned to glance at Sirena, amazed to see delight in her eyes. Rosemarie just became my sister-in-law not long ago, nevertheless our relatives were kissing and dancing. "Let's not disturb them, I see they're very fond of each other, I'll call her later."

I had a surprise before we walked away from the shoreside, that softened Sirena with a huge smile. Queen Dionysus and Sirena's sister Dianthus were waiting at a nearby dock, farthest from any humans. I reached out to her through the conch, the only way I knew how, and I pleaded with her to bid her farewell to Sirena, as the Queen now gave us blessings. As I walked away, I only heard how much they loved each other. It was hard for Sirena to talk about romance with her mom, even her sisters. To them it's war and lust. But Queen Dionysus saw some sort of quality in me. The ladies didn't weep, nevertheless they looked like they were having a delightful banter, despite the Queen's sour face. "Goodbye, Dianthus. Goodbye, mom. I love you," Sirena said again, her being the only one to cry as they hugged.

I was waiting at the top with the flight of stairs. It appeared like an incredibly promising image to me. As Sirena met me, she gave me a huge hug and we swiftly looked towards where the ladies were, we scanned the beach at the nick of time to see the sirens jump into the ocean without being spotted.

As an alternative to rice or floating lamps, everyone sent off a message of a hope or reminiscence to us newlyweds, and hurled bottles into the sea. Gramps brought the yacht around to another nearby dock, as everyone congratulated when we surrendered our one more binding kiss before the honeymoon. Then we slowly turned to face our guest before I rushed her to climb on board.

The yacht remained embellished along with more orchids that tugged in ribbons alongside its span. I grabbed the ship's wheel and was ready to take it in full speed, as Sirena waved away at the rear deck and yelled out *"So long, thank you all"* towards the beach, as everyone waved back.

Finally, Sirena stood in front of me as we sailed off, the woman I loved with all of my soul was before me, while I had an arm skin-tight about her waistline. As I continued steering my boat imagining our new life together at that moment. This was the start of our first voyage as a newly married couple together, it was going to take some time before we reached our destination.

We've experienced many hues of affection, mellifluous at this very moment. A few days later, we made a stop. "Puerto Rico?" Sirena asked, lifting her eyebrows once we arrived at the marina.

"Only a rest area near the way," I promised her with a smile, she hugged my hand saying, "I love you." I bent my head beside her, "Always and forever." We stayed at a marina near the yacht, before seeing some of Puerto Rico's remarkable sites. Later I kissed her, I gripped her within my arms. As I went a little overboard with Sirena's bikini, my lips wandered down further as she persuaded me to carry on. My heart was sprinting as I had hoped that this was just an introduction to what awaited us.

I slowed down the yacht, pulling the exactness keen on view alongside one of Jamaica's marinas it would stay in, for a while. Cutting out the engine, there was not anything other than the ripples, spanking gracefully opposed to the yacht. I began telling Sirena to carry her bags. She was thrilled. I surprised her with an overwater bungalow.

"There's houses over the ocean?" her tone of voice became concerned, although it even sounded so enthusiastic as if she desired one for Carolina.

* * *

I glide across to her and she radiates with that wonderful beam of hers, as a replacement for taking her hand, I hauled her up and about into my arms. Carrying my beloved across the threshold of our honeymoon bungalow.

Walking the beach, the moonbeam remained vivid on snowy shore after that, as a handful paces apart from the bungalow, shimmering swells. But I hardly even emphasized that portion. I was further centered on the extremely massive pearly silky bed at the heart of the chamber, with rose petals around the shape of a heart.

Sirena laughed and said, "This is silly, you are carrying me. I never saw such a thing, what does it mean."

I grinned. "It's old human traditions of beginning our honeymoon."

"I thought that was when we make love." She looked baffled and whispered to herself, *humans are amusing.*

The space was humid as well, drier than the Caribbean darkness near the waters. I followed a trickle of sweat moistened on the nape of Sirena's neck. She strolled leisurely ahead up until she might stretch out then stroke the rose petals. Maybe for whatever reason she felt the necessity to ensure everything wasn't just a dream.

I wanted to grab a bottle of champagne and hang about the private patio with my new wife, but I couldn't find her anywhere. I was making my way inside the room, until I heard movements in the ocean. I turned away from the bungalow, to gaze at the vivid sunset of the vibrant swirls of reds and golds I saw my Sirena alluringly swimming around in. Though when she saw me her human half moved upwards slowly and sensually. Her long, wavy wet hair was loose and covered over her breast as she calls me in. "I was pondering," Sirena smoothly answered, "but...perchance you'd be fond to unite me to take on a night's plunge with me?" She drew a heartfelt gasp, and her tone was beyond serene as she spoke for a second time. "This seawater is incredibly welcoming for such a human."

"Looks wonderful." My voice cracked as I swallowed hard as my eyes combed around her erotic encounter, then staring at her naked breasts swaying at the surface of the water. She was dazzling and charming, otherworldly mortal melding with ancient myth. I quickly got rid of my clothes, fastened a champagne to my waist using a satchel, and said to myself, *this was happening.*

"Before this day, I dreamt of every single imaginable way to make this...take place," Sirena confessed. She stayed where she was and in the calmest, irresistible voice, said, "I want to show you something." She kissed me giving me air, holding my hand as she began swimming. It was around the island...a very exquisite cove. It was part of a café, where people cliff dived into the cove. It was wonderous and unusually vacant at this time. At sunset, the waters as we swam above the surface, was for the most part— a magnificent magic. What I saw, was an electrical phenomenon around us. The dark body of water was shimmering as if I had vivid neon beams. Similar to a little child, I clutched a handful of water and speckled it back watching it sparkled like stars. It was whimsical and we stood along the surface of the ocean drifting still, I only thought about making amorous pleasure to her, passionately. I don't know if it was some sort of animal instinct, as I was consumed with the desire to make gentle to wild, spontaneous, fiery passion with her underneath the deep just as she was. I swathed my arms graciously around her back, then tenderly yanked her into my embrace where our skin's touched.

The oval moon stared upon us with its whitish light. It felt immensely wonderful being inside Sirena for the first time ever. I've stroked and savored her before, but never had I emerged myself inside of her. I lightly pulled her hair clear of her shoulder up until it uncovered her neckline. The scent of a light fusion of eucalyptus, Rosemarie, and lavender on her aroused me while I bent ahead. Her bronzed skin was silky, and graceful. Each second was delicate, raw, as well as blessed. It was worth the wait. We went all night, and when we stopped, we kissed and talked and drank champagne, and continued more on the sand of the cove all night long.

As she fell asleep, I whispered into her ears, "Mrs. Hanks, you take my breath away. I've never seen you look so lovely. Thank you for making me the luckiest man today and the rest of my life." The chills I had each time I named her as my Mrs.

CHAPTER 16

In the morning, mesmerized, I studied with bliss as she floated with ease all through the sea water, her physique rippling along with the tempo of the returning currents. Awakening to my wife here and now, seemed as if she was an all the more magnificent creature I had ever seen. Something is occurring all over again to me. I feel a marvelous phenomenon appearing in my chest. Suddenly the whole lot all around fade away— our room, our bed, as well as our bungalow. For moments I am in perfect brightness, and the only core appearing in the room that is more important than anything, is Sirena.

"What are you thinking about?" I questioned, difficult not to swallow her up with my gaze. The gust propelled her hair to the fore, pressing alongside her angled cheeks. The split ends stroked counter to my upper body. She was dressed in no more than my lengthy white T-shirt that was floating the underneath of her ass-cheeks. It was awfully difficult not to come into contact with her.

"How does Jamaica look on land, besides the bungalow?" she answered, and afterwards she stared up at the hills pondering what was above. "Josh? Are you there?"

I heard every word; this wouldn't be a real honeymoon if we hadn't gone sightseeing. "Definitely, I have a handful of sightseeing ideas." I told her with a smirk as if I had laid out wicked arrangements for us. I was hoping that we wouldn't smack into any land-dwelling seafolk, but then I wasn't going to allow my concerns to appear on my face.

We plummeted through the waves and sneakily went back into our bungalow. The next few days, Sirena and I have breakfast on deck most mornings. We've taken so many beautiful pictures while walking on the beach during the sunrise, horseback riding in the morning, a few nights we went dancing, and nights we had romantic dinners. I grinned a full smile that gleamed each day I woke up to her wondering about my next surprise I had for her.

We had many couple massages and the most fun was snorkeling alone while taking pictures undersea and looking for treasure.

We went back to the bungalow and each night ended with a gleam of moonlight on our naked sweaty skin as she sat on top of me face to face. Her delicate voice drifts as she pushes her warm skin onto me and exhales into my ear. Every single night was different, but every single night I passed my fingers down, all over her bump, lay down her leg after that back up. To me, it was like pinching myself to see if it was all real.

It was invigorating as well as liberating.

One fine day, I asked if Sirena would come with me fishing, but she was behaving so fickle recently and shouted no! I didn't want to be in her way at the bungalow, so I planned on fishing the rest of the day. Hopefully, get something I never would catch at Carolina. I looked into Sirena's outraged eyes; she was wondering if I would leave without saying goodbye. Of course not, she's probably on her time of the month, it's understandable for her to act like a shark. I gave her a huge kiss and jumped on my yacht.

I asked if she would come with me, she was behaving moody and shouted no. I didn't want to be in her way at the bungalow, so I planned on fishing the rest of the day. Hopefully, get something I never would catch at Carolina. I looked into Sirena's outraged eyes; she was wondering if I would leave without saying goodbye. Of course not, she's probably on her time of the month, it's understandable for her to act like a shark. I gave her a huge kiss and jumped on my yacht.

After about an hour later, I came back to the bungalow. I carried one after another, three 20 lbs. and one 50 lbs. Caribbean spiny lobsters. I reveled in feeling like the king of the island, without notice I heard the voice of my Sirena shouting out, "Help, HELP Joshua!" I dropped the lobsters and ran to save her. Although, there was no need for saving…she only had a nightmare. She grabbed me like I was her only safeguard. I took her to the kitchen and started making some chamomile tea, but as she began describing her dream, I saw her looking intently at the lobsters. Her story about the moon, blood, and sorrowfully a young one being burned at the stake while Sirena prepares for the burning staying around crying; began drifting off. She then grabbed all the lobsters and began clawing them. Ripping their crustaceans' long bodies and muscular tails, peeling the raw flesh out from the lobsters. She begins eating quickly as if she hasn't eaten at all during the honeymoon. After eating all 110 lbs. of lobsters. I was astounded by how greatly she ate, but she was more curious of a sound.

* * *

Jamaica had a deep, dark secret that a cavern hidden so well that only Sirena could hear. She insisted that we followed the melody but before we did, she needed me to grab a few ingredients; seashells the crown jewels of the sea, a small jar of ocean water from the magic deep, and sand where the ocean meets the land. It sounded like it was exceptionally urgent, and I'm surprised because Sirena didn't want to help find these treasures. For the first time she felt unlike herself.

Sirena closed her eyes, as she paced herself hang on to a tune only, she could hear. She believed it was setting out to fade the nearer they were on the trail. In short, the drops from the drizzle that had fallen on us during this trip turned into a hurricane soon after we entered the cove. I can hear the crash of the waves against the rocks. It was dry and kept us safe from the huge pour, but I was wondering where my wife was taking us. Following Sirena into the cove was so treacherous, I nearly cut myself a few times walking through the mist beneath that swayed and swung every bend and every tight corner, uncovering the jagged pillars. The cove laid out another exit with a staircase that led into an ordinary grey stone cottage.

Sirena said the entrance of the cove was meant to be clear for us. My heart thumped noticeably hostile to my chests, along with my breathing appearing to become wedged in my throat. She didn't explain much, just continued walking or following the whisper she said she heard. However, looking into Sirena's eyes, I saw she had almost the same panic. As if she was in a trance…I worried she was tranced by Caribbean sirens. Rosemarie told me ahead of time that she knew each of the siren pods, so we were safe in Montego Bay, but I with the way Sirena was acting it was like she was human.

Now a shivering Sirena had bestrode up the slender trail. We had to hike a further wonky hill leading us to a cottage. Thus far, it seemed like fate. Just as though we were destined to be here. However around was nothing, not a bit of commotion inside or in the overgrown gardens of the cottage, simply the icy winds. The doorway appeared as if it had never been moved in months, ancient roots were grown as well as entangled in all places across the door. Sirena said, "We should get inside and light a fire. Let the storm pass, I won't be able to swim with you in these waves."

I peered through the dusty window beside the entrance; it certainly looked vacant. "What made you lead us here, are you okay, hun?" My words were unsteady as it clattered through my ranting teeth. "I wonder, if there's somebody in there?"

There was an interesting mysterious beach sanctuary into a small shop called, *"Avery's Readings."* I got rid of my concerns after that attempted to sound hopeful. "If we must, we'll break a wooden chair into pieces to burn." The door handle unlocked without difficulty and the tiniest of bumps bursts the door open. Absence of screeching and creaking.

A voice appeared, when we saw a woman dressed as a gypsy hauling open her kitchen screechy door. Her hair was dark as night and her skin was of a caramel complexion. She had big, slanted doll eyes, the kind that look ravishing on a woman but also made you wonder how scandalous she was. She was about the same age as me. The gypsy woman had on a finery, vivid graceful skirt, along with a lacelike top. Gold earrings, bangles on her wrist, and necklaces around her throat.

"I am sorry, ma'am. We were out walking around…it's our honeymoon you see, and suddenly the weather just turned on us. That's my fault for not listening to the weather report. All right, we bumped into this cottage, and it appeared vacant, and we supposed we could get dried up and hang around for the rain to pa—" I felt I appeared extremely respectable, or else pathetic enough for a person who didn't reside in her island, what is more just committed a crime breaking into a woman's house. Nonetheless, it didn't look as if she worried very much about my confession, if anything the more quickly she may possibly get me to shut up, the change for the better.

"YOU! Would you shut up please? Both of you can stay. Must stay!" The mysterious lady walked away after looking flustered. Why did she look so nice, but her cottage outside looked abandoned? I felt like we were in a trap, it could be a land-dweller seafolk. Sirena wasn't safe.

"Who are you? And what do you mean by, *must stay*?" I grabbed a lamp, ready to knock it on the lady if she didn't give me any answers. Good answers.

"My name is Avery, jerkoff put my lamp down, before I throw this teapot in your face! I'm a seer and yes, I overheard all the questions you had for your wife. Like the one about my house. Rude! You didn't mind coming inside when you were freezing your nuts off, but now you see me and you're pissing your pants!" Avery poured us tea and glared at me until I put her lamp back, "It's an illusion charm, a friend did it on my flowers… to make sure not everyone goes poking around. Only the ones invited, like Sirena here. She heard the melody." She looked at Sirena with many feelings, wariness, admiration, and fondness.

"It sounded so familiar, like a melody I've heard in the past. It sounded like home, but I don't know it. None of the— my sisters sang this before." I assumed Sirena was close to calling her sisters a bunch of aggressive man-eating bitchy sirens, but I think she wanted to be careful just in case.

"Darling, it's not from your adoptive family. Every call-in message to the seafolk is the first song or memory, deep with their memory from the first closest one when they were born. Your message was your mom singing. YOU…Sirena, I only call for you my precious ocean pearl, not the human. He can stay in the lounge, you!" She said forcefully after pouring us tea, then pointing between me then Sirena ordering us around like she known us for a long time. "You come with me, into the back patio." Shit! She does everything and why can't I come along.

At the cottage, Avery showed Sirena through the kitchen. "Wait a minute girl," pinching her eyes shut to pay attention to the aura around the kitchen. "This is sanctified ground, I just wanted to make certain no further visitors were invited." The ladies then sat across from each other at the round table in the back patio, and Avery just scrawled as she spoke. I saw them speaking for a while, but then I sneaked to listen. I saw Avery just drawing sketches that looked like horrible ink blot test that supposedly she can read from. "We can speak freely right now; I see the *moon* shining on *the tower* in the ocean, but painfully I see something, it hurts but it's too blurred for me to tell you…" Avery stopped her scrawling and closed her eyes. I figured she was far too drained to attempt anything further, therefore we left after putting her on her bed, leaving a note that we'd come back to see her.

When we got back to the bungalow, Sirena had only just stroked the water and whispered out her sister's name, *Rosemarie*. I begged Sirena for specifics, but then she hardly understood anything. Along with, saying that Avery's visions were vague about all the specifics, it was unclear like her own visions were abandoning her. Before this day we were going to leave early, but now it seems we would stay a few more days before going home. At this point, right now Sirena needed her sister, Rosemarie, to fulfill finding out the whole truth.

As Sirena went to bed, I stood up drinking a corona thinking to myself; it's not the same as I wouldn't intend to help her find out the truth ourselves, that's the infuriating thing. The reality that so a great deal of her that I need to get into my brain, is that her way of life revolves around the supernatural. The irritating portion is that she needs her sister a lot more than she needs me, because I can't do anything around the magic realms to get the answers my wife deserves. Even the human seer saw me more human compared to her. I want her to rely on me more, I'm struggling to see it because perhaps I don't want to realize it, but I know deep down…I won't always be her savior.

CHAPTER 17

The ocean carried the name, and as Rosemarie was coming out of the beach, she heard the calling. The calling was transferred instantly, so she swam ahead, to her sister wish as rapidly as she possibly will. I could imagine that for Sirena she soared in the open of the sea a handful times, spiraling upward as well as down into the surge of water only so she could get here on time.

"Wake up sis," Rosemarie said when she cuddled in the between Sirena and me. Rosemarie never had her limits when it came between my wife and I, it was like I was sharing her with Rose. If Sirena never kept me a secret in the past, I wouldn't be surprised if Rose joined our dates.

"What do I have to do for you my favorite mermaid sis?" I was so glad I had my bottoms on, I got up and said I'll leave them alone and make breakfast.

Both women smells like seawater and heat. Rosemarie pauses to take a decent glance at Sirena. "I can't imagine how much I've missed you already."

We were all up in the early hours that daybreak and sat all around the tabletop, eating breakfast, along with discussing just about every detail of yesterday's journey. Sirena told Rosemarie, "I need you Rose, she made everything sound important. She literally said I was the ocean pearl she called for."

"Ready?" Rosemarie shouted from across the ocean, all too hurriedly. I began to stop embracing Sirena's neck and I finished preparing my underwater gear.

"Ready," I whispered out at the ocean, not trying to catch any attention as of any neighbors on the bungalows. Rosemarie scowled at me from the ocean's surface.

"I don't think you're really need to come, if the seer didn't want you then, what makes you think she wants you now." She was already starting with me.

"Not at all, I'm going, I know the direction." I retorted, unperturbed.

"Nonetheless—"

"Nope, now way."

"Just—"

"We're done talking," I finished with her, before grabbing Sirena's hand and jumping into the ocean.

This time I smirked at her bitterness and shrugged. The ladies followed me through the underwater forests, and I overheard Rosemarie scrutinize the stunning glistening blue of the ocean surrounding us. After some time, she embarked on right, selecting her course across the ocean floor. Which didn't make any sense to me; as there were still secret tunnels that we had to swim together in, and most importantly the sunken pirate city at Port Royal which was the pinpoint where Sirena and I found the cavern.

I memorized the paths over the seashore for the reason that it had a very distinguishing cavern with a very distinctive trail to the seer's cottage. I was capable of leading the way, meanwhile Sirena was fairly in a daze when she found the seer. The scenery was intensified from the last time we plodded through the forest; the heat had doused the essence of all existence, cherishing everything living, vivid green leaves in addition tropical red and orange colors, admiring brushwood. Regardless of the moonlight the breeze seemed echoes and joyful. We parade through the warm rainforest like wildfire, only pausing on every occasion Rosemarie slashed marks on alternating trees; she didn't trust my direction and wanted to be sure we could find our wake back at least to the cavern.

I was flabbergasted once we got there, everything we well-defined to Rosemarie about the spine-chilling hut wasn't there. In its place, it essentially looked like a decent cottage. There was even two seagrass salted cocktails, I had guessed that seer lifted the cloaked charm for her probable guest now. The seer opened the door with high spirits when we arrived, especially the ladies. She ignored me, instead of the part when she demanded me to sit in the lounge again. Only this time, Sirena was with me, and Avery had Rosemarie all kept to herself.

"I'm super happy you've come this night." She rested her fingers on Rosemarie's arm, and she didn't yank away. There wasn't any necessity to, besides the siren did value the seer's admiration. Avery said she hoped this day would come, she saw it in the past but hoped it would come when she would meet Rosemarie, she longed to meet the witch of the sirens. Rosemarie spoke about how she appreciated what the seer had going on for the ocean folk. "I advise you begin speaking. What do your visions have to do with Sirena?"

"Isn't it obvious? So many things are coming, and the sea will be dangerous. More dangerous than it is now with the realms of sirens and mermaids fighting each other." Avery showed Rosemarie the ink blots, as well as made clear of their meaning, "When your sister passed to the core of these waters, I unpredictably had the visions, then I saw what was approaching. She has a unique link to that human."

Rosemarie begins to look annoyed, and her voice becomes irritated, "Yeah, yes, I know! They're married and they're star-crossed lovers, what is it? Are they going to poison each other with belladonna?"

"Apparently, throughout these days of the honeymoon they had an exceptionally enjoyable time together. One thing led to another and now our mermaid, the one that your family wanted so bad to be Queen— is pregnant." Avery said with a worried expression, even if with seeming cynical.

Rosemarie glanced over at Sirena beyond the corridors where she was staying with me in the lounge. I could see the sisters grin at each other from across halls. I pondered what the fuss was about. Only, catching sight of Rosemarie's gestures which were confusing…one minute she looks cheery, the next minute she looks bemused.

"Oh, my goodness really? Hang on, n-n-no! Does Sirena know' because she didn't tell me anything about this when I arrived."

Avery was a significant seer, and she was frightened of her own vision and also baffled by it. "I didn't have full vision yesterday, until my dream last night. Rose, you understand that I am telling you this is dangerous. Her baby cannot be royalty! And there is still more but I cannot read that yet, something is shadowing those parts of the vision. It has never been done to me before. But like they say nothing is possible. You have to be its protector. Let them in."

Inside the kitchen, ignited with numerous candles on the edges all over us. I was just as excited, hearing of my wife's pregnancy. "SO, what's the big deal? Should we be celebrating" Though, Sirena looks as if she was in a mistaken dream-like state finding out she was pregnant.

Avery said, "Everyone sit down, lets join hands…all of you relax, especially Joshua, open your mind to my voice, I can show you,"

In the beginning, seafolk and humans…over thousands of years ago, knew how to coexist with boundaries. But then, there were times when seafolk tried to carry half-breeds with the ones they loved from land. But it nearly happened, and when it did…dangerous things occurred. Half-breeds were reasons of hurricanes, typhoons, and rogue waves. War and bloodshed followed them. Desperate to protect each other's realms, laws passed of seafolk never being pregnant by a human. And past half-breeds were separated from their families then slaughtered. Many were slaughtered, and more wars increased, wars against sirens and mermaids, seafolk and humans, and half-breeds against whoever. If mermaids ever bared any half breeds; they were stronger than the average mermaid, had greater abilities, and were able to stay on land and procreate easier. But when sirens ever succeeded, which was scarce, their half breeds felt a hunger on land, and they siren more than usual.

I looked at everyone, "Sirena…ladies come on! Our baby would not be like those babies were. They didn't have direction of what family is or who they were."

Rosemarie looked at Avery and said to me, "The half-breeds was the results of a thoughtlessness that ocean folk had took advantage off. Rather it was an affair or used to gain power."

"Rosemarie, this is your niece or nephew. It is like the keywords you said, recklessness, affair, power! Those words have nothing to do with Sirena and me. Now, passion, marriage, and love…that's the keywords that made our baby." I continued arguing over the fact that everyone was wrong, I can see in Sirena's eyes that she wanted this baby just as much as I did, unless she was in shock.

Avery looked at Rosemarie, "I have an idea…now, it hasn't been done in a long time. But Rosemarie, I can feel your aura and it's strong as the siren witch. The only thing you need is my seer abilities." Rosemarie said she never studied that form of magic. Yet, Avery stated that it was something you were born with, "But with you being a siren, we will try an old ritual, it is a form of blood magic, you have to take a bite of me and drink. Enough to transfer some of my sight magic to your abilities, but not enough to kill me."

Rosemarie laughed flirtatiously and said, "Sheesh, you could've at least taken me out on a date first, besides I'm sort of seeing someone."

Oh, my goodness, was Rosemarie really flirting right now and is she talking about dating my cousin. Gross, I did not realize she was a freak!

Rosemarie looked away from Avery and said to Sirena and me, "You guys, are in luck Avery called you in and confirmed your pregnancy before you went back home. The siren realm embraced your love and unexiled Sirena. So, help me, this is going to change everything. I'm worried Sirena and you, won't survive for quite some time to know its sex."

Sirena began crying, so I jumped up and I started talking, "Enough of this. And how dare you intimidate me, with the life of my love one's. Can't you see, you're scaring my wife. And I mean it when I say it, that we will cherish our baby. We cannot act like this; we have to have a clear mind and a clear plan that we will follow as soon as we get home. And since there are rules, we will tell the Queen, that would be the smart thing to do. But there is no way in hell, she's taking our baby for power or slaughter!!"

Sirena was flustered she left shouting, "Screw this. I'm going back to the bungalow." As Rosemarie ignores her sisters leave and she begins drinking the blood of Avery. "You taste different." She was simply overly pleased to receive Avery's blood.

Avery explains, "It won't give you all of my powers, but you will be able to sense more than you do now. At times you might even be able to scrawl like me and read the images. But unlike me you will not have nightmares or dreams about people. If anything, if I have any dreams of you all, I promise to let you know."

When Rosemarie got to the bungalow she spoke to Sirena on the side, "What is it about the baby?"

Sirena held her stomach, "Hmm, about conceiving a blessing in disguise with a human during a romantic honeymoon night…"

Rosemarie looked at her and said, "Regarding life as a mom. I mean look at our own mother."

Sirena laughed and then sighed saying, "You should know this, Rose. I— I was abandoned by my own mother, my own family and realm when I was an infant. I appreciate everything *your* mother, *my adoptive mom*, tried doing as I grew up, but I always wondered. What if? What did she look like? If she loved me? I don't want my baby to question such things."

Rosemarie looked at her, "I understand sister, I will always protect you. You are my kin no matter what."

CHAPTER 18

"Can you please take care of Rose for me, I'm too exhausted to go anyplace honey." Sirena said worn-out and, in her flattery, girlish voice. She did this in order for me to say yes, especially the things I loathed the most.

Rosemarie was by now plastered at a bar on the island, I sat beside her, and she spoke, "The seer left out a few things about the halflings. If any seafolk without doubt was with child by involvement of a man, she would be ostracized as of her clan on behalf of treachery. Defiled, she will instinctively despise the half-breed deep inside of herself, in the same manner that her entire species loathes humans as a whole, what is more specifically the halflings. Be that as it may, she will furthermore deliver the child. She will shortly abandon the newborn on the seashore to perish, however. As a matter of fact, it is even reputed that some seafolk, disgusted, will impulsively slaughter their newborn after initial glance."

I wasn't sure if it was only the alcohol, but it felt like Rosemarie was intentionally attempting to rile me up. Perhaps even trying to test my sincerity for Sirena.

"Well, I know Sirena…she would be maternal, sheltering, amorous and be devoted to the baby. She wouldn't even think about doing something like that." I said with all my heart, eagerness my voice was further influential than ever. It was as if she was seeking to perceive if everything, I had put my confidence in was altogether ramshackle beneath my feet. But I didn't exactly think so.

And in the fullness of time, you equally will plunge aside from being engulfed by means of the unending blackness as if hibernating under…

Rosemarie's mind was spiraling wild as she recited the words the seer spoke. She then eyeballed me for a very long time, studying deep-rooted keen on my soul, it would appear. But at a given point I no longer cared anymore. Her eyesight was becoming ever blurrier after drinking so heavily. It appeared as if the hollowness prowling within her in all instances had matured so far and gripping her. That she possibly felt the same as her innards melting into oblivion. It was definitely time for me to take her back to the bungalow, I picked her up and about into my arms and taken her all the way.

Throwing down my stuff, I tossed Rosemarie on the bare bed. Tilting her head to the side, she heeded for a while. "Where's Sirena?"

"Your sister is swimming in the ocean, as she usually likes to do before bed."

"Don't you know your wife's presence shouldn't be in the ocean?" She yelled, stepping into defensive-sister mode once again. It never ceased to astonish me that the instant she is comfortable, she disregards I have managed lacking her all these months.

I strode back, fingers almost ripping my hair. "Fine I'll call for her, but you still don't give me plenty trust as her husband. Did you forget Sirena is remarkable with her combat skills? And you know that as a mother, possibly an even greater force to be reckon with."

The next day we were leaving, I never thought I would live to see the day, but I asked Cheryl to use the yacht for the rest of Sirena and MY honeymoon! I asked her to enjoy bringing it back home, we were leaving early by plane. On the plane, it was just me and Sirena and I began to contemplate…life after honeymoon together with life with a baby, during the same period. When my parents got married, they didn't except my grandparents' house. As an alternative, they made a great effort before they even got hitched so as to buy their own home. Before I didn't have so much to worry, when I thought it would just be the two of us…in fact, I still didn't have anything to worry…a baby is so small. The guesthouse is perfect, as so I presume. But I know Gramps would say otherwise. And I know that Rosemarie would naturally agree with him, so that Sirena wasn't as close to the sea. But now, I was wondering…what is a mermaid's pregnancy like overall?

As we got nearer to our house, I could see her throat tightened, and hear her heart slowed down from the distance inside the car. I tried making her feel comfortable like we were when we were just leaving to our honeymoon, but the more I babbled the more I mentioned the baby; "Gramps is going to be so happy to hear the news." Her grip on her dress seemed to get tighter. I decided it was best for us to still get non-magical normal pregnancy test. Once I explained everything to Sirena, she thought about how silly and disgusting it was. I made jokes about how she was right about the disgusting part; I told her how some wives liked surprising their husbands in the weirdest unsanitary ways possible. Like cakes!

"This is the second one I did; the two lines means—" Sirena began asking sounding very confused yet again.

"That the seer is not a joke, you're indeed pregnant!" I thought I may possibly fall over with joy, However as I resumed watching Sirena's face, she gazed out the kitchen window at the trees back from Carolina, gleaming leaves in the gentle wind.

I was in euphoric delight for something like ninety seconds, before I sprinted to tell Gramps, and then it ultimately struck me; a flood of remorse along with fear blended in together that had me all choked up. Pregnant? A halfling? Expulsion? Have I done wrong? I pulled my hair out of disbelief; I marched a handful steps backwards. Strolling closer to Gramps, I was encountering my own reality check, which brought me even closer to the precipice of absolute panic. I fucked up my wife's life again!

"Gramps, we haven't even married that long, and I already messed things up?" I sat at the dining table looking all screwy. "She's scared I can tell…"

"What are you talking about champ?" I told Gramps everything. "Let me go check on her, I'm pretty sure it's better than one you think…do me a favor and continue painting the basement, it'll help keep your mind busy."

Be that as it may, before Sirena could dissolve into tears and dash yelling out of the room, Gramps drew her into his arms. "You are gonna be a wonderful mama," he said to Sirena, to her troubles. The family's affection flooded her, and she began to weep massively, dripping tears onto his much loved ivory shirt.

After talking to my wife and me painting the basement. I just realized that Gramps has been working on something since the honeymoon. Gramps explained that every memory of Hanks' history in that home, that dusted in the basement was moved into his shed as well his fishing gear. He was working on a project just for Sirena and her sisters, whenever they needed time secretly alone. After some days, we grabbed the tools and finished the saltwater pool he started. It was halfway done, so by this time we would complete it in a month, my only thought was how this was happening at the best time for Sirena.

Each day we worked on the indoor pool, and each day I just thought about Sirena. On days I couldn't work on it, Rosemarie, who knew about the surprise pitched in. Sirena would walk back and forth from the house to guesthouse, but her thoughts were so filled she never really wondered what was going on downstairs, if anything she appreciated the odd behavior between Rosemarie and I, she wanted to dwell in space. Though when we were done, Gramps gave me the keys to the main Hanks house, and he did exactly what I believed him to do. For Sirena, we took it for now, but I did wonder if he would be safe that close to the sea. Rosemarie mentioned she knew a potion to protect the whole area from any uninvited guest. Sirena hugged her sister and Gramps softly, but she still looked so sad. She was missing the ocean. That's when Rosemarie put her hands over her eyes and we began walking down to the basement, "It smells like, like home…' Gramps revealed the surprise. It was Sirena's own lagoon of ocean seawater, with seawater plants, and seawater fish. That's when Sirena jumped in and cried happy tears.

* * *

Already parked from work, I see Cheryl parking ahead of the Hanks house, yelling a voicemail on her phone while she fixes her makeup. I can't get out of this car; I don't want her to see me. But shit, I know Sirena is in the house, I have to save her.

Sirena, inside, hears her voice and rolls her eyes looking bothered as if she was just enjoying the saltwater from the indoors basement pool that Gramps and Josh made for her.

Cheryl was leaving another complaining voicemail, "Rosemarie, if not replying to any of my calls is some sort of factor of your cunning proposal to have me in your life, well let me remind you we have been done since you've disappeared on me…Nevertheless, I'm at the house, and there's no sign of you. Right now, pick up your goddamn phone, or I'm driving away without you having a taste of me."

After Cheryl walks into the house, Sirena walks upstairs from the basement up and says, "What the hell are you doing here? I mean, oh, what a surprise…I wasn't expecting you here" Smiling wryly, dressed in a one piece maternity dress like swimsuit, her tummy hardly looked like a bump.

It was everyone's fear, once Cheryl found out about the pregnancy, she would want to constantly update the entire pregnancy trimesters on her blogs. She would say, "Pregnancy is trending." My cousin did it all on our wedding day, as she declared herself the reason for all the greatness that day.

Sirena complained about how the honeymoon made her feel like a cow and she wondered if Cheryl knew of any diets. She looked down at the baby bump which was slightly hidden with the dress. "Ri…ight, I'm no fool…darlin' you're not fat, you're knocked up from the honeymoon. Sweetie, you should've waited a few more years before getting preggers."

Sirena gave her another wry smile, "I see what my sister sees in you… has anybody told you, you have got your father's behaviors."

When Cheryl smiled, a little flame within her turned into an enormous beam of light, "Darlin' please, I have a better temper than that, Carolina knows who to watch out for! By the way where is Rosemarie and Gramps?"

"Beats me. Rose is getting something for me to eat, and Gramps is long way away."

Sirena grew quiet once again but then she left Cheryl pondering.

Cheryl frowned. "Hell, you mean, long way away? That old man is always here and your sister message me to be here."

Sirena was bursting of mounting hormones and felt further than disturbed, "Well, just a moment ago, he was here making ambitious vows about caring for me as his own in this view, making promises that no parent of mine would make— he was every bit of imaginative in relation to how we're family— and then I don't know, he seemed frightened and I'm not sure what happened after a few bottles of Scotch. I suppose that's what I make for entrusting any paternal figure."

Cheryl looked at Sirena with a fierce attitude, I didn't have enough time to get them apart, but I overheard everything, "Hey, that seems more akin to your sister to me. Gramps is not just some old man with paternal instincts, and he will certainly not break a vow. Which means that there a man out there, at his old age most likely secretly working to support you and Joshua with that bun. So don't you go bad-mouthing about that old man."

I finally opened the double doorways that lead to the grand living room. "Ladies, ladies, what with the whole hollering." Once they quieted and before Cheryl spoke, I timidly said, "Cousin Cheryl! My— wonderful beloved cousin…You came back from my honeymoon already? So soon."

Cheryl begins looking like she's burying secrets herself, even as she speaks with teary eyeballs although keeps a gigantic springy smile, "Well, yes. I was having the time of my life, thank you Joshie, however I knew that my Rosie was missing me."

CHAPTER 19

ramps, having lived his whole life in the Hanks Victorian beauty, which outside made you feel like you were living in a storybook setting on the beach. A massive house that had an enormous wrap-around southern front porch that held each family members secret. During my great-grandfather's time, the basement was famous for the Hanks gentleman's club where they smoked cigars, drank their bourbon, and spoke politics while playing cards. After my grandmother's passing, the basement transformed from a social place to a colossal storage room for Gramps to leave every piece of memorabilia since his young times and so forth. Now, Gramps was so inspired by the love he had for my wife, that he transformed his storage room to a beautiful humongous indoors seawater grotto.

The white froth had tapped only her toes, after that she tearfully chuckled. She plunged into the pool; however, she wasn't shifting. She was just swimming absolutely exposed along with only her legs. She appeared as though she may possibly bathe in there forever, remain under water continuously, immerse while playing as well as studying in the grotto endlessly. Nevertheless, we all stared at her with shocking misunderstanding. I couldn't tell if she noted it herself. The way she swam, Sirena obviously felt fortunate enough to feel the saltwater touching her skin, dancing into the seawater she then sat there on the stony steps as she stretched out slightly further, up until the water slapped at her knees. Yet, still not noticing.

She remained sculpting her legs forming a fin illusion, but then yet again it was simply an illusion that she didn't recognize wasn't there. She glanced at myself and Gramps, along with an enormous smile that I hadn't seen in a while, she expressed her thanks so greatly. As she rinsed her face with the grottos water, with a nervous energy I hastily spoke, "Sirena, you're in seawater; how come you haven't changed?"

"What do you mean? My tail is ther— oh, um, maybe there's something wrong with this water."

Gramps said, "Trust me darlings, it's not just salted water that I made. Joshua helped out and constructed two pipes, that they apply for a number of aquariums. They're placed just over the seafloor. By doing so, it's the exact ocean water you're naturally swimming in."

Rosemarie then leaped within the area examining the water. But despite the fact that she concurred as soon as she felt the sea water, above all her tail approved after it splashed all over. But then she looked closely at her sisters' legs. "Look, she still has her glossy tangerine scales, shimmering and scattering around." I started getting closely enough to recognize that from her thighs to her ankle, like flower-patterned designed stockings, Sirena had scattered scales around her thighs, a few sparkled like shimmering dust on her knees, and even more around her lower leg. Though, soon after something aroused all of our attention…within Sirena's "Lily Pads" inside the inner thighs the scales was fluorescent.

Sirena looked horrified, as if she had felt like her body betrayed her, her fin wasn't appearing. She remained sitting panicked, speechless, dumbfounded, as a consequence in her bestowed form there was only demeanor. She then listened to the voices coming as of the sea water while she was beginning to weep, "I suppose I am the subject matter in the ocean. Not exactly a very pleasing one, I understand their fear, but it is impossible to contribute to it. I don't want to believe the baby will be reason for tides as well as bring about corpse to ride the waves."

Gramps pretended to stay settled down. At which point, he began speaking of something which I had no clue of what he was referring to, "You know, Sirena my dear, before my wife was pregnant, she hated mushrooms. The texture and the smell made her want to vomit. However, when she became pregnant with our first child, mushrooms was all she wanted to eat…pregnancy changes women. In many ways…"

Sirena and Rosemarie stared at him with puzzled smirks, I soared in saying that possibly the pregnancy is changing Sirena in a manner that even Rosemarie have the faintest idea. Come to think about it, the mermaids and sirens have their immense gap from each other. It would explain why the siren Queen never gave the *talk* to Sirena.

Still though, afterwards she wanted to be left alone in the grotto. After I gave her a kiss, I looked back at her, Sirena's periwinkle eyes were dreary. No indication of bliss or positivity could be observed in her expression.

* * *

The grotto was an extremely fine idea. Not merely to keep her alive and well from anyone who would want to make sure of her harm, but what is more to stay away from me. Some night, I discovered her side of the bed deserted, as soon as I sought for her, I was uneasy, although not enough to scream everyone awake. I had a feeling to go down the stairs to the grotto, when I did, she was sleeping in a colorful coral reef seabed. So, I laid next to her, brushing her hair away from her face and I whispered, "It's my fault, not yours. When I figure it out, I will do what's right. I promise!" I didn't want to disturb her, so I disappeared back into my bed.

Sirena didn't believe that I understood. However, I am competent at envisioning, living even as being mindful of your own inevitable misfortune, while staying kept away from your own home has been difficult to cope with.

The oceans laws go by all the way through Sirena's mind during the course of the latest days. The phrases engraved in her attention. She was brought up, have being educated of the history of her ocean depths better than what was demonstrated. Even, increasingly more than the royal family she lived with and those who ruled it long ago. She was able to rehearse the family name of the ocean's ancestors, after the woman who given origin to the siren realms, from the woman who given origin to the mermaid realms. Then all the way over into the Goddesses who gave birth to the oceans, lakes, and rivers. Her heart and soul was borne from the ocean, but as of her pregnancy she saw herself becoming a tainted stain from the ocean.

An abrupt dread smacked upon her. The reality that she was expecting was tense plenty, nevertheless the concept of notifying the Queen of her situation discouraged her all the more as she considered the notion of becoming a mother. Sirena recalled the way her mother looked at her the day of her marriage, she remembered the hug and love as well as being pardoned from her exile. Her worries held up with her in one fell swoop. She started to remove herself from all of us since the moment her fin didn't show, along with the disturbing stress triggered by an unwelcome pregnancy. Pushing us all away as she was feeling her world had been turned upside down and uncontrolled events were happening too fast for her. She needed to be alone in her mind and think. But I was worrying that she was pushing us far beyond into the abyss, that she wouldn't be able to find us when she most needed.

"Listen here, Sirena! I understand what you're going through, we all do…Now, I may not be from the sea, but I am the man who loves you, and who married you, and who did hope for all future surprises with you. Perhaps, I didn't think about it being sprung up so early into our marriage, but that's what love is about! Taking the risks of jumping together into the adventures." That was beginning to make Sirena feel a source of shame for isolating herself from this family her. But knowing my Sirena, she was stubborn, therefore, I persisted onwards, "And no, I didn't think that if we had children, that we would end up on your mothers' bad side, AGAIN! She seems to be the hardest entity to please. I understand that it's devastating not being able to step into your own home, being an abomination to seafolk. I empathize with how you're feeling. We all do! If you weren't so closeminded you would realize your sister, has been traveling back and forth trying to arrange a meeting with you and your mother in one place." She stood silent and I can see she was embarrassed and wanted to cry. "And I am promising you this, if we start avoiding each other now, it doesn't matter if you're human or from the ocean, but that is the way that you'd not only ruin your marriage but ruin your child's future. Can't you see! WE can be the doom to our baby's future if we don't stand by each other and if we stop appreciating each other as usual."

⁎ ⁎ ⁎

Sirena kept on listening to the footsteps from the kitchen, the pacing from side to side was bothering her as she attempted to read sitting in her most comfortable living room chair. As she glanced over the turn, she was shocked by what she saw, "Rose, you don't have to stay here. I'm surprised you didn't call an uber to make you something."

Rosemarie drifted in opposite of the kitchen booth, chopping a salmon clean. After slapping her book on my head, Sirena asked me if I would put her up to this. I didn't. Then she whispered to me, that in all her years, she'd not once witnessed Rose cook anything in her life, other than her brews. She turned out to be worried and asked me to double check what Rosemarie was truly doing.

Rosemarie apparently eavesdropped, her mouth jerked up until her lips gave approach to a partial smile, "That Uber food delivery constantly gets our food incorrect. Moreover, earlier I noticed these luscious looking seaweed, and magnificent salmon. I just had to try, who knows I feel like it might be in my nature, beside I might have to learn a thing or two about being a baby's...what is it again Joshua?"

"We call it, aunt! And also, being the baby's protector and all, we want you to be the godmother...um or goddess mother?" I forget sometimes they prefer saying goddess, their belief is that their goddesses created the ocean, lakes, and all other types of land water.

Rosemarie looked at me as if she just finished looking through a statistics quiz, "What, now I have two titles? Really, what is the point of an Aunt Rosemarie and goddess mother Rosemarie?"

As I started explaining, I wondered how many titles for their family did they gave each other. I guess it didn't matter so much when you had to live in a world that had to fend for itself. "Well, being her aunt, identifies you as not only our baby's family, but also, it's mother's sister. And the other thing, well it's kind of an honor...in case something bad was to happen to us...you'll take over. But you aren't the only godparent. SO don't worry you have back up."

"Well, let's just hope that never happens, cause I'm not ready to be a parent. An auntie sounds fine enough." She grimly laughs and turns around to the refrigerator.

Sirena jumped up really quick, strolled around Rosemarie, "I guess it would make sense to be a cook, in both concoctions and cuisine." She then seized a slice of fish from the chopping board and shoved it in her mouth.

Sirena gave a kiss on her sister's cheek and then caressed her stomach, "Baby desires, I fathom. This little swimmer desires to munch. Ooh, can you please combine a little sea cucumber on the side."

"Yes, anything for the one I'm intended to care for." Rosemarie then glanced at her stomach. "I'm sorry, the seer said to protect you, and the quite parasitic baby, but Sirena I can't even imagine that halfling growing inside you."

"Fuck you! I'm not hungry, I don't want to eat your crappy disgusting shit!" Sirena snapped at her sister, I knew from prior occasions that it was most excellent for me to pay no attention to the bickering and to not get myself caught in between the sibling arguments. They had abilities, I didn't. "Rosemarie, you only got to know the seer Avery for a few days. You don't have to obey her commands. YOU don't have to HOVER me!! I wouldn't want you to feel gruesome thinking about my baby!!" A winter of trepidation freezing over seeped along my backbone. I turned over to face them, however my own face was dazed with panic.

Sirena would rather behave like this, then admit that she'd been scared out of her wits deep down of finally meeting up with her the Queen and discussing her pregnancy.

CHAPTER 20

irena couldn't take it anymore that she sprinted out of our house and jumps into the ocean. Ah, how lovely it felt. It was just like before she thought, instead of the small belly bump and the fact that her two legs wouldn't transform into her fin. But she could breathe perfectly as long as she could, and she didn't care of her nudeness.

Suddenly, something swam quickly right by her. A tone of voice at the back of her frightens her more and she twirls around.

It was the dark seelie, grinning disturbingly she says, "You're not meant to be around here."

Sirena questioned her name though when hearing the name, Undine, she became absolutely terrified of her.

"Oh sorry. I didn't intend to panic you. I'm Undine. Rosemarie knows me, very well."

"You're her tutor. You're the head sea witch she told me about."

Undine stared around at the mermaids that began to appear lurking around the coral reefs of the siren's territory, "Rosemarie just requested me to come keep you company after you stormed out furiously. You understand, they're more and more drawn to this area. The baby you're having is part human, part mermaid. You and Joshua created something extraordinary, as well as something fatal."

Sirena didn't want to say too much about what the seer said in Jamaica. It was menacing in the past; it would be petrifying in front of the head sea witch. "You sound like the seer from Jamaica and even Rosemarie. The seer thinks the baby…well I rather not carry on. I'm not even sure what…*it* is."

Undine looked at my body and smirked, "You realize, I know how to do something regarding that if you feel like. You know, find out if it's a baby Josh or a baby you."

Afraid Sirena speculated, "In the ocean or out, I'm not going anywhere I don't know!"

"I think it's a better idea to do it above, too many mermaids are watching you. You're not supposed to be here, remember? And you could be putting them in danger. It's a fast secret. Come on, you have to be a tiny bit curious."

On land, Undine and Sirena sit on the dock next to the guesthouse. Undine begins chanting something under her breath, resting Sirena gently on her back. She clutches Sirena's stomach before bringing out her crystal necklace and circles it above Sirena's stomach. When it stopped, Undine whispered the sex to her. Sirena wasn't even showing, she wasn't even a week into her pregnancy.

She explained everything when she got home and calmed us down with her apology included. Although the following day things were fairly off. She was dressed in my old loose clothes from high school that she most likely recovered from the shed. At that sunrise her smile appeared to be so forced.

"What's wrong?" I asked when I saw her, "Are you okay?"

"Oh sure," Sirena said short of eagerness, "People don't trouble. I just don't feel awfully well."

I looked at Rosemarie and whispered in her ears. "Sirena looks worse than she admits. What's wrong with her? Is it magic?" She was so slender; I couldn't think of her being with child. She even began to look too weak; you could see the dark circle under her eyes of her now pale skin.

"I have been feeling extraordinarily ill, Sorry I can hear all your whispering concerns from afar." Sirena admits to all of us.

Rosemarie said, "Welcome to living the life on the human side. You should've swum faster the instant he proposed." I shot a glare at Rosemarie. But then she took a look at Sirena's ear, it was leaking out blood, "You've been significantly cursed!"

"Who would do such a thing?" Gramps was grabbing the phone, as I rushed to clean the blood from Sirena's ear.

"Now don't touch it! I need it." She instantly took a shot glass full of her blood. After chanting something, she drank the blood. She warned us ahead of time to leave her alone so she can use the seer magic. "UNDINE! You can't escape the Carolina's barriers."

Sirena sweating bullets yelled, "Stop it Rose! Besides if I was important to the ocean, then why would the sea-witch put some kind of curse on me. You're saying that, so long as I'm keeping this baby, I can't get away from Carolina. If I do, the curse will murder me."

Rosemarie scrolling her crystal around her body, said, "Well that's what happens to you when you don't listen to us. We're just trying to watch over you, now I have to find the source of where she curse you. As you keep on baking the halfling in your tummy. Leave it to your sister to break the curse." Rosemarie sprints off to resume her study in concoctions, leaving Sirena to contemplate if keeping the baby was worth both their lives.

"Although for the moment, we have a visitor to speak with and Sirena you ought to unwind."

* * *

Soon after Sirena is rummaging in Rosemarie's Garden patio, "I can't find it anywhere," Sirena yelled, distressingly. "No worries. I found it," she said, dragging it out of Rosemarie's plant shelf where she had hidden it. "Wouldn't you know— it was before my very eyes."

"By all means, it was," Rosemarie muttered as Sirena rose upright and placed the book lying down on the chair.

Sirena lifted up a brow. "What were you meant to imply sis?"

"I'm simply pleased that you discovered it."

Sirena sniggered wryly. "No, that's not what you said. I'm not hard of hearing. Are we in a bad mood these days, ROSE?"

Sirena glared back at the tall, slender female with the curly, scarlet hair. As much as Rosemarie had stayed rattling on Sirena's tensions recently, she knew Rosemarie had just been protective. Rosemarie walked away, as Sirena, sitting cross-legged on the floor in the garden patio, began reading through each page of the leather- bound book of concoctions.

But there was no concoction found to make the baby just secretly vanish. As everyone else prepared to protect the island.

* * *

Dianthus glared at Rosemarie, "Best of my knowledge a change has developed in our siblings, in the whole realm if you ask me!" Dianthus couldn't step by the spelled barriers, although her sister Rosemarie was simply an inch across, and I noticed how interested she looked around. "Our connection stresses under the gravity of our existence being in the palms of this creature, our adoptive sister carries. Day after day, we are becoming all the more separated from our genuine nature and steadily reaping kills we once possessed. Our sweet sisters, Nerilena and Kalidelia, have matured rather enthusiastic to the increase of viciousness.

Dianthus ensures everyone a recovered memory even from the farness. Her vision revealed to us, the sisters with other sirens. They were savagely drowning anyone from their boats, without luring them with a siren song. They were rebelling by exposing themselves, and they were overfeeding. Even for sirens, that was against the ocean's laws.

"However, the genuine difficulty persists in our sister, Sirena." In another vision, the eldest siren sister shows them me during my weeks prior late afternoons. I began shouting out to stop showing this, I commanded, "Change the channel," but Dianthus was not giving in. The vision showed me on the yacht far away from the beach, I was throwing evidence of severed bodies that sirens left around. In the ocean and some on the beach. Since the sirens overfed, they didn't feel too hungry to complete their meals as usual. One of the pieces of evidence was a couple, they were naked but wrapped around each other, as if they didn't want to let go to be the last thing they did. The worse evidence I found was a toddler herself in a bathing suit.

Everyone gawked at me for a long while. They all were offended by me. I shouted and cried out at them, "I couldn't send each of them to the hospital, there was evidence all over their dead flesh. I wanted to give them proper burials, I did!!" I kept crying, as Gramps walked to me patting my back, "I thought that I probably could have poured gasoline over their bodies and burned them to ashes. However, I found them in various locations while fishing for Sirena's craves. The only solution I had was the sharks. I'm sorry!! But I was honestly freaked out. I'm still in pain, like fuck, a baby!!" I cried on Gramps' shoulders. "The sirens were sending a message and I didn't want to freak anyone else out. I'm sorry; but it was either that or send them all to the

E.R end up looking like a sick murderer, get caught burning all those bodies, or throw them in the marshes where the alligators will later shit them out and it would eventually rile up a murder investigation. What the fuck was I supposed to do?! Please, tell me!!" I knew I was being hysterical, but I had this on my shoulders for a while. I didn't want my Gramps and Rosemarie to see that, but it was eventually going to pop up.

Dianthus grins a little, a dark grin, "It was going to eventually pop up. Now, the Queen is a different story. She remains to conceal her detachment with harshness, as she continuously has. However, she isn't doing much to prevent her daughters and the other sirens from their rebellious behavior. The other siren pods around the world are in riots, some want to join our pod, and others want to rid mom from her throne."

Rosemarie began to speak, "Even so, we must hold on to the likelihood that this child is very hopeful. What if the baby is able to lead the seafolk back on the right path, a route indicated with the influence of how siren realms should traditionally behave? If all else fails, what if the baby was the restraint to our family's empire coming to an end in obscurity."

Sirena must've stopped reading along with seeking to explore for "cookbook recipes," as she was currently messaging Rosemarie and I to join up with her at the garden patio for an essential conversation.

Then Rosemarie grimaced staring at me hard, "And you Joshua…I thought we became friendly enough to the point that you can share those sorts of things, I could've helped you dispose of those bodies with a use of my potion. I could've helped you cremate them in seconds."

"Was I expected to leave them behind floating in the ocean, resting on the shorelines and rocks to decay? Anyway, with the rapid thoughts traveling around through and through my mind, at that point in time it was my responsibility." I sneered at Rosemarie and Dianthus, "Let's not fail to remember, that they'll strike my vulnerable pregnant wife who's bearing our baby!"

Dianthus rolled her eyes as she said, "Oh, I remain so pulled by your newly discovered idea of fatherly burdens to our mermaid keeping your halfling crab in her shell."

Rosemarie exhaled while trying to shift matters hastily, "The strategy to bail out Sirena. You know, our mermaid sister? As the sirens mortal enemy because of her condition."

Dianthus smirked, "Bail out?"

Rosemarie said, "You called me saying that you would get back to me, with a plan to clear the water. Therefore, it there a plan, or anything?"

"Fine, fine. Well, first of all, she is not ultimately the siren's grave enemy. I wouldn't be able to be here. The Queen isn't that diabolical, that's still something that needs to be in court. And secondly, that dialogue is between the sea witch, the Queen, and Sirena. And thirdly—" She turns to me and ask me to guess.

Rosemarie cut me off, which was great because I had no clue. "And thirdly, the plan, is that you demand Sirena to simply be left alone…right??"

Joshua being especially unconvinced, "That's…that's not the entire strategy, is it?"

Dianthus scoffs as she rolls her eyes, "The third plan, well obviously battle. Sister, if that happens, we don't know if it would be amongst us and humans, our realms against each other, or just everyone against Sirena."

Sirena's voice entered all of our minds, "Dianthus, this mermaid wants you leave, Rose and Josh, I need you at the garden patio." Before Dianthus left, I apologized again to the siren sisters.

* * *

Sirena looked distraught and bothered as she was prepared to explain, "I would like to know whatever the ground plan is. Frankly Josh…honey please don't be saddened with me, but then I attempted to discover something that would make the baby go." Rosemarie previously knew; however I stared utterly feeling broken and blindsided.

"What the hell, Sirena? You didn't think of speaking to me." Sirena looked like she felt bad. "Well, by plans, that depends by what plan you mean Sirena— we apparently didn't use the protection plan, too late for the Plan B plan, you secretly have plans for termination, and I'm the only one who have plans to keep the baby!"

Rosemarie takes her spell book from the table at the side of her and tosses it in my face. It slaps my face so hard that it implants my face with the stamp of the siren's emblem.

CHAPTER 21

I found it irritating that Sirena wouldn't allow me to go with her and discuss things with her mother, I felt that I was just as much to blame for as she was. I didn't want the marriage between family to get off to a rocky start, but she insisted that if I didn't want to die, I'd stay in the house. Therefore, when they left, I hid in the lighthouse to listen in, knowing very well that the Queen wouldn't leave too far from the ocean.

"Ahh, mother!" Sirena squealed, throwing herself into the seashore as the Queen was just beginning to start drying up. She reached across then gave her an indecent gigantic hug. The Queen began to sigh from feeling a sort of atrocity from the absence of manner as well as the fact that Sirena didn't burst out a tail. Rosemarie on the other hand strolled up to her mother with grace, and as a replacement for a hug she offered her a dress wrap.

"We can skip the most part, the story about your atrocity in your belly is all over the ocean. I'm so ashamed of you. You should be ashamed of yourself." The reaction from Sirena's mother was snobbier than I expected.

Her mother's face unbends with indifference, along with her hands descends along and moves, so softly, the area just beneath her belly.

A very unexpected sniffle tortures all through Sirena's mother, crushing her ideas, and the sisters look further than stunned, terrified at the same time, being unsure what it implies, just then her mother's sobbing alters into merriment.

Sirena became so nervous and hysterical and grabbed her mother's hand, trying to see if she could feel the same thing her mother had felt,

"What's wrong? Is the baby OK, is it dead, why are you laughing, you never laugh?"

"It's quite healthy for now, it's strong just like I am, I can hear the sea rushing through its veins." Sirena was happy to hear that, though Rosemarie looked concerned still.

"Even though she was cursed by the sea witch Undine. Do you know anything about that…mother?" Rosemarie gave her own mother a tensed look.

"Yes, of course I know, I asked Undine to take care of that myself, that way Sirena wouldn't have any crazy ideas. She can be so immature." She chuckled just like many Queens did, it was so elegant and still very egotistical.

Rosemarie became furious, "And what in the right realm would make you do something that preposterous?"

"Oh, Rosemarie if you girls are going to react so distraught of how I take care of things I really don't know how I can have this conversation with you."

Sirena responded more serenely particularly because she yearned to salvage the relationship she had with her mom, "Can you help? You're the Queen for the Goddess's sake!" she pleaded. "Or do you want me to continue living hating you? I want this baby badly; it was made from love. I should hate you for not trying hard enough"

"You're breaking my heart," the Queens answer was.

"I can't hate you," Sirena wept. "How can I hate someone who mothered me? But why would you accept my marriage but not allow me to have a baby!!"

"I haven't said you can never have children, did I? Ungrateful child." the Queen replied. "I only thought you would have common sense and have a child with a tritone at least."

"What, what sense would that make? So, you can take my child away from me and take care of it as your own? In order for you to still have a mermaid in your realm." Sirena looked at her with disgust "How could you mom? I trusted you; I loved you."

Then Queen spoke, "I'm sorry, but Sirena you're having a halfling, which is exceedingly dishonorable within our realm, and what you might called, baneful." Sirena wept as Rosemarie held her hissing at her own flesh and blood. "We know why I have trusted Sirena, a mermaid not of my blood, to be in line of the throne. It was her true powers out of all of us, that would make our pod stronger than any other siren pod." She looks up at the Hanks land, "Unfortunately, the one I mothered didn't take what I given her. And though, I had approved of the marriage, I didn't approve of her having a halfling…until now!" Rosemarie demanded why, "A halfling beholds enormous devastating powers, but if contained and educated properly, well, it can remain untroubled to us all and take it's line in the throne."

Rosemarie continued restraining Sirena back, but as she came into contact with Sirena's stomach it seem like she saw something. She then changed to attack mode, screeching, and hissing at the Queen. She had a warrior posture as she stared down at her mother with an aggressive encounter. Rosemarie had sensed an eager responsibility of reacting overprotectively, specifically following a feeling she sensed amongst her mother and the baby.

"Oh, dear Rosemarie, since when have you've reacted so sensitive. You know the duty of the royals and our realm. I'll forgive you." The Queen was so patronizing that she wouldn't believe her own daughter by blood could have separate emotions from her own species. Forgiving Rosemarie was better than believing that her most dependable daughter had actually changed.

"I don't care about your kingdom! I don't want another woman carrying my baby. I want to the mother of my children and yes, they will be confused by our lineage but again I will never lie to them, and we will get through everything together as a family."

"You're so gullible, why not? It will grow up strong. This child would act on warrior instincts and hunger…what are you trying to do poisoning it with idiotic schooling that they teach on the land?" Queen Dionysus asked as she seated herself at the elegant tea table on the dock sipping with a crooked smile. As Sirena and Rosemarie remained soundless with shame, forgetting that they had tea, their mother continued, "It only makes sense that when you already have something, that would be born savage you must contain it. And the only way you can contain it, it's within the siren's realm. It will be taught how to survive and rule like a siren."

Sirena's eyes lined with tears, "You only want my baby, so you can convert my lovely halfling into some sort of tri-breed." Rosemarie looked at her bewildered, just as much as I was as I overheard, "Mother I'm not foolish as you say, during my royal training I've learned from the past lore of conspiracy of silence. Feeding a mermaid halfling blood…distorts it even greater. Everyone is now scared of my halfling, imagine a tri-breed. You're not having any guardianship of my baby."

Queen Dionysus straightened up in her seat, took a sip of her tea, stared at Sirena from her legs and swiftly looked deeply in her eyes as she snapped, "I know what you all are wondering about. Why haven't you turned yet? Your legs haven't changed since your pregnancy, have they?"

I felt Rosemarie's anger rise as she jumped in front of Sirena, "It's just the sea-witch…I'll reverse that!"

"No, you foolish girls, haven't I taught you anything? The reason why you're poorly sick is because of Undine's curse. The reason why you haven't changed is because you have to live in the water during the pregnancy. It's the only way for your halfling to be born, is in your mermaid form." Queen Dionysus stood up looking into the ocean as she didn't let her dignity go astray. "Have you ever seen dolphins running around in human legs whenever they feel like giving birth…no! In order to make sure that baby is healthy inside of you need to live inside the realm, or at least inside the ocean. You may be a wife on land, but you were born a mermaid and the ocean runs deep inside your veins!"

"How the hell is she supposed to do that if she's forbidden from the ocean, she couldn't even take a plunge for a while," Rosemarie spoke disagreeing with her mother's explanation.

"Well, I am still the Queen of my realm like it or not. They won't be expecting either one of you, however that's when your older dexterity of defiance falls in, so sneaking in the realm wouldn't be a problem for you both." The sisters continued to feel the weight of Queen Dionysus' eyes as their mother resumed talking with an unflustered tone, "She would also have to stay inside the fortress. Only Dianthus and you can know. The rest of the sisters and even the servants can't know. It will only leave a target on Sirena's back. That's the only way this baby will be born safely, in the ocean. Not through her human form but in her mermaid form. And Sirena would regain her nourishment and recover."

* * *

"Mother, how do you even know such things? How can I believe you're telling the truth? I'm protecting Sirena's child, but what if you're the one I have to protect it from."

"Many years ago, before there was war between mermaids and sirens, I've seen it happen amongst them. The ones who stood on land didn't transform into their natural forms, and ended up having miscarriages. However, the ones who desired to live mainly underwater transformed and birthed healthy babies that were born. But later on, of course the law was passed and that no longer happened, that's another reason why we need to keep this secret between all of us."

I ran outside of the lighthouse where the ladies were standing. "This isn't happening, not if I have a say in it! Do you have any fucking idea what you two have done? She's taking away both you and the baby away from me." I looked at Sirena and Rosemarie as if they backstabbed me. Suddenly I became hysteric, "I'm sorry mom-in law, but you're not taking my wife! You just want OUR child, YOUR grandchild, so you can somehow find a way to raise it in royalty. Then marry it off to another power-hungry pod and conceive superior force. Just face it, you're not her real mother and mothers don't do things like this to their children. You're not looking to save her." I pleaded in tears. "You've made it so I can't be around my own wife's pregnancy. I bet that pleases you, does it?"

Sirena hangs her head, "We'll talk about this later, I really don't believe she wants to hurt—"

"Don't bother talking to me tonight, I need to clear my head, GOOD FUCKING NIGHT, YOUR MAJESTY!" I began turning away but then I said, "You know, I thought we were actually coming together…you know as family. I thought you would appreciate our baby but again, your Queen siren attitude that kidnapped me and stole my girlfriend before, is right back in action!"

Before she left with a grin as chilly as nightfall, Queen Dionysus rested close and caressed her daughters lightly on the cheek. Her face appeared to float ahead of me in the sunset. Her eyes was filled with red, as her smile was always a bit contemptuous.

Rosemarie and then went into my head, "You have to control yourself. Sirena's not doing this because she wants to, it's because she has to for the sake of your family. We both believe is true, especially if I'm going to literally babysit. I'll look after her for you, and I'll make sure you'll see Sirena."

I was livid, I shoved Sirena's and Rosemarie's hands away from me. I ran up towards the house to my office. After smashing the door closed, I then sank next to the wall after yelling my lungs out and tossing my lectures all around the floor. I was trembling in wrath, with dread, with melancholy. That vile, fucking sea creature.

CHAPTER 22

t night in the dining room of our home Sirena tells me that she's leaving to go back to the realm during the pregnancy. I want to say something, but I don't even know where to begin, especially after Rosemarie gesturing to me not to. Gramps is just wondering if we still get to see her every now and then. He's up to speed as I explained to him everything when he found me in the office throwing all my books and papers, being upset at the world.

"This is not a normal pregnancy," Sirena says. As if she had to justify why she was leaving me again for her mother her fucking wicked mother.

I continued on eating my dinner, I have no say as usual. Plus, I'm afraid to look at her in the eye. Instead, I'd look at the plate. I noticed the steak could have tasted better with espresso butter. Next, I started to think about how since my grandma passed, dinner has never been executed perfectly.

But later I walked up, and I turned to my wife, and I gave her an embrace, not lightly but splendidly, and you can say proudly. I need to show her exactly how greatly I cherished her as well as grateful for her. I wanted to show her that I was here for her just as if she was in the ocean. Sirena's feet appears straight up away the flooring as I whirl her about.

Joshua says, "Sirena you're right, we've been discussing about receiving this type of adventure for so long, we only never knew it would come with a cost! But I'm with you love!" Rosemarie and Gramps begin to aw.

"Just a minute," Sirena says, "I haven't been expecting to have this adventure so soon. I'm unsure whether I want this baby by any means. I've been going about this, back and forth still. I'm sorry honey but that's the truth."

I knew what she meant; Sirena had plans to finish her basic education in a community college and start her business in aromatherapy with Rosemarie in town. As well as going on living our lives together. That plan went out the window when Queen Dionysus stepped on shore.

Between noon and sunset, Rosemarie spent her night with Cheryl without telling her anything, while Sirena and I spent time together deep into the night. Sirena traced her lips beyond my mouth, and we were connected. I wondered to myself exactly how long would it take for us to devote this moment with each other yet again. As I made love to her, I kept wondering; when would be the next time I would see her smile, how can I be that supportive husband to her, and most importantly how am I going to develop a relationship with my unborn baby.

The next morning, I woke up to Sirena packing up only her ocean projection necklace and the underwater case for her phone. The things she took with her made me wonder if she was holding on to her promise and keeping me close to her heart, the projection necklace was a picture of me and her and if she didn't want to see me, she wouldn't care about a picture of me. The waterproof casing for her phone would give her some sort of connection to me and her and hopefully the baby's growth.

Rosemarie argued, "So you are serious about this? We're truly going back to our home in the ocean, even though our own mother did everything to make you forget Joshua, your husband and father to that baby. Which we still don't know if she has anything else capable for that unborn!!"

Sirena looked at her as though she was a confident child. "She had explained this very well to us— if I am planning to keep this baby it needs to live in the sea during my pregnancy, there is no time to spare you see how sick I am."

"So, you're letting your husband just say goodbye to his pregnant wife, is there any chance you will be getting to see him?"

"Rosemarie, I thought you never even liked him, stop doing this to me. I bet you're only caring about you and Cheryl. Trying to make this burden even harder than it already is on me, of course I'm going to try my best that I can, to see him but right now it's about the baby. And it's better that I leave him for a little while, than to end up dead!"

Sirena picked up a few of her things and went outside, striding boldly across the beach. Rosemarie followed; they both noticed that Dianthus and I were together chatting with Gramps.

Dianthus turned around and first stood frozen with shock thinking of how her sister got involved in this, knowing that the newborn would be attacked by their cannibal sisters daily.

I didn't worry any longer that I was the man hollering out at my departing wife. I grasped onto her, staring straight into her eyes and I said, "What would I do if something ever awful was to happen to you?" Giving her a kiss, I added, "If you don't leave now, I'll end up regretting it, living my life as a widow and fatherless."

As I caressed her lovely stomach, smooching it as well as telling my baby how much I love it and can't wait to it. Sirena teary-eyed and said, "I'm grateful you appear to get it. I ought to go. I am unhappy about leaving you this way, I promise it's not eternity. I will have my mother and my sisters to take care of me and I'll discover a way to see you." I caressed her resting on the forehead, then again bend over and softly press my lips to the little rising heap at her stomach.

That's when Dianthus notices that throughout all this time I was holding onto Sirena, her footsteps were wet and into the sea, she desperately freaked out, "Why haven't you change Sirena, how are you going to swim with those legs?"

Then Sirena looked up at Dianthus, before plunging into the sea "My Goodness Sister, it's the whole reason why I'm staying in the palace during my pregnancy."

Rosemarie then transformed when she plunged in and surfaced, "Her baby isn't getting the sustenance it demands, her fin will come out the longer she stays, the scales will somehow benefit. I thought mother told you everything! Come on, we have to hurry, the tritones are usually switching duties."

I can tell that Dianthus didn't know what to think of the pregnancy. Even though I couldn't go with the ladies to the palace, I made sure to at least travel with them though Rosemarie's secret tunnel.

As Dianthus and I swam in the back, I had some time to speak with her short of her actually feeling disappointed with me. She confusingly said to me, "A mermaid with child by a human, I didn't even know that was still possible? You understand how dangerous this could be, right?"

Dianthus looked at Sirena, then began asking me, "how is she able to be a mother for this baby, she's uncapable to transform which means she's not being able to provide or protect herself?"

We were finally at the hidden tunnel near the realm, where Dianthus swims into action, preparing to distract the guards away from the palace and leaves looking up so furiously and offended by Joshua, that it saddens Sirena. Dianthus is only absolutely terrified and enraged that she called Sirena and I, *reckless*. As we swim though the tunnel in a line, I overhear Sirena whisper to Rosemarie, "I knew you lied to me Rose, you could've made a brew to get rid of the *matter*, which could've saved everyone the problem, but you didn't!" Rosemarie looked in back of her, we were both devastated to know that Sirena would still want to get rid of her baby, even after she fought for it.

* * *

There was a moment when I stopped receiving messages in bottles and calls from the conch. Once I arrived at Lake Orchid with my Gramps, suddenly something big was swimming towards us. "Hey boys, I know it's not who you expected or hoped. But I came to give you our first month's update. I know you're worrying about the less communication; she's just feeling completely sick lately. I'll explain why the halfling is better off being incubated undersea, however she needs to eat like a human. In other words, more fruits and vegetables compared to fish proteins." I looked at her, like I thought you knew that, then I started thinking what the heck did they eat then when they were pregnant? "When we are pregnant with our own kind, it's safe for us to eat all types of seafood. Now that I have answered your question, the problem is our mother. It's not her, ever since we got home the big problem has been my mother. She won't allow us to go out like she promised Sirena. The reason I'm here, it because I have more leeway, I go on land and hunt animals and steal from people's grocery or farms."

Gramps looked ashamed of her, as if she was his daughter, "Rosemarie, sweetie why didn't you come to me? You shouldn't be stealing, haven't you thought what could happen if your red-headed self got caught or if someone shot you?"

Rosemarie cried a bid but turned her face away trying to hide her tears, "I'm so sorry Gramps. At the time I didn't want to worry you, about my crazy mother. She's always asking where I got the source, as if I want to hurt my own sister's baby. Then she gets frustrated whenever I have to refill on the nourishing ingredients that is like an oily lotion for Sirena's fin. I have to travel to Asia for a week's long to get Chinese swamp eels, mudskippers, and a bunch of sea slugs."

I started thinking it was too much of a coincidence that my cousin had been traveling to Asia every now and then, "Hey, you have been around! You take Cheryl with you. She loves travelling around the world, but to be travelling to one spot only it must've been a good reason…like her girlfriend!" Rosemarie finally admit that it was true, "If you could sneak yourself to meet your girlfriend, why couldn't you sneak me into the palace yet??"

"You're right, but you don't understand how much our mother has been hovering. Obviously, we came back home for Sirena's protection, so truthfully, I'm not trying to ruin any chances of that. And honestly Joshua, I know Sirena feels it too. Every day, I see that she has not any openness, as well as a great deal of weight from our mother. Everything you're intended to be doing as her husband, my mother is doing. We can't tell if she's lingering out of devotion, out of nursing, or if she's seeking to be the baby's mommy."

Gramps cuts in, "Listen that doesn't matter right now. Whatever your mother's attention is, for now let's not care, as long as you Rose are safe, and Sirena is stronger and healthier for herself and the baby. For you to stop thieving around, I'm going to grow a farm inside your garden patio and buy whatever meats you need ahead of time. Talk to me when you need me! Other than that, how else is she doing? Do you think she's becoming detached?"

"Some days yes, some days no. She has her entire day scheduled. It might sound weird but ever since she heard that mommies take swimming classes, our mother and her have been doing a 30-minute mermaid exercise. It's actually very useful since most days Sirena lazily doesn't want to get out of her sunken bed. Then she's scheduled to go on a piece of land when the sun is setting so she can read a baby book to her bump. My mother believed it was so ridiculous, and all of it was absolutely pointless to her, but she kept some sort of openness that we were dealing with a halfling. Whenever Sirena has her eating times, she goes up on that same piece of land. It's a secret cove, not even the tritones or any other sirens know of it." I began to think, but then suddenly Rosemarie jumped, "Oh no, I gotta go…I wasted way too much time here. I'll let you know anything the next time I come by. Don't lose any hope, I promise you I'll protect Sirena and your baby."

* * *

Once Gramps and I arrived at the Great Dismal Swamp, you would never have expected there was a hidden cove. However, as Rosemarie led the way I spotted a few captivating things that grabbed my eye. There was the smell of the wetlands not too far, some snakes that found their way in, then there were empty cupcake boxes and a small number of my shirts all over the area. It looked as if a drifter had lived there. Then, a familiar voice whispered, "Hello? Who goes there?" We spun around, and the most stunning whimsical wonder ever, Sirena. My love with an enormous belly. I nearly imagined she was carrying more than one seahorse in her cove. "Josh is that really you?" she asked.

"It's not a seahorse," Sirena began giggling. "And I really hope not. I think one is enough! I'm so happy to see you guys." Gramps and I looked at her, wondering if she was really only in the end of her first trimester. She looked like she was going to burst the baby out.

"Okay, Champ, how are we effectively going to do this? This is one fish I've certainly not experienced catching before." Gramps began chuckling, "I'm sorry dear, usually you're the size of the Leopard Seal but now you're the size of an Elephant seal, which I thought would take a little more time."

Sirena laughed hard, she agreed. She said even seafolk naturally don't gain this much weight so fast. "Gramps, you're the notorious fisherman here! I assumed you had a strategy."

"I'm afraid not, Champ, we took a small boat here. There's houses from the entrance we came from, she came be noticed. You're going to have to swim on the other end with her, it leads to the sea. Rosemarie has to go too, make sure she helps you get safely somewhere I can find you."

I stared at Sirena, she was still so beautiful but how was Sirena going to be able to swim she looked so overweight, "Okay I understand Gramps, but Rosemarie how dangerous can that be for her?"

Rosemarie looked at her and nodded, "Well, it's like your grandfather said she looks like an elephant seal, that's still a mammal that even do it's clumsy on land it can swim great. She just needs to use her upper body."

As soon as Gramps gets the small boat running, Rosemarie, Sirena and I get ready to start swimming out. Then Rosemarie tells us in her mind in a frighten voice, "Dianthus is on to Sirena. We need to hurry and get home! Hurry, if we get caught…well I don't know what would happen." I missed the first three months of my baby's incubation; I wasn't going to lose the next six.

Once we were halfway home, Sirena mentioned she would have to stay in the grotto. The only thing now, I was questioning how the fuck were we going to carry her to the house. Last time, I checked was that a female elephant seal weighed up to 1,500 pounds. Sirena beamed at me and snickered; "Don't worry babe, I can waddle most of the way there. Just keep watch for me." And so, she did, it was quite comical, but she shuffled her tail back into the basement's grotto. I helped out by pouring sea water on her tail and the sand.

In the grotto I stared at Sirena. She'd at all times looked gorgeous; nevertheless, motherhood for some purpose had a stunning nurturing look upon her. Her skin became more radiant. She looked exquisite. I stood blissfully. I would become a father; my grandfather would become a great grandfather. Only I still had so many questions for Sirena.

When she feels the baby move, she also feels a major shift in her life as she introduces my hand to the baby's foot. Suddenly she shows me more how much she loves and wants this baby just as fiercely as I do.

Sirena looked at me; "Well my mother wasn't lying about keeping me healthy, even when she was hovering. But my love for you, Joshua Hanks, was too excruciating. Even more now that we have a little one, I had to come back home." Then she elegantly provided me with a kiss on my lips, so gentle and so sweet. "And to answer all your questions, our baby won't be born with a tail, it'll happen during its adolescent years. However, it will be able to breathe underwater. Behind their ears occasionally are gill slits, and on occasion may perhaps have webbed toes or fingers. Josh, it's essential to organize our cove since I am going to deliver the baby there, it can't be in the grotto. It's tradition for a mermaid to deliver in the ocean water is responsible for a healthy blissful labor." I thought to myself, *that didn't sound like a wicked ritual.* Then Sirena continued, "The minute our child matures into its teenage years, it's natural that it'll question, even more, about its powers than its body. Our child will have a tremendously more prevailing power than I. We're going to have to express the actuality about mermaids and sirens, about their seafolk side of their family." I laughed as I had not once imagined this being the sort of parental conversation I would have.

Sirena looked worried so I asked her what was wrong. She said, Undine paid a visit to Sirena. Like a gynecologist nurse she was there to begin tracking the pregnancy's health, especially after Rosemarie said she felt something dark. By the end of the conversation between her sister and the sea witch, Sirena suddenly feels severe pain and agony, as she cries in the cove. Rosemarie's facial expression reciprocating the agony. As Undine leaves, Rosemarie reaches out to Sirena. "I'm okay, what did you guys discussed about?"

"Death…" as Rosemarie stares and holds onto Sirena's baby bump. The concerns were even that Undine wasn't able to see the meaning of death, giving red flags to everyone.

She mentioned how worried the Queen was by how severe the mere presence of the condition was. Supposedly, the Queen went to see the seer Avery, however left without any thorough facts. As a result, the Queen provided her instructions and told her that she better follow them or else the sisters would be well ordered to execute her baby. Sirena wasn't sure anymore if she trusted her mother, there was a time the Queen wanted the baby to carry out the throne, now she herself was in fear of the baby.

Giving up our baby like the Queen ordered, would be like giving up an enormous jewel from the deep sea and perhaps the ultimate coin toss of its destiny. Sirena had other plans though, she had so many dreams of her baby that she was incredibly more careful and protective of her baby in her belly.

CHAPTER 23

osemarie pulled me aside and took me to the lighthouse, "My sisters and I come from the same bloodline as the sirens from our pod in history. About 100 years ago Carolina became our home that our pod migrated from occasionally. But I find it interesting, possibly almost stunning, how the mermaids are returning every now and then drawn by a halfling that is half mermaid. However, Seelie's court seeks to use the halfling as leverage to safeguard. The question is now how much of a threat are we facing Josh? It's become bigger than the baby."

"What are Seelie's?" I asked her. This was my first time finding out that something else wanted my baby.

"Let me guess, Sirena didn't tell you. Well, they're part of the fae realm, which explains why they don't have fins like us, and they live in air unusually in the ocean. You can call them enchantress of the sea; we see them as much more. If sea folk didn't believe in the gods and goddesses of the oceans, the next thing we will believe in would be the Seelie's. They know everything and all. They're royal to royalties. They are politics above all the sea, they can change any law any realm creates. You never want to look like a fool in front of a seelie, I'm serious. Undine, she's different…she's a dark seelie or unseelie. So, she threw out all of the rules, but since she's made her own, she's dangerous. Our magic from all seafolk realms come from them. They have a museum of grimoires that no seafolk has ever read…spells that we never practice or maybe that our great great-great-great-parents have."

Okay that did sound very impressive, I had wondered if I ever swam by them. I also wondered how they look. Then I begged Rosemary, "I need you to go back home," she hissed at me and grilled. "You're meant to protect the baby, how are you supposed to protect the baby if you don't even know the plan at least from the siren side?" She looked at me as if she was impressed.

"Oh, no! I must be liking you too much if I'm listening to you." I smiled. "Or I just really care for that baby's future." Rosemarie always knew how to punch me in the gut, but I knew we were like great friends. She told me she'd only be gone for three nights, then she left without saying goodbye to Sirena. She didn't want Sirena in worrisome which meant I had to keep Sirena engaged.

* * *

Rosemarie sneaked into the palace when she saw her three sisters; Dianthus along with the twins Nerilena, and Kalidelia sitting in front of each other in a triangle, listening to the whales singing, while nourishing their scales in seaweed and blue-green algae. A dead human girl in her bathing suit is drifting in the room, her body pale and faintly shedding blood as of the numerous penetrated wounds around certain areas.

Rosemarie entered the rooms, "So this is what we do as sirens? Psychotic-killer under loose sprees, as we leave our food in the rooms, since when we allowed that?"

Nerilena continues polishing herself, "Sissy, the greatest gift to yourself it's a spa day and beautiful scales require commitment it's not a miracle. Isn't that right, Dianthus?"

Dianthus looks up from buffing her fin and says, "Yes, that's quite right, Nerilena."

Rosemarie then nods to the lifeless girl hovering above them, "Then whatever's this just about?

"Nerilena and Kalidelia, together discovered everything about our sister, Sirena, staying here. This happened to be their approach of a, symbol of peace of some nature." Dianthus stated as she motions in such a way that it looked as if she's still seeking the right word for it.

Kalidelia sighs as she says, "I believed, after dwelling that long on land theoretically dehydrating oneself, along with carrying her own remora fish, perhaps our mermaid may possibly be rather famished." Nerlinena scuffs a chuckle with her twin sister.

Rosemarie watched her young twin sisters. They showed no remorse for their kill which was very known for a siren, however they played with their food, drank all of its blood, and left their food remains in the realm. Matters which were sloppy and unusual might as well stick out a tail for a group of humans to follow. It was pure bloodlust!

Dianthus looked at both young sisters with a face of hierarchy, "Then I made clear to our sisters that mercy cannot be accepted with a human sacrifice. More than ever, with Sirena who doesn't eat flesh. I repeated to them that she would've appreciated it if they ended overfeeding and Sirena obviously desired to find a shift in their routine that specifies carefulness combined with self-growth. Nonetheless, as an alternative of bringing the girl back to her home like I ordered, they secretly consumed on her."

Together girls rolled their eyes blamelessly. Nerilena and Kalidelia smirk then in absolute harmony said, "Well, needless to say we couldn't let her death been in vain, could we?"

Irritated I informed Dianthus, "Well, I suppose you'll be the one to tell mother the reason why there's sharks lurking around this area." The blood had lingered earlier staining the ocean in the siren's realm, around that private section. It was going to be noticed.

Dianthus asked the younger sisters to go away. Dianthus could not help but become aware of Rosemarie's reluctant visitation failed to mention her reasons. Nonetheless, Dianthus took Rosemarie's arm, and together they swam across quite a few of the palace's rooms to its veranda which encountered the forests of long brown kelp. Rosemarie's eager judges yet again give the impression of examining the rooms beyond anywhere they pass by, and once more, on obtaining any certainties in relation to the siren's methods. They spoke for hours but it felt as if Rosemarie was slightly unaware. So, Dianthus continued to speculate what secrecy was at heart in all of this, then with royal inquisitiveness even though she had to question Rosemarie herself. The echoes of the deep sea drifted all over them through the wide gaping towers, faded in the space. Dianthus sat down and motioned Rosemarie to sit beside her. "Now," she said, turning her graceful face full upon her, "Why have you really been here? I want the truth, the real truth, and no excuses."

"I just want to know what our pod has against Sirena, and what they might be planning." Rosemarie just blurted out, but it felt so foreign to say out blaring in front of her other sister. But the future Queen did have to know something. Nevertheless, she simply knew only of the plans for her coronations, and the most was that their mother was still speaking to the seer.

* * *

Meanwhile, as I made calls within the three days between Rosemarie, using the ocean conch. In the grotto, Sirena only asked about her sister whenever she was hungry, but I made it seem as if she was always occupied or with Gramps. She looked inside the little fridge.

"Good morning my lovely wife." I said to her, smiling as I leaned in the doorway of the grotto as she smiled.

Sirena had just taken a brief swim and was now coming up to the surface. The grotto was renovated when she stood at the palace, Gramps and I imagined that possibly when things came to an end, just maybe she would enjoy an entrance to the sea from the grotto. The construction helped limit the despair that was in our mind. "Good morning, take note I understand I'm the one and only in the house that truly enjoys downing vegetable juice, so would it destroy anyone to make absolutely sure it's on the list? I'm trying to cook a healthy baby, you know."

I dipped myself into the grotto kissing and hugging her, I asked her if we could take a swim together and she was more than happy. We pushed ourselves through the ocean's entrance deep into the water and swam. As I gazed before me, I saw how the oiled silk mirrored the sky so strikingly in this sunlight morning, and how gorgeous my pregnant wife looked swimming more relaxed. We had a wonderful morning, until mysterious mermaids surrounded us. We weren't looking for any trouble, and we weren't sure if they were friendly, though I noticed Sirena looked very intrigued. Swimming as fast and as intense as I could I had Sirena by my side and we swam back, closing the gates entrance behind us.

Rosemarie came back home, "Hey sis, I very much hope the humans were heeding to your every desire in my absence."

"In your absence, as you like to call it— which is a way to cover for saying you were in the siren palace these past few days." I didn't tell her anything, how did she know. Rosemarie looked at me, but then looked at Sirena's belly.

"Your baby has abilities, great…now you see things without needing to ask." Rosemarie said with a sarcastic grin. "SO, your baby has an ability of clairvoyance…great!"

Sirena then had a serious bitch face that I never seen on her, especially towards Rosemarie, "Wow, that's amazing, obviously it's still developing. I didn't get to see everything, if I did then I would have known the reason why everybody is convinced my baby is Cetus!" Then she began speaking in a mellow voice, as if her mind was dwelling on it, "Mind you Josh and I were probably harassed by mermaids, not that I know for sure since all they do so far is be seen and look intently."

I grin sensitively when I shove the vegetables aside then get hold of the vegetable juice out from the mini fridge, and then pours Sirena a glass. After Sirena recognizes that she had vegetable juice the whole time, she appears vaguely accountable and humiliated.

"Listen, you weren't even supposed to be swimming in the ocean like that. I'm just so happy to see that you're in one piece. I have some concerns and I still don't have the answers." Rosemarie gazed at her feeling ashamed that she didn't do as much as necessary for her sister and the baby.

When Rosemarie told Sirena about their mother still trying to find answers from Avery, Sirena sensed sandwiched between feeling loved or terrified. "Everyone is just evil and superstitious. Additionally, my baby's life is still at stake as long as I'm supernaturally connected to Carolina, which isn't reassuring?" Sirena's voice broke as she spoke.

I then looked at Rosemarie, "Absolutely, I believe it's time we attend to that predicament for you, Sirena." Rosemarie smiled at me and agreed.

"I am all in favor. The moment they're unlinked, she can find a safe cove out of Carolina that she can prepare. Does this mean we're torturing my tutor, Undine?"

After considering my fate amongst a dark Seelie's hands I said, "Yeah, we probably shouldn't think about doing that. Do you have any brews for telling the truth?"

Sirena gives me a significant look of disbelief. I was only human, but she needed me to stand up for her, "We might dehydrate while dosing her with your truth serum. Hopefully she cooperates, if not, well you might have to siren that amnesia song before we ship her somewhere far."

Rosemarie looked forward to the idea of siren her own mentor, she said, Undine had way more to teach but wasn't trying to help a siren's capacity to learn that much craft. She said she'd hope that Undine would forget what she was, wind up somewhere that was full of sun, and shrivel into dust.

143

CHAPTER 24

"Wow," Rosemarie says as she enters the grotto, "You look dreadful sis," as she sits next to Sirena on the steps, "Perhaps it's time for the unborn of Armageddon to eat its ceremonial dinner!" She begins cackling as Sirena glares at her. Even when she moves in to slightly embrace her a bit, she continues laughing like a child as my wife battles to get her off.

Sirena giggles, "Yes, and it'll save you for last…Rose, *really* no more names."

Later, as the moon rose, we were together eating with Sirena at the grotto. We were having our usual laughs until, as we all stopped pulling on our barbequed ribs because there was a vision in the grotto's water. It was by Queen Dionysus and Avery.

Avery was chopping up the onions at a ferocious rate before poking her oxtail stew with a wooden spoon, while she continues speaking ecstatically to Queen Dionysus who was sitting on a chair as if it was her own throne, partially naked wearing only a wrap around. For an older lady, especially one who loathes me, she did have a pleasant body, but I tried not to think about that, especially with all the seafolk abilities around. The seer turned around as she chuckled, joking about how she was so sorry this wasn't close enough to palace for her.

While staring into the vision we were all asking ourselves; was this the past, the present, or even wilder…the future? The Queen and the seer looked like they seemed to be comfortable around each other, their sarcasms and discussions showed it. Which I found unfair because I have tried everything to be on the good end of the stick with the Queen as a human, and she still doesn't like me. Yet, she meets this seer, every now and then, who is still human, and they are laughing like best girlfriends. They both began speaking about me, sharing their thoughts of how I intruded in their lives, as if I were their famous plaguing joke. That piece was embarrassing as it felt like it lasted for an hour.

Avery at times had to pause their conversation when she had to work with the clients, I wondered why the vision continued showing us everything. That's when I figured it had to be present. If it wasn't, then a mystic vision could've been edited. Once I told the girls, we started wondering if this was something Avery wanted us to see, did she know something was coming up. How were the visions getting through the grotto water, it was only plain seawater? There was no significance other than it traveled through the house. Then we all began to look at Sirena's massive belly, it was hard to believe that the baby was showing this picture to us. Gramps left saying he felt like a weird peeping tom. Rosemarie and I stayed because we knew it had some importance, as Sirena, who also felt the same way, fell asleep.

"I suggest you go back to calling me, Queen Dionysus, no more referring me as Dionysus, I don't want your witches to call me without my title." She continued speaking about exactly how it was already inconsiderate as well as unbecoming for her to be in Jamaica, while she ought to be ruling in her realm.

Avery stop stirring her oxtails before turning to Queen Dionysus, "Don't begin getting all high maintenance with me! I'm the only witch who still likes working with seafolk. I didn't even give you the call and you came to me, honey. Not the other way around. Remember that! You want a witch's help, well here I am. Unless you know how to do what I can do then you can try yourself." I tried to stop myself from snickering for the reason that finally someone was able to put the Queen in place.

"Well, it's been days that I've been leaving the sea, to come here and speak to those witches I'm supposed to trust my life with. To have some clarity. Where are they? Can't they tell I'm a Queen that's trying to do more than save her own realm." She was beginning to feel that there was no need for hope, her despair was setting in.

The seer held her hands as she tried to keep the hope alive, "They'll come around. They're just old-school. And scared."

Queen Dionysus scuffs, "Scared of what? Your prophecy about the baby? I'm pretty sure if they see the prophecy themselves there would be second opinions of the meaning. It's just a tiny thing, if anything the most it might want to do is hate me as a *nana*." A tear slowly rolls down her cheek, then I felt the strong emotion in her words.

Avery shakes her head, "I can't help what I see, Dionysus. Sirena was meant to be called for a reason, and though it took me awhile I learned most of that reason."

Queen Dionysus said, "QUEEN! Anyways, it's like you said…most of it…not all. The baby probably has no importance at all." The Queen then walks towards the countertop and reaches over to grab some crab. "Move you're in the way, you should get a bigger place." Of course, even if Avery was her only friend, she wouldn't stop being a narcissist.

Avery then listened to the roar and the shrieking of the wind, she paused with an impulsive nervous wistfulness, "Queen Dionysus perhaps it's best if you just go back home, I'll call you once they'll made up their minds."

"No, I came here today, to Jamaica, to try to find out the truth of my daughter. I'm staying at a cove; the sirens there are actually hospitable. I'll be back tomorrow." She was quiet for a long moment, after that I could tell that her trips had made her feel more than anxious.

"Please do!" She said in a way that made the Queen feel nervous. So, they said their goodbyes, and just when Rosemarie and I thought it was over, apparently the Queen decided to be hidden near the garden and trees.

Avery quickly began drawing something, fast as if her life depended on it. Then she saw a dark shadow on the side of her eyes, that made her stop scrawling. Immediately after, Undine and her servant dark seelie, grabbed her after throwing a paralyzing powder into her face. The Queen wanted to attack right there and save her friend, but she also felt confused. Undine had protection and worked under the sirens realm because Queen Dionysus made it so. But why was she snatching the one person that can help them with all the answers. Was this the reason why Avery's witches didn't come, perhaps they felt something bad in the air just like Avery did.

She was a Queen who didn't have many guards. Suddenly, as we watch her touch the water calling out for *Rosemarie*, the same way Sirena did on our honeymoon, the grotto wakes up Sirena with the sound of her mother's voice echoing Rosemarie's name.

* * *

I looked at Rosemarie, "Wow, weren't we supposed to trust that seelie who linked my wife to Carolina, who now can't choose her own grotto for her own childbirth. No matter how far. And now kidnapped a seer!!"

Rosemarie said she knew who the other dark seelie was and where he lived, she asked me to give her 30 minutes. I wasn't sure if she was going to knock on the door, I wasn't sure what her plan was until the grotto's water appeared with a present image of her.

Rosemarie had found him in a dark fae city full of seelie's, she entranced him to come out to meet her in the back balcony of his residence then she made him gobble down a candor serum. She began asking him where Undine was, he tried to find tricks up his sleeve to overlook answering the question. His first true answer was, "If I say to you where she is, she'll just kill me!" Rosemarie resumed to probe, asking him what she was up to.

The dark seelie was speaking to Rosemarie, in fear but trying not to show it, "Listen in, I make that to further seafolk, Undine seems a little overwhelmingly wicked and darkness even for still the bleakest seafolk. But to us dark seelie's, she is our ruler. That might not be significant to you, since she's not precisely an empress, nevertheless it means loads to us dark seelie's…we don't have anyone. Undine is the only one of us, who understands vital critical incantations, and we know she is taking care for others, not just dark seelie's."

"Like kidnapping a human seer?" Rosemarie looked like she was timing how long she'd been there as she listened to the waves.

The dark seelie looked tense then with arrogance said, "Listen doll face, I did it for Undine. You have nothing on us…besides it's nothing worse than what you and your sirens do. At least she's able to breathe."

"Don't ever call me that. Oh, you'd be horrified by means of the events I had to do for Undine. Right now, tell me where the human is! Or else…" She brought her poisonous tails stinger to his throat slowly…the dark seelie then whisper something in her voice. She smiled and wrapped him up in her tail seductively, as he thought he was getting a frisky thanks, Rosemarie was actually giving him an amnesia siren song to forget she was there. Then she was on her way.

Ten minutes later, Rosemarie informed me she knew where Undine was hidden at, as well as what the strategy was.

Leaving Gramps to mermaid caretake Sirena, "Who made them the duo in charge?"

Rosemarie and I went to the siren realm to rally a group. This time I had my harpoon gun and ear plugs, so I wouldn't get siren. We really just need a tritone and three of the oldest sisters, besides Rosemarie, which meant Dianthus, Petra, and Valerian. Enough for robust siren songs.

I swam up to Rosemarie's old room.

Rosemarie became furious, after a few times of saying it, she then slapped my head, then I realized it was the ear plugs that made her mute for once in my time of knowing her. She wanted to know what I was doing looking through her things. I knew since she was the only siren of her sisters, that were *witchy*, she would be the one to hold onto a grimoire, even if it meant creating an air bubble for it or chiseling one of stone. I was half correct, only that she kept hers above in the hidden cove near Dismal Swamp.

I tried reading them, but sirens used ancient symbols. She asked me what I was looking for. "Well, I was thinking since we're going to Undine's territory, perhaps a lot of sleeping potion." She knocked me on the head as she said she was already prepared.

"Now, time is ticking, we don't know what Undine's plan is with the seer, and she is very impatient?"

"Let's not forget the seer can't breathe under water." The sirens laughed before each gave me a kiss, pushing more air to my lungs. And Rosemarie said in my head, *seelie's don't need water, they have homes with a bubble around them. Once you walk in, you're not only dry but it's full of air. Some homes, you float, some seelie's can make it so glamourous, but the more glamourous is what kills you.* After that I didn't want to go, I was scared while swimming. Until we reached her home. From the outside you couldn't tell there was a bubble. Either way, what was between us and Undine's home, which was a wrecked ship that wasn't glamourous as I pictured. It was cold, grim, and might as well have been a mausoleum in the crack of the ocean.

Rosemarie led the way towards the back she said in all of our minds, *swim quietly.*

CHAPTER 25

t hand was a stir up of dread as we all entered through the transparent dome, the fear of not knowing what was behind the crossing. Even as the tritones stood outside, with spears aimed in case of an ambush. Just like Rosemarie explained they would, the siren sisters appeared dried up and were now walking around in the nude, and I too was dry. Soundlessly we moved to the back of Undine's home, sneaking a quick look through the shattered glass window of the bilge we saw Undine and of course Avery.

It was a cruel revelation. The seer was struggling against the shackles and chains on her wrist and the ankles that clanks around, which gave her enough height, which made us wonder if that was Undine's sick approach to cut her victims throat for her unique blood properties, she could do it now. But she didn't.

Her surface had tear smudges all through her damaged cheeks, although she wasn't in shock by any of it. Avery then cried out, staring directly at the ladies, "What do you think you're doing? You don't need me Undine, let go of me!" She was toiled with delirium and her requests for clemency were passed over as Undine fled away.

The sisters began to leave quietly as they seem to get the same message that Rosemarie received, as she whispers it to me, "She wants us to leave her…she doesn't want Undine to find us." Damn, we had all those sirens, the amount to put her to sleep and they swam their tails away.

Undine laughed and lifted her hand to Avery's face, "You humans… it becomes extraordinarily unnatural when a few of you are born with these unusual gifts, like you." She sets a basket on the counter. "I need more answers."

"Slaughtering me to get to Joshua and Sirena— or their unborn— is certainly not the response you want!" Avery said appalled, "But of course, you're only a dark seelie, you know so little. Having you as a mentor..." She spits at Undines feet, "Rosemarie probably just learned the basics from you."

"Bitch, you'll want to speak about basics. How about the fact that before kidnapping you, I disconnected little Sirena from Carolina." She begins filing her nails. I look at Rosemarie like, *yes, we don't have to go through the hassle in trying to make her undo the hex, she already did it!* Then things altered entirely as Rosemarie concentrates even harder on the counter and Undine, "Yeah, I reckoned the mermaid should give birth to the little apocalypse anywhere, outside of Carolina hopefully. Nevertheless, while you were asleep, I linked you two together...almost certainly she was sleeping too for the hex to work. Your premonition was vague, but we both know that baby will bring death...to who...we don't know. But it is my duty to figure out the whole premonition. I need you alive and close."

With a petrified voice, "What are you planning to do?" Then she gives a stiff stare at us, *stay away, I don't want your help, I just need you to get to my house. The answers is on the music sheet. Check the music sheets, don't worry about me, this was the universe's plan.* Hearing the message with Rosemarie didn't make it as comforting, we couldn't leave just yet.

Undine looked at Avery, "Are you trying to call in some witch enforcements? I'm afraid, they won't be able to find you here." Holding up a hefty vintage syringe with a long needle. Avery gave the impression that she was familiar with it as the sight petrified her, and she frantically strained to draw back in spite of being shackled up. I felt Rosemarie's hand squeeze, I continued to watch as Rose buried herself into my shoulder.

It took more than a few wrong turns before the needle made its way to her skin. Right before Undine pierces the needle right in Avery's stomach! The seer looked at us, trying to keep a brave face but if we dug deeper, she looked like she was not only in pain but also in fear.

Avery cried out, "Why would you do that to her, you know for fact the baby can't live through that!" Oh my god, I moved a little closer to see what it was. What was it that she did, that might hurt both my wife and baby?

* * *

Rosemarie gets a vision of the grotto. Sirena without warning, cries in agony and as she's evidently hurting more and more, she naturally reaches her stomach. As soon as she draws her hand away, she observes the blood on her fingers as of a slight wound that is even now beginning to restore itself. Gramps wakes up from reading a book, when he overhears Sirena yelling, he gets to his feet so instantly that he tips over his glass of iced tea and then hurries down the stairs into the grotto.

Gramps runs waist-high into the salted water, not caring how her fin looked as if it cooked knock him over, "Sweetie, are you okay, what the hell was that? Is the baby, okay?" Gramps sounded alarmed, checking the belly, and holding Sirena's hand, as he was then prepared to call up a family doctor.

Sirena began shuddering as she spoke, "I'm not sure Gramps, it felt like I was being stabbed in my stomach, and I'm sure it's not the baby kicking. Now everything feels normal. Do you have an exceptionally large conch shell? Anything to hear if it's swimming or something? Where is everybody?"

Gramps eyes at Sirena and stares at her with comfort. Then takes a deep breath before he worries her, "Oh you mean a stethoscope, yea we do, I'll get it…darlin you sure you feel well?"

Sirena shivers and shakes her head, "I don't know, just feeling fatigue and a chill." Gramps found that peculiar as his eyes hold Sirena's in place, while she still felt no change.

Gramps then places his hand on Sirena's forehead, "A slight chill, in all reality you're freezing over." He begins rubbing her arms like he used to do with me when I was younger. He stared at Sirena as he began to worry, beginning to get an emerging insight that something serious was occurring. "Maybe I should call your family, someone might pick up, right?"

* * *

Dianthus looked at Sirena laying in the grotto suddenly breathing in and out heavily, the sisters looked at her and mentioned how cold she was, "Relax your breathing, ladies sway the waves with me, we must all bring the temperature up in the water ladies." Dianthus told the ladies as they began warming up the water, that even Gramps jumped out just staring. "Sirena, we need you to relax, don't worry your husband will be here."

Sirena shuddering as she said, "Don't tell me to relax Diane, I feel like I should be an Alaskan mermaid."

Dianthus paid no attention to her and her pregnant mood swings; "Hey! Simply because you're keeping a halfling doesn't imply you bring about torment like one!"

Rosemarie and I then swam quickly to Sirena, Rosemarie pulling my hand as she swam like a bullet home, to the grotto. Where they just found Dianthus and the two other sisters from earlier, humming while circling their hand around their uneasy sister's pregnant belly. Gramps ran up to us, "I didn't know what else to do, so I used your conch shell."

I gazed up timidly at what seem to be like a seance, "What the hell is this, what happened to my wife?" I quickly got up as I tried to stop them, but they continued.

Rosemarie examined her sisters, "It was what we saw with Undine." She begins rubbing Sirena's head, crying and rubs her belly. The sisters continued to make wavelike motions with their hands, now changing their humming into a soft siren song, I was concerned with what they were they doing.

Rosemarie looks at the music sheet and looks at the scrawling in the back as she plays the song. I was worried about how she looked; she looked like she was locked in a trance. And I asked her if she was okay.

"I feel a little strange…this is creepy. I'm absolutely just the seer's charm." Rosemarie said as she repeated the music song once more.

I was uneasy with what she was doing, for me it seemed frightening, "Make sure whatever you're doing, doesn't kill you. I'll never hear the end of it from everybody, if I never bring my baby's aunt back home." The last thing I needed was some sort of missing route with my sister-in-law's face stamped on the picture, with me being the last known person to be with her. I was really fond of Rosemarie and genuinely imagined her as my own sister, although she didn't feel the same.

Rosemarie laughs and blushes a little as she read Joshua's mind, she began to think to herself how all this time she always been used to being overprotective with her sisters and caring about their thought…she never thought she'd actually gain a brother, "As you may recall, since we met,

I figured you as a true…what are the humans slang for a male's penis… oh yea dick!"

I smiled listening to the melody of the piano, "Aw, that almost sounds like a compliment compared to what I thought you were going to say?"

Rosemarie laughs, "Oh, I've just grown to like much more about you." But then as she continues trying to pay attention to the song, "I don't understand the music sheet and the scrawling…"

But then I search inside the piano, when I find more scrawling. It took a while but then we realized that since the day we met Avery she was seeing more and more visions, in which she kept. It later began to look like a huge puzzle, which we began to start solving on the floor. For the blind like myself, the scrawling had to be a full puzzle for me to understand the meaning. Which was opposed to a seer like Avery and recently Rosemarie, they can see one portion of the puzzle and understand the meaning!

Finally, we had it all! Rosemarie then explained it to me. Avery saw Undine coming the same day the Queen hid, she saw herself in shackles, Sirena in incredible pain, and the needle which was something Rosemarie paused at. "Oh, my goddess's! I can't believe what Undine did. She's creating a monster…and for it to die through Sirena."

"What the hell do you mean?"

"She injected essence of a siren and seelie, in Avery…who is connected to Sirena and your baby. Hopefully, the sisters have finished unlinking Sirena to Avery. We need to go, like yesterday."

Rosemarie then felt the energy from the baby that it was unlinked from Avery. She demanded her sisters to leave and thanked them very much while telling Petra that their mother might be worried, and to let her know everything was okay.

Sirena insisted Dianthus to stay, while the other sisters left. She then turned to all of us, "The baby has siren and seelie blood. And Sirena partially has it for now, she's only the carrier since the spell was linked to her primarily. The seer wanted to show that death isn't the only premonition, fortune and peace have also been the premonitions of the baby's birth. The premonition of Sirena is that she surely lives. And there is a drawing of the waves rolling together."

Everyone was astonished, though the premonitions were still foggy they sounded a bit better than before. However still, seafolk had grim tales about halflings, what about how seafolk would react about a quartet hybrid?

Rosemarie then whispered to herself, "Damn it, I can't leave the human with her I need to save her you Josh stay here, Dianthus I know you don't care about humans, but this human care about us…please?" They were off, as I kissed my wife and her stomach, still feeling like a regular bless man the grotto flipped its channel again to this now Rosemarie and Dianthus.

CHAPTER 26

The sisters kept swimming, all the way to the bottom, as they headed through the tunnels of kelp towards the immense crack of the deep. Rosemarie indicates to Dianthus that the seer was down in there. Rose acknowledged her sister with a gesture, as soon as they settled their strategy and got moving. Upon arrival it seemed that Undine appeared to be absent from her vessel. Dianthus decided to stay outside of the ship to keep watch over Rosemarie back.

She hesitated at her first sway into the vessel, when Rosemarie begins to hear the wails and moans of agony coming from the seer's brig below. This was the first moment in time that I've always seen Rosemarie moved about as if she was afraid of someone other than herself. Once she went below and whispered, "Wake up, please! I'm here to get you somewhere safe."

Avery spoke in a feeble and woozy way from who knows what Undine did to her in a full day. "Undine, are you already back to torment me, you have to at least feed me if you want to keep torturing me."

Rosemarie looked at her miserably, "It's me Rose, remember, *ugh don't tell me she erased your memories*, I got you babe. You'll be eating a lobster in no time." Rosemarie first takes out her potion that helps smelt the hinges, and as it begins to melt away, she uses her fin and blasts it in one shot on the brig's door. It splits and Avery hurries on the way to the siren and drapes her arms all over her, trembling and sobbing, "I tried Rose…I really did try. I'm so sorry. I thought I told you to go Rose?"

Rosemarie withers aways still, not sending back the embrace; it was obvious that she still didn't like most humans, friend or not, caressing her. "Oh, aren't you human enough to be capable to simply say a thank you?"

Rose ignored the vulnerable seer and dragged her out of the wrecked pirate ship. Just then, Avery glanced at the outside of the dome, gaping into the intense navy space, and watching over the creatures swimming along, "How am I getting out of the depths without wasting my breathe and freezing up to death?"

"Easy, like this!" Rosemarie then held her hand and promptly gave her a lengthy kiss as she strolled her outside of the transparent dome, and suddenly they were in the ocean. Avery was able to breathe, and she didn't feel frozen being at the bottom of the ocean. The seer looked differently at the siren, to her that sudden kiss felt magical. Though Rosemarie only saw her as a friend to keep alive.

Dianthus continued to keep watch, but every moment she watched her sister she felt disturbed. It was understandable when Sirena had emotions for humans, but her true-blood sister was gaining more emotions than Rosemarie would believe since Dianthus last lived with her on land. She felt more and more appalled by it. The vision disappeared from the grotto, I calmed Sirena down because she was worried if they got out on time, without Undine finding out.

As time went by, Sirena and I were just beginning to talk about the future of our child when Rosemarie came through the grotto with the seer in her arms. Rosemarie panted as she ordered me and Gramps to leave her on a bed to relax and cook her a lobster meal that she had promised. Sirena eyed worrying as she asked where Dianthus was, Rosemarie thumps with rampage as she explains, "*It was too many emotions for her to identify with. She felt mortified.*"

* * *

I carried the seer into one of the guest bedrooms. Gramps remained waiting next to the bed, then he smoothed out the sheets, and tucked her in. Now go to sleep, I said. The seer took a deep breath, as she rested her head on the pillow trying not to touch her wrist. Gramps said, "Poor girl, she went through a lot, she's human and she was tortured because she tried not to give that bitch what she wanted. I hope she can heal from this."

The next Avery opens her eyes to sunlight sifting in the windows. After looking in the vicinity of the house, feeling the walls and floorboards, as well as looking out of the windows, the senses of the seer informed her that she was alive and well. Before she followed the seawater scent coming from the basement, she decided to refuel with the meal that was left for her.

We then listened to the knocking on the basement door, and then the footsteps coming down the stairs. Gramps went ahead and approached to the woman's voice that yelled out, "This is so divine…ohh, good morning, everyone! Rosemarie, thank you my dear I'm so sorry if I was a little pest. And who made that delicious meal I woke up to? It was delicious so thank you so much. That seelie somehow made me starve all in one day." She groaned as Gramps helped her down the stairs and settle down. We all had questions, and I was sure even the seer knew we all felt like we weren't going to like what would happen next.

Sirena went ahead and began speaking, "Is everything you have written on those music sheets true? Everything is very confusing." Rosemarie looked at the seer as if she shouldn't have given the seer a kiss of breath and she almost wished that she had never played that piano. I, on the other hand, wished I had never found the rest of the scribbled articles for that unsolved puzzle. If we had known the outcome in the first place, would have wasted so much time to save her?

A slight gentle wind turned as of the ocean's entrance as well as breezed past Avery's face. Abruptly, she appeared as if she was conscious of all of our thoughts. She turned away sluggishly as she felt extremely devasted. When she had the impulse to turn about and watch from the back of her, she saw everyone's glare looking beyond at her.

In order to try to alter the emotion of everyone's ideas, Avery just laughed a little and then looked sad at the ladies, "Well, I'm sorry my dears. What I see or feel…I draw…and it's destined. No matter what path we want to choose in life, for our friends and even ourselves, there's only one destined path that already chooses us." Everyone set out to ponder if freewill had already escaped the Sirena and the baby and wondered what the troublesome cause for Sirena's reaction was earlier. Avery then continued trying to explain, "Yes, she stuck me with a needle which is a blighted object, I'm actually uncertain how she even attained it. You see, it's actually an ancient witch's item, so it seems that as soon as she found out about the baby, she had a few ideas. The puzzle is very confused, I'm still baffled whether it's annihilation or if it's showing me harmony…"

Sirena cuts her off, "Just please jump to what the actuality of what the syringe did? Because I felt like I was freezing to death."

"The purpose of the syringe back then, was for witches who wanted to broaden their community for humans who wanted to be in the coven and for those covens who wanted to have stronger magic. It infused the magic into another, just like Undine infused the genes of a seelie and a siren. Both, by the way, are powerful and dangerous in their own ways. As we were connected, you were infused with the very powerful and dangerous genes mainly in the core of your baby." She looked disheartening. "I couldn't run away, I know that's what you're wondering, Undine could've used any seer if she wanted. So, I sacrificed myself, I knew Rosemarie would find my music sheets. There's one more thing, the universe wanted this to happened, so I believe your baby is born for greatness, there's no concern about correcting this." Sirena began to cry realizing she had no way to stop this from happening to our baby. "It already did what it was meant to do. Trust me, it did work, and I know someone separated the union. I heaved a black spew which indicates that not only it was finished, but that our knot is broken." Rosemarie breathes in relief. Sirena begins to settle down, as I look dazed.

I hold Sirena's hand and kiss her stomach, then smile into Sirena's eyes with hope, while me and Sirena gaze at each other for a long-lasting moment. Rosemarie observes our mutual glances, so she immediately told the seer, "Come on, let's go." Avery was too terrified to leave, there was a bizarre emotion within her. She then tells us that she can't go back home, she imagines that she'll get snatched there again. She's worried about Undine still looking for her. She wants to stay in Carolina for a while far from the ocean until the baby is born, she'll know then that Undine can't do any harm.

Sirena got pissed off, "Are you telling me that bitch of an elf, was just using me to save all the sea-folk of the oceans, I'm going to rip her to pieces with the abilities still in me!" She then storms out of the grotto and swims towards the dark part of the ocean. Rosemarie swam right behind her as fast as she could in order to stop her. Finally, she caught her in time, in order to take her back home and make her think straight. "I want to leave pieces of her around the ocean and have the sharks feed on her. She turned my baby into a monster?" Sirena shouted out to Rosemarie as she held out her stomach.

Rosemarie looked at her fiercely and held her stomach, "Your baby is no monster, and if you go to Undine, you will only give it a greater chance of dying."

She broke down in tears, "Having this baby, being ostracized from the sea, I told myself that I would do anything for my baby to remain safe. I told myself it would never be anything, but a halfling…just a regular halfling. Now look at what's to come!"

Rosemarie understood her emotions, as she was slightly shunned, although considering a mother's misery must've felt harsher, "What's to come is a beautiful baby, as you remember the seer saying it would be marvelous!"

"Well Undine deserves something more ghastly coming to her!"

"Sirena, you don't want this, what you need is any type of compassion you're searching for, that's all. And you need maidens to oversee your baby." Sirena scowls at Rosemarie as she respects it. After a split second, Sirena takes it in and stops swimming in the direction of Undine's ship.

"Since when you've been the noble sister who warns me not to do something dreadful. You eat humans for the goddess's sake."

Rosemarie stares at her sister's eyes, "Oh, who said I was being noble."

Rosemarie swam to the nearest group of seelie's as she sang her heart out. In her siren song she told them to do everything they could to assassinate Undine. That their dark priestess was a threat to all seelie's, that she wanted to forsake her own kind, and that she was a force needed to be dealt with. This was the kind of song which the seelie's would be obligated to remember up until the deed was done, it was also a siren song that the seelie's would pass along the siren's message to the other seelie's. This was a siren song that effortlessly produced an army. Rosemarie did this because she too was angry, but she didn't want any blood spilled on their own hands. Sirena grins proudly at her sister thanking her.

CHAPTER 27

The next day, I searched around the house and into the grotto to find that the Hank's house was completely empty, "Sirena?"

I used the conch shell to call Rosemarie, and she answered sounding extremely fussy while she was by now preparing to give a severe speech to her mother. "Joshua, can't you see that I'm dealing with something a little bit extreme?"

I began looking all flustered said, "Is she with you?"

Rosemarie was tremendously confused, "What the hell are you talking about? Avery?"

I began to get so aggravated as I bit my lip and softly shouted, "No, not Avery! I'm talking about my wife, she's gone! It's been a while since she doesn't hunt for food that long. Do you know where she is?"

She stood silent for the first few minutes and began stuttering, "Wha-what th-the fu-uck? Th-this is-isn't her e-even u—sual f-feeding time. I-I'll be th-there soon!"

I nervously paced all around the grotto expecting for her to turn up from underneath the sea water.

"There's only one special friend of ours that I know who could find Sirena. The only thing is getting to her before something bad might happen to Sirena. I'm just keeping it real." Rosemarie said as if she was getting sick of all the drama within the family, especially her sister Sirena.

When we finally found Avery, she was with Gramps, I passed her Sirena's favorite plush toy, I wasn't sure if it was going to help her even better, but I had to ask, "Do you think you could find her before anything happens to her?"

"Most definitely!" The seer began scrawling and mentioned coordinates on the ocean, Rosemarie gave the expression that she knew where that was.

Rosemarie began to tell us, "She's in the ocean where she was born…in Brazil."

I knew in my head what she was telling me, but I didn't want to believe that I was actually right, "Oh goodness, please tell me she went to Brazil… as in the city in Indiana."

"No! Brazil as in the largest Latin country." Rosemarie looked saddened as she said it. "I'm nervous that she's there…"

"Are they going to hurt her??" I was pulling my head because this was taking too much from me.

"No, I don't know, honestly. I'm nervous because she's going to learn more about my siren ancestors, and how they ambushed the mermaid realms, mind you my sisters and I were babies just like Sirena. But the sirens had shrunk each mermaid realm from a thousand to a hundred. Usually leaving babies alone." Rosemarie looked disgusted as she thought about it, wars were reasonable, but ambushes were inconceivable.

"Why do you think they would kidnap Sirena?" The seer looked at everyone.

Rosemarie said looking uncertain, "Honestly, I'm not sure. Hopefully, they thought they would get hold of their kind before something catastrophic happened. Possibly they want to get rid of her after hearing about her pregnancy. Most certainly they wouldn't hurt her, she has many warrior's poses…that definitely comes through blood."

Gramps looked down, "What if there was a chance, that she went out looking for them, instead. Like a mother's unique instinct to go back to her native land."

I seem to fall into discouragement as I stated, "Apparently, Sirena desires to grasp the relationships that are more akin to herself. I suppose our family was not up to par for the Brazilian mermaid." I felt the concerned eyes of Rosemarie and Gramps fall on me.

Rosemarie gave me a long kiss of air before beginning our search for Sirena near the Brazilian realm. She said their realm was known in, *Baia do Sancho*, a little further isolated than the part of Brazil I thought. The way she charmed me before we swam was to move just as fast as her. Then I asked Rose, "Can you sense her anywhere? Like on the seaweed or the ruins nearby."

Inhaling in the briny air, filtering through her gills, Rosemarie swam toward me until she moved toward a boundary on our way. "No, but I can smell the strong scent of mermaids nearby, so let's pick up your pace."

"I'm still in curiosity, why would she have any interest in them or else why would they abduct her," I still couldn't see clearly in frustration.

Rosemarie then said, "I hope it has nothing to do with revenge about the past, they probably already know she lived with sirens, especially the whole royal realm."

I was getting too sick to my stomach to hear this, "Rose, please don't continue with your guess's and just hunt for her!"

* * *

Sirena awakens in a garden of corals, feeling a little drowsy. The pounding on her backbone along with her head was submerging on an enchanting underworld kingdom full of mermaids before her. She looked around wondering where was in the ocean imagining in which direction to escape. But as soon as she finally grasped where she was, there stood merfolk that Sirena hasn't seen for almost all forever, curiously beginning to turn up.

The merman with tribal markings all over, with a tiger barb fin began to look at her enraged, "No, this can't be?"

Sirena realized the tiger barb merman looked at her as if he looked forward to meeting her, but then was disappointed by not only the fact that she was pregnant but the fact that he could feel it was mixed with more than its human half. She began preparing herself in a stance that the sirens would do when they felt attacked.

"Why are you behaving like this? Calm down, I just need to understand. Plus, I would never fight a mother." Sirena wanted to believe him, it was the first time she had seen someone similar to her, her own kind of race. He had a gentle face, with a long silver beard. It felt genuine, up until other mermen locked her in a cage persuading her it was just for her own safety, and to ensure she wouldn't leave.

It seemed like in the garden, nobody outside knew about her. Only the same familiar intrigued merfolk she would see every now and then when she went for a swim. The ones who were compelled to her pregnancy as

Undine said. Maybe it was just their pure curiosity, or maybe it was the fact that they felt frightened after seeing her siren style stance. Either way, Sirena wanted to get out the old fishing cage, "Who are you, what do you want from me? Let me go!!"

A mermaid with a tail of neon pinks and yellow, yelled out of the small crowd, "She shouldn't even be here, she's not like us, she's an abomination!" Sirena knew how to stay confident but the first time she was in the same area as her own kind, the word *abomination* got thrown at her.

The tiger barb merman with full faith opens the gate and ask for Sirena's hand as he pulls her in to his broad shoulder, "She is like us, and we don't turn on each other!"

"I'm Cato, and as you probably can sense it in your scales, this is Brazil!" He laid out his arms wide sharing the open space, the vibrant colors of the ocean from the city to the empire was amazing. Sirena can even here the music from around, how was that possible weren't the merfolk worried of any fishmen or divers?

Sirena asked him, and she said how a long time ago the first king and Queen knew witchcraft and put a veil over Brazil. Sirena was amazed by everything that she saw but then she became worried but the reality, "This is so beautiful, but why have you brought me here? What are you planning to do with me?"

"I am not here planning to do anything, that would hurt you…or the youngling. Wow, you look just like your mother…we'll talk about that some other time. Don't worry, the merfolk around are just fascinated as well as a little bit anxious of what's to come. Someone wants to meet you, someone that wants to help." Cato said as he tried to broaden his chest out, showing the merfolk that there wasn't anything to worry about.

Cato looked at Sirena with interest, "May I ask you something, you do understand you are a Brazilian mermaid…so why for such a long time have you lived with sirens?"

"Well, I always thought that if somebody actually cared for me, they would be searching for me. And if they knew where I was at, then they would easily take me home. But no one did. The only reason why I knew I was a Brazilian mermaid was because my mother told me everything, she found me during a war, and she raised me instead of killing me. Why should I treat her with any disrespect by leaving her?" Sirena told Cato and she looked at him wondering, was he some sort of family that had been searching for her.

"Do you think I'm just here because you're pregnant? With a sort of crossbreed baby, well I'm not. You are the daughter of the emperor's most talented royal guards, a legendary royal guard of this region of mermaids who I was an apprentice to. And because of that last war, we've become a very small minority than you think. We were humongous once! But almost all of the adults went into battle, because sirens from all over attacked mermaid realms one by one. Most at what you're looking at, were children and babies like you who were protected as they parents hid them to fight."

Sirena looked around and she couldn't help but cry, was she supposed to hate the sirens that she known as sisters. But the more she looked at the mermaids she realized they were all about the same age as her. Instead of Cato who looked like one of the adults who survived. And Sirena still didn't forget the fact he called her mom a royal guard. It always seemed that when Sirena tried so hard to get out of the royalty lifestyle, something was always trying to pull her back in.

Another merman with a black fin with dark silver spots, Wyatt, appears, "Is that her?" The small crowd around bowed their heads.

After bowing his head, Cato says, "Yes, Wyatt. Her scent can change over years, but her scales have been the same since birth."

After feeling that was just personal information released. Sirena began feeling so scared and cried out, "Cato, who is this? No, please don't harm me and my baby! Please, take me back home!!"

When Cato swam toward Sirena asking her just to listen. Wyatt swam to her, "You're not in any harm. We know what the baby is, it's a hybrid of four."

Sirena gave the expression that nothing from the sea would ever be kept to herself, "Wow! News travel fast in the sea, don't they?"

Wyatt had broad arms, also had markings that Sirena began to think were warrior markings, but she didn't understand the bow. He says, "No, we did not hear it from the ocean, let's just say we have our own seelie of the sea. She's here now if you want."

Sirena looked at him like, *seriously*, as she began to say, "The last time I trusted a seelie, she turned my baby into a monster."

Wyatt laughed with a manly voice as he said, "Undine is wicked, I've been trying to arrest her for years, but she outsmarts all of us. Well, this seelie is also half mermaid who you can trust, just like you trust your sister. She won't do anything…she'll only give you ingredients, so your sister could do the rest if she understands what they are."

CHAPTER 28

n old two-legged mermaid swims towards her, as she smiles, she speaks in a native tongue to Wyatt while brushing her hand through Sirena's hair. Wyatt said, "You have to forgive her she knew your mom; she said you look just like her. And she could feel the heart of gold, just like she felt with your mother. The ingredients are ginger, a pinch of dandelion, half of thyme, half of sage, oil of rosemary, a dash of seaweed, one drop from of mermaid's blood, and all in a teacup of natural spring water."

"And how would I know this would work?" It seemed that Wyatt translated everything to the seelie mermaid, who continued speaking in a native tongue.

"She is saying that when the tea turns purple, you'll know it's ready. If you're worried about the ingredients, your sister will know. It will neutralize the extra abilities of the baby, in other words the siren and the seelie in her." Wyatt said, and he continued, "I hope it works. I can only imagine how you feel, it must be tough when everyone in the sea feels like you're carrying a ticking bomb whose blood is transfigured and so many have questions of future armies…oh um let me shut up."

Sirena felt furious, she was finally with her species, her own kind, yet secretly they were all wondering if her baby was going to become the end of the days, when to her it was still just an innocent baby.

Wyatt then ended their conversation, "I must go but there's so much more I still have to tell you. By the way, I'm sorry if I have offended, sometimes when I get nervous, I don't know how to shut up. Which is a paradox in my role for our people. Nevertheless, your baby is nonetheless a blessing and I know you would find a way even without a potion. You have the same tenacity as your mother, and it was my honor to have met you. Cato will swim with you home."

As Sirena said her goodbyes and thanks, Cato and Sirena began swimming away, "What did Wyatt mean by *his role to our people?*"

Cato said, "Oh well he is our prince, I'm so sorry Sirena for forgetting to tell you. It's hard to explain, his father was a warrior who also loved your mother. We all did and loved telling the prince the infinite war stories. He fell in love with the idea of becoming a warrior, more than a prince. He also fell in love with your mother and made it his life's duty to search for you. The babies conceive period is what made the search easier."

Sirena swayed as she set out to think to herself of the things she never thought would happen. Sirena never thought she would meet her own realm, she never thought her mother had an ounce of love for her, and she never thought that her realm actually held that much love strong enough to still search for her and keep its small real intact.

I swam into Rosemarie as soon as she said we were getting closer just behind the ruins. I readies out my knife just in case, but Sirena was just staring straight at me swimming with another merfolk. As I caught my breath, irritatingly I smirked saying, "I'm sorry! I believed my wife's life was in jeopardy. It seems that we were wrong."

"Yeah, I was abducted, oddly all for good reasons. As soon as I tell you all at home, you will be surprised by the most remarkably bizarre day I had." I disbelieved everything she was saying.

I stared at the big merman who was swimming with Sirena earlier, "She's just saying this, so I won't hurt you, how could you go around threatening a pregnant woman? How could you!"

Sirena go in the way, "No! This is a friend, he's from my realm. His name is Cato, they searched for me since I was a baby. I'll show you everything in the grotto. They didn't hurt me."

I didn't want to believe it, I felt like if I did that meant that she was warming up to the idea of going to her realm. And if that was true, that meant she was taking the baby to her realm too. I didn't want to shake the merman's hand, I didn't want to say thank you for taking care of her, in my head it crossed off as if something nasty happen all I did was say, "I'll take you home." and the swim home was silent.

At the grotto we saw everything that happened in Sirena's realm. Rosemarie remembered everything the seelie mermaid told her as for the tea ingredients, she said it was a neutralizer. Rose wanted to ignore Sirena and complete her task for a bit, she felt the burden of guilt of her ancestors ambushing her sister's realm, especially knowing that her siren realm was the reason for Sirena's mothers' death. Sirena swam to her and said, "Rose, the sea gives and takes things from us, in different shapes and sizes. The siren Queen didn't have to take me in as her own, but she did. And if she hadn't, we wouldn't have been sisters." But Rosemarie still got out of the water to fetch the ingredients with Gramps. Of course, he went with her to help her with the land ingredients, also to help her understand that sometimes there isn't enough we can control.

On the other hand, I was dealing with things too, I couldn't take the fact that merman, Wyatt, kept looking at Sirena, as if she was his. I couldn't help the fact that I felt jealous…by many things, she found her home, she found her people, and there was even a prince who devoted himself longer to her than I have. "It doesn't matter how long he searched for me, you're my prince Josh, and this is my home." Damn it! I hate that with her pregnancy she read my mind faster than normal.

* * *

The following couple of days, Sirena daydreamed as she whirled all around into the deep. Wandering as she allowed her body spin without direction through the deep sea surge. One day I followed her, I saw her spinning below the surface of the deep indigo ocean, she was delighted as she soared alongside a gravelly sea floor. She crossed the boundary that we all agreed on since she came home, there were vibrant groups of fish sprinkled ahead of her and then she stared into the void when I decided to leave her, hoping that it was just extra space she needed.

The next day, I was on the beach digging for clams, Sirena then stood above shore. Laying on top of a rock, she turned back away from smiling at me, leaning her hands on the battered rocks. Staring far into the direction of the ocean she just recently visited.

Then she popped up from nowhere when I continued digging, she appeared with two sea lions who have been helping her swim far depths, when Sirena said to me "I made my decision, I want to find my birthing cove around, *Baia do Sancho.*"

"Wait, what?" I looked at her with confusion. "Don't I have any say in this?"

"What do you mean, *by your say?*"

"Well, I'm the father of the baby and your husband. I want to be a part of the birth, how can I, when you're almost a day's way from me?"

Sirena ignored me as she jumped back into the ocean swimming away with the sea lions. I dropped the clam kit and went right after her, not caring if I could breathe or not. This wasn't fair to me at all, and she needed to know that.

I caught up to Sirena, and gently entwined her by her arm, whirled her over to face me. I hardly had any air left in me when she helped swam me up to the surface. After gasping for air, I saw Sirena glaring at me like she never felt so furious in all her life, she loved me and needed me to see that, but a long time ago she was a mermaid who was unaware of her realm and who she was, now that she did her heart sank among Brazil and Carolina. Night and day while Sirena believed her mother neglected her, in actuality her mother sacrificed her life protecting Sirena as a baby, and for the reason that she had never known that until now, her birth mother remained a part of her even greater. It was enough when I could see the sorrow in Sirena's eyes as she explained the truth of her mother's wellbeing, however Sirena didn't know how to express this to Rosemarie and her siren family without making matters harsher. "Let go of me Josh!" she wept seeking to pull back from me.

"I don't want you to leave Sirena please…I love you!" I pleaded, all of a sudden terrified I was going to lose both Sirena and my unborn baby.

"Whatever do you mean, I'm not going anywhere?" Sirena cried out vulnerably.

"Your mind is! I see the way you have been daydreaming in the deep. You want to go back!" Without realizing it I shouted back at her, knowing that I was right, and I had to fight for it.

Sirena was determined to make this happen, "Well, we're going to have to make it happen because I want to give birth where I was born, around the merfolk who my mother protected!" That became the end of her argument.

"It is my baby too, Sirena! don't I have some opinion where our baby should be born?"

Getting the impression that I couldn't influence her to stay, I let Sirena go on and flee into the empty space. Finding herself set free, Sirena galloped back in the direction of the deep.

After Sirena vanished into the dark, Rosemarie turned to me. "Sorry Josh, the moment she settles her brain to carry out something, there is no shifting it. I'll go after her to make sure she gets there alive and well. Perhaps give her some girl-to-girl talk, whatever you humans like to say."

Later that evening, Rosemarie returned to the grotto explaining that she couldn't allow herself to go inside the realm. However, she did explain to me that the ladies spoke.

That night when Cato and Prince Wyatt dropped Sirena off, they were not only invited to the grotto, but they were in the presence of one of the siren realms descendent. The prince also brought us a midwife for Sirena, granted as a gift.

Earlier I left Sirena on a bad note so I had to make sure tonight we could least say goodnight on a good one. So even with our new visitors, I decided that they should join in on our discussion. I wasn't sure if she would change her mind, however perhaps we could meet somewhere in the middle. I told her how much I did understand her reasons she wanted the baby's cove to be in Brazil. So, I discussed the fact that for the next few months we would stay in Carolina since I needed to work enough hours before I went to take off for the ninth month to Brazil. We all agreed to at least see it through as time went by, keep the midwife so she can determine how much time we have, and so forth.

"I'm thinking of a beautiful Brazilian birth cove." Sirena pushes her hand into my shoulder along with delivers me a grin, was this serious...is this the unrealistic nesting brain?

Beyond from the grotto where I was relaxing with Sirena, our new midwife, Aline, raises her eyes gently from painting the scallop shells with Brazilian paints.

CHAPTER 29

irena was staring into a dark reflection of herself into the ocean. She's dying, dying while giving birth to our baby and the light of the lighthouse— I woke up, soaked in night sweats. Not this again. I've had the constant nightmare night by night for weeks, perhaps the rest of the second trimester by now. And it constantly ended the same. Since the grotto, I slept in a glittery sleeping bag shaped like a mermaid tail near Sirena, and I did the same thing as I did after every dream, I ran to the water to check on her. She was already up and about since I screamed out her name during my dream. I began to cry as Sirena swam to me and sat on the surface, I lay on her fin as she tried to calm me down. With my wife being pregnant, I was never going to allow myself to tell her about my nightmares. Sirena went through enough challenging experiences already, and me stressing her away was perilous for her and our baby.

I'd had a bad feeling, like something horrible was going to happen, and I just couldn't shake the feeling that something was coming or waiting for us out there…like there was a tsunami coming. Though unhinge was mystery blistering at the Queen's crown, for once this nightmare tsunami didn't feel manipulated by her.

Pain clutched my heart, as I no longer wanted this *thing* in her. What if my wife died overwhelmingly trying to deliver ourselves a forceful hybrid baby? And, what if our hybrid baby did grow into a virtually indestructible child that broke hell to us all, as the seafolk legends goes? Perhaps I was only having these nightmares because this mermaid midwife hadn't done a single ultrasound, which didn't make me feel great. All Aline did was use her abilities to tell us Sirena's weight gain, give her a proper nutrition, and proper exercises but never even told us about the sex. I was worried about my darling Sirena.

Much to my surprise, the grotto's water glimmers. Sirena shows flashbacks; from when we first met, our very first kiss, the first day I saw her transform, our lovely whimsical wedding, and even some memorable parts of our honeymoon. It was stunning and made me feel a whole lot better. I asked Sirena if she could do that again, unexpectedly Aline was wide awake all this time across the grotto and she replied, "Sirena, doesn't do that. Your baby did, it has magnificent abilities. It seems like it still has further abilities, especially since it use the seer's ability to read Sirena's past memories and combined her seelie and mermaid abilities to assemble those recollections appearing in the water."

All I could think to myself was, *WOW* my baby could do that? I didn't even care at that moment that it had multiple abilities, because right there it felt like my baby was trying to tell me something; tell me that it loved us, it adored its parent's love and devotion, and wanted us to stay confident and remain strong for our baby like we have triumphed for our love. It wanted to remind me what I've been fighting for, and so I did.

Aline then walked towards me, and said with a bit of a stern voice, "Joshua, I am known as a professional ocean midwife so don't question my ways. The reason I couldn't see the baby's gender and even due date, is because your baby is still able to tap into its hybrid powers. My echolocation abilities can't see pass that." I was appalled, she read my thoughts and now she was giving them to me. However, I was also confused, what about the tea that Rosemarie made to put the hybrid abilities asleep, "Yes, I wondered about that too, but it seems, that your baby would do anything to tap into its dormant abilities for you guys. And seeing that your hybrid baby is listening to your emotions and is willing to show you something with this much potential, I can see that next month is the babies last incubated month."

* * *

Sirena's birthing cave was smacked down in the middle of where she lived all her life in Carolina, and where she was born which was Brazil. Prince Wyatt helped with the birthing caves with approval from the mermaids residing in Puerto Rico. The one that was available for her was a hidden cavern in *Cueva del Indio*. Prince Wyatt had to persuade the mermaids all together to consent to the one and only siren, Rosemarie, into the birthing cave deprived of any harm.

During this occasion, Gramps and I learned something new; a birthing cave is required to be decorated by her loved ones with all the things the birth mother had been collecting and decorating. That explains why Rosemarie and Sirena kept inviting the siren sisters to collect treasures, like painting seashell curtains and turning glass bottles into beautiful stained-glass sculptures. Avery also stood around the house during the nesting stage, knitting baby clothes and blankets. While Cato and Wyatt no longer cared about who was what anymore, they continued coming over inviting me to go spear fishing with them. And some days when we felt the grotto became crowded, us three would swim to *Cueva del Indio* to drop off some of the finished treasure.

* * *

Close to the last month, we have finally completed decorating Sirena's birthing cave, she was going to love it. We had one more week before our leave. At the moment, were several more days now that I come from work from an extra hard day's work, to support our even greater family tree.

It was three days before our temporary moving date, when Sirena started to feel something. She couldn't sleep well in the grotto, and she rolled in pain. However, the same sunrise she had awakened to smell of coffee while everyone were all preoccupied, was the same morning she felt rather odd but turned a blind eye to it. Gramps was at Fire Island, to dig up something special at the cove that he had given his own first born. While I was at work preparing to take a month's vacation, Rosemarie was with everyone else at the birthing cave.

Later Sirena began to feel agonizing; though, she remained utterly alone, she sensed the must to hurry to her birthing cove. If it wasn't for the midwife, Aline, who was only hunting nearby, she wouldn't be able to find Sirena at the last minute. My wife wasn't able to move any more, especially while Aline kept track of the rate and length of her contractions. The instant Sirena gone into labor, it began to come down with flash of lightning and rumble of thunder. The weather began to act very peculiar and bizarre.

And Sirena grabbed the ocean and she started to scream, "Help, help, Cato, Rose," and Sirena screamed so loud that though nobody on Fire Island was around to hear her, everyone from *Cueva del Indio* had instead of myself. I suddenly had an unsettling sensitivity stirring within my stomach.

Aline then leaves the ocean water and after drying up, she uses a conch shell to call Gramps. She tells him that everything is okay, but not as to plan, that Sirena can't be moved and it's too late for her to go to her birthing cave. She also mentions that if the people she cares about aren't around, then it'll definitely become a doomed birth. Sirena is trying to sort through her lonesome emotions, but then becomes distracted by her constant vibrations of the ocean as she calls everyone out. I didn't have to be a mind reader to know that Sirena was missing me as well as expecting that I would be present during the delivery. She would be brokenhearted if I wasn't present.

By the time we arrived at the cove by the side of Fire Island, the moon stood out. Aline and Gramps were thanking the gods. Gramps was trying his best to soothe the contracting mermaid, as Aline said she wasn't far enough along. However, possibly if she whirled in the cavern, it would inspire the baby down.

Later Rosemarie stood by one side of Sirena and Aline on her other side. All of a sudden, a gooey secretion came out of Sirena's scales, and the fin folk began getting extremely excited preparing Sirena for the moment. Everyone's act became extremely eager and alert, that Gramps and I realized, this was a mermaid's giveaway indicating that her water just broke! Sirena had low expectations of what was to come as I tried not to think about what could go wrong. However, when she saw the soothing tides of the pool, she swam in slow elegant rings inside the cove's seawater pool; then she hung on as her contraction intervals became shorter. Suddenly, a very pearlescent glow and unearthly and nonetheless fastened with deeply entrenched keen on the sea waters.

The moon was arising to twinkle above the opening of this dormant volcano, which made the water shimmer other than shifting snowy white. As I dived into the cove's pool to be by her side, Sirena seized onto me as the moonlight shined through beaming at us. She tightly held onto my hands, while she remained weeping tears streaming down her face. Rosemarie shouts to Sirena, "Come on Sis, one last push! Push! The baby's almost there!" A few minutes before the moon became full Sirena kept behaving hesitantly, crying out no! Moments later Rosemarie says, "I can see the baby, gently push, and wave you fin!" At that minute, Sirena let out her last cry, our baby swam out toward the surface of the water. The moon's shine created a snowy hue of the baby's hair. Gramps yelled out, "It's a girl! What the heck? She has old, tinted curls and elfish ears! Are you certain she's not full pixie?"

Once she held our new daughter, she began to cry and uttered to her, "I will always love you, my precious. I will make certain you stay with us always. Josh, she looks similar to you; but she has my eyes." Outside of the cove, the siren sisters made tides grow smoothly, and began delivering a harmless serene siren song at Sirena. They were open-handedly giving Sirena their blessings, and more, cautioning her that she better be watchful as the Queen summoned tritons to destroy the newborn.

* * *

After receiving that announcement, the Brazilian mermaids swam off promising Sirena not only a safe home but a merman in the name of Cato whenever she pleases. Rosemarie left before us to check if there were any tritons on the prowl. And as for the newborn, Sirena, and I, we immediately spun home. Sirena embraced her baby into her chest and swam.

When we all finally got on land. Rosemarie began running after Sirena, I was actually trying to catch my breath, since Sirena only had time enough for one kiss of air. Rosemarie followed Sirena, running in the direction of the closest church with her newborn in her arms; she knocked on the doors crying out loud. The fact that Sirena was in the streets in utter nudeness wasn't her concern, the fact she was holding her baby behaving absolutely petrified, was. Sirena was caressing her baby farewell now, setting the baby away on the doorstep, hoping someone in the church would take her in. The minute I caught up to them, I couldn't believe what I saw. I virtually accepted the fact that I had to grab my baby and stop her; but I didn't. Sirena took one more gaze at our daughter, and she knew she couldn't give our daughter up. With our baby in our arms, she sauntered to us and asked for forgiveness, assuring us that she just wanted her safe.

Policemen overheard reports of a stunning red-headed nudist lurking around; police were all over the area, looking for Rosemarie. Later two officers found her, I was anxious she was going to *siren* or attack. Instead, briskly she ran toward the ocean and plunged, leaving the police officers stunned and confused as they couldn't spot any sign of her after that.

Hurriedly we arrived at our house, as Rosemarie had moved to the Lake Orchid cove where she could still be near her niece and sister while protecting them. By the minute we got home, everyone already agreed on the name for our daughter, Luna. The name was given to her because of her snowy hair. Luna was gorgeous. She did look sort of similar to me, but she was fortunate with Sirena's magnificent eyes. This little girl had snowy white hair, which was curly like mine. She didn't have to some extent webbed toes or fingers; on the other hand, she had these sweet adorable elfish ears. Our Luna was exquisite.

CHAPTER 30

ver the few weeks, Sirena and I embraced parenthood to our beautiful hybrid, but we were all frightened for Luna's destiny in life. However, at some point we had to tell Luna the truth. Someday she's going to be aware of her powers. One of these days she's going to realize that her mother doesn't age normally, and maybe sooner or later, she might even catch her mother or aunt with fins.

When Sirena and I looked up to check on Luna, we noticed huge tidal waves coming in, which only meant one thing: Sirena's siren family. I sprinted toward Luna and hurriedly snatched her out of the water. As for Rosemarie, she swiftly leaped into the sea where she found her sisters eyeing her dreadfully and repulsively. The siren sisters were upset to see Rosemarie again who was banned from the pod because they failed to execute Luna.

Once Rosemarie was already undersea and I had my baby girl, I knew what was happening undersea was not respectable. The further irritated the sirens turned out to be, stronger the tides became stronger. The wind started howling, lightning began setting off, and you could make out the loudest shrieks approaching from down below. I knew those shrieks from anywhere, and trust me, they weren't Brazilian. They were from the siren sisters.

Each young parent copes with challenges that aren't entirely planned such as, being denied sleep as well as the emotional anxieties concerning the well-being of the baby. However, our challenges were even greater without a doubt, as we had to protect our Luna from seafolk that didn't understand her since she was a baby and didn't want her alive. Parts of the ocean had always felt threatened since Luna's birth; they never enjoyed the four years from the pleasures we had from her.

"Good morning parents! So as the godmother of my beautiful niece, I would be keen on us to adjust for whatever could come about." I was swaddling my baby girl as I looked concerned looking at both Sirena and Rosemarie, from left to right as she continued to explain, "As the sisters warned us, they revealed that the siren realms nevertheless felt dicey regarding the baby's birth. Hence, I have an only some notions although they're going to take time."

Sirena then looked guarded as she said, "No, they can't have my baby, I don't care if I must fight all the realms of sirens, I'll die just as my mom did to protect my Luna."

Later that day, I decided to take care of the baby as Sirena took a swim, she was having a hard time breastfeeding and needed time to relax. As she did, I planned to find out more about Rosemarie's ideas. Though Rose and I bumped head, she always was the type to care more for Sirena than herself, maybe even more than Sirena, on the plus side she was brilliant with her charms.

Though we had to lock the gate for the grotto, since there is water still plumbing in it made it easier to take care of Luna that way. Every time she got fussy, I sat on the steps of the pool and cradled her as the water touched her toes. Rosemarie was beginning to describe every detail of her charms, when suddenly Luna was behaving fussy once again. I went through the parental guide in my head and checked everything I had done for her. She suddenly wiggled her hand out of the swaddle blanket and touched the water. Where Rosemarie and I began to see another vision starting. My sister-in-law then yells in my ear, "She wants to show us something, let her swim in the water!"

It was an image of Sirena swimming with Cato. I began worrying that Sirena was in danger, but as Sirena swims around she looks very confused while talking to Cato. All at once she stops speaking as soon as she observes that the vessel from far afield is usually nearer than it was. Sirena looked so flustered that she prefers to ignore it and just continues swimming believing it was just her. "Cato, I have been swimming in this ocean for years, this vessel— doesn't belong here, no not here...we're meant to be within earshot of the Hanks beach, I'm not sure if this some sort of postdelivery brain, but am I going daft or are we going in the wrong direction?"

Rosemarie gave an evil laugh and then yelled out, "Yes, it worked!" I wanted to ask her right there what she meant by that, but as Luna kept swirling around the show remained appearing. "Hold on, lets continue listening, I'll explain soon."

We watched, while Sirena and Cato reflected soundlessly as she explored the vessel and the pillars near them, "These pillars are too close to the Hanks beach, they wouldn't even be around the coastline, everything is wrong…hold on, I'll be right back, watch my back Cato." She swam immediately above the ocean, in one direction where our house was meant to be sited, only to find out that mysteriously they were a long way from the Hanks. Sirena dived back down realizing she was on to something, they should have been home by now, yet it felt like they were swimming in circles and still not getting anywhere closer.

Cato makes a joke saying, "Well I know for sure I didn't give birth, and I know I'm seeing the same thing as you are." After Sirena laughs, Cato becomes serious and says, "Your family doesn't happen to have any witches or any ties with unseelie's? Besides that, last one that I heard of, don't they? Because this is starting to feel like a concocted trick." Sirena stared perplexingly as she sought him to enlighten more, "Personally, I've seen this turn out in heaps of combats, many unseelie's specialized in illusions, if they sought to make the opposing side go livid or if they wanted to change the way the opposing side saw things for a siren's advantage, they could do it easily, it was always terrifying to save our kind from those illusions, we never knew how to undo it."

As I looked at Rosemarie, she began to look ashamed, "I was going to explain it to you both, I didn't know it was even working." I began to feel worried, and she continued "I have to go and get them, open the latch! The fastest way is through the grotto's entrance. Leave Luna in the pool so you can watch over us."

Looking back into Luna's vison, Sirena falls apart and then spins upwards to the surface once more, attempting to get a better view while throwing seashells at the fake visual before her. When she looked around each corner there was our Hanks beach stretching out everywhere as soon as her eyes enlarged in panic, she began to feel completely woozy, she almost sank to the ocean floor until Cato caught her.

Rosemarie then plunges into the ocean and meets them, "Oh, I was so anxious this was going to take place. I was intended to show you just in time, however at the moment my labyrinth didn't hold."

Sirena gaped unbelievably at her sister appearing to be utterly distraught, "What did you do to the ocean?"

Rosemarie was trying to explain, "Sirena, I told you there were things we were going to have to do in order to protect the baby! I thought about this soon after the sisters gave us their warning. It's one way to block many siren realms from getting on your land for the meantime."

Sirena became more agitated, "How do you expect me to swim? or Cato? What about Josh!"

Rosemarie didn't like the manner in Sirena's tone, so she hurried as she clarified, "That's the thing I didn't think about everyone else. I just spelled four objects and buried them around the ocean of South Carolina. I could see through it because I created the charm. If I wanted to lift the labyrinth enchantment, I would have to simply unbury an object, for good I would have to break the objects. Joshua won't be affected cause he's human. Outside of the labyrinth Cato will be able to see pass the illusion."

Sirena was too uneasy to accept Rosemarie's reason for anything, "Still Rose! Rosemarie you should've spoke to me first, how is my family supposed to see my baby and how am I supposed to swim round when I want to?"

I saw the image, I felt Rosemarie's heartache, she only had tried to do what was best for the baby. That was all, now she was being treated harshly, "I thought I was your family, the Brazilians come in and all of a sudden— you know what that doesn't even matter, what matters is Luna! If you would let me finish, I was just finished creating the charm bracelets for anyone who we entrust to go through the labyrinth and see clearly. That means not even the siren sisters could have one. Knowing them, they carry loads of trinkets they'll misplace a bracelet, and that could be a gain for a foe." Rosemarie was infuriated as she was troubled, chastised, and demeaned all together. Other than being taken for granted, "So Sirena if you two could follow me, I could show you the way. By the way, I probably didn't think ahead of time as soon as I thought of the idea, but I still thought of something then leaving your baby vulnerable."

Sirena began following her sister as she regrettably replied, "Rosemarie I'm sorry I didn't mean it—"

Rosemarie cut her off, as she wiped her face swimming ahead towards the Hanks beach, "Let's just get you safely home to your family."

As they got on land and began transforming, the vision disappeared, I took that as a sign to grab Luna from her swim and premonition. When the sisters came home, they continued bickering, while Rosemarie finished chanting as she dripped her concoction on three bracelets. She then gave two to Cato, for himself and prince Wyatt, and threw the other at Sirena.

For the rest of the day, Rosemarie wanted to give Sirena the silent treatment, so Sirena just left her and took Luna from my arms. "I'm feeding Luna, and taking a swim one more time, dropping Cato halfway to his home.

I walked up to Rosemarie, "That what a very genius tactic you have, using the ocean as a labyrinth…if Gramps saw that he would've agreed with me that it was very clever."

Rosemarie smiled a thank you, "But there's much more needed work to take care of." She mentioned that Avery was at the house and saw something while looking over Luna. This was the reason that Rose had various ideas. As she shared them with me, she ripped apart the nursery door from its hinges. I was confused at was upset until she explained. "Avery, saw a shadow of an uninvited guest, at the nursery's door." Rose begins to leave me feeling frightened as she paints the hinges with an aromatic glue she continues, "Apparently, after I asked what I can do to prevent that from happening, she said it's meant to happen and that we can't alter what's coming. Therefore, if the uninvited guest is coming and she only saw them at the nursery door, I'm going to make it my best to stop them from going in." She asked me to screw the door back, as I did, she begins painting symbols around the door borders. "The glue is visible only to us, made with the seer's shield brew, with a pinch of all of our blood. If you remember yesterday, when I pricked you with my dagger, I did that with Sirena, Gramps, and myself as well." A prick…I thought she was trying to slice the blood out of me.

I looked down at Rosemarie as she even painted a strip of the shield glue on the doorstep of the nursery's entrance, "How do we know if it's working?"

After Rosemarie finished, she stood up and glanced back at her work. She didn't look at me, just continued to stare at the symbols as she said, "The sweet scent. It's the sign for only the invited that the glue is working." When she finally looked away from the door, she said to me in a dismayed whisper, "I'm not supposed to say this, Avery told me this in confidence. However, if Sirena feels too unnerved, she may perhaps take Luna and move to Brazil."

CHAPTER 31

Sirena is rocking on the nursery chair, holding her swaddled Luna, and staring into her periwinkle eyes. When placing Luna along in her cradle then observed her with fascination as she pulled her little hairs back. Queen Dionysus sneaks up the stairs while humming an eerie soft song. As she was just about to stroll into the nursery she freezes, barricaded by an unseen wall that Rosemarie had put up.

Standing before her mother, Sirena glared up at her. Queen Dionysus had barely moved. She twisted slightly, shine off her knife edge cheekbones as she watched the mothering beaming off of Sirena.

The Queen gave a careless smile as she said, "I will take good of her, as I did with you."

"You are not going to turn my baby into a monstrosity, she is my sweet Luna. She won't be infected by your ways."

When Sirena had finished her mother said, "I do say, it's very queer. Very queer indeed. I do say this is not my forte. But my dear she's already a miscreation more than you think."

Rosemarie appeared behind their mother and said you are not going to take the baby, "I'm thinking that half the ocean is going to side with us" Queen Dionysus scuffs in the open in back of her. "Once the mermaid realms hear about you trying to harm a descendent of theirs, they will come here in Luna's favor. At the worst time for you when your daughter is becoming Queen."

Queen Dionysus's self-righteous grin slips off of her appearance, and she becomes beyond perilous, "What, is that a threat? How dare you speak to your mother with that tongue?!"

Suddenly Sirena looked up at Rosemarie, "Get her out of here, the baby is heating up!" She started yelling as I entered the house, Rosemarie was telling her mother to plunge into the sea and never come back. Then she gave me a wink. I handed her what she asked for and walked into the nursery to stare into my Luna before things would unravel.

* * *

I woke up thinking about what today had to offer, I left my beautiful Sirena in bed for a few more minutes of peace. While leaving her lounging, hips lifting upward.

It was the morning of Dianthus Coronation Day, the day she would become Queen of the siren realm. But sooner than they announced the words, "Queen Dianthus of the siren realm" Rosemarie submerged in the depths to meet up with her mother. Sirena waited at the dock, bawling her eyes out as I tried to calm her down. I left her and began to snap throwing things all over the place in the house.

After Rosemarie took a sip from her flask, the same flask we all did earlier, she began crying as she swam to her mother. "Mother, I need you to come with me up shore."

"But you said you never wanted to see me there…Rose are you crying??" Queen Dionysus stared at her with a disgusted glance.

Rosemarie wiped her face, straightened her back and continued, "Like that would ever stop you, this is serious, trust me you'll still be in time for the coronation…right now Sirena needs you!"

When the ladies revealed themselves above shore, Sirena pressed a decorative chest as she stared at her mother with swelled red and wet eyes. I saw the Queen and ran up to her, screaming, "It's all your fault, now nobody gets to take care of her, you monster!" Gramps wasn't around when I needed him the most.

Rosemarie dried off and ran to me, "Relax Joshua, hurting my mother won't solve anything!"

"She needs to see what she did!!" I bent and softly tugged away the chest from Sirena. "Beautiful, embellished chest, right? The sort you would collect in your treasures, well look inside, because this is your doing!!" I dropped to my knees and broke down crying. "Take a good look! You could've just left our baby alone, she'd still be swimming in the water, or wrapped in someone's arms. The siren realm should know what you are capable of!!"

Dionysus was confused at the sand she was looking inside of the embellished chest; she didn't know what it was. Sirena cried as Rosemarie stared at it as she said, "It's called cremation…that sand is actually ashes of Luna. Her body's temperature burned up when you last arrived, and then she scorched up into this. Ashes to ashes. Her small figure wasn't competent of carrying every one of those abilities you made she'd have."

"And how can I know this is her for sure?"

Rosemarie demanded her mother to taste a pinch of the ashes. I looked at Rose with revulsion, I began screaming, "Don't you dare lay a finger on her!" However, it was already too late, their mother tasted a pinch and her eyes turned foggy. She looked pale as she stared at us almost remorsefully.

Sirena see that Prince Wyatt and Cato are arriving, "We need to begin leaving for Brazil. Aren't you proud mother? You finally found a way to break me. Now while you convert your daughter to a Queen, as I will be paying respects to death of mine." She says as I mournfully stare down across the ocean. Something was making the ocean rattle.

Sirena stands and reaches out for my hand to stand with her, she snatches back the urn chest from her mother's grip. Queen Dionysus looked as if she wanted to say something but knew she didn't bear the right words.

Dianthus approaches looking distraught at Sirena, "There's merfolk around the realm swimming towards here. Then I heard everything said, is it true sister? The baby?" That was the cause of the rattling ocean, hundreds of merfolk swimming from different realms, as they sang a melancholy song paying their respects to our daughter's demise. They didn't take any notice of the sirens that Sirena was related to.

Dianthus gasped in horror as Sirena said, "Ask our mother why, it was her doing, Luna passed a few hours after her visit." Dianthus wraps her mouth along with her hand before she erupts into fury and cries all together.

"Sirena, you must understand this was just as much as your doing, having a hybrid for instance." The daughters weren't surprised she wouldn't take any fault.

Sirena ignored her mother and told her sister, "Dianthus, I appreciate you being here, but you must go home and become Queen now. Hopefully, you can be a better ruler." Queen Dionysus sighed and grunted that Sirena was being childish, so she disappeared back towards the realm. Afterwards, Dianthus gave her sisters huge hugs and wiped Sirena's tears before following her mother to her coronation.

Once they left, I jumped into the ocean where merfolk were hiding in all places. Sirena and Rosemarie gave me a kiss of air, including three Brazilian mermaids although they seemed to be appalled about the concept. I swam in the front with Rose, Sirena, and Prince Wyatt. The mermaids continued singing the song of mourning as we swam to our Luna's birthing cove at Fire Island.

In the candle lit cove stood our family and new friends, and each merfolk carefully placing a treasure or a seashell inside the embellished chest of ashes. Giving their blessings for us and our baby girls short lifetime, including the little memories we shared with her. The ceremony was lovely beyond measure, in the revealing of genuine sincere emotion. After digging the treasure chest, the sun went down, and the merfolk left. However, something came over Rosemarie, Sirena, and I.

We created a bonfire in the cove and Rosemarie spelled a border for no one to hear us. When she completed the barrier, she then nodded that everything was fine. I instantly embraced Sirena, "Oh my goodness, that felt so real. Do you think your mother in fact tasted our daughters' memories from the ashes of the stillborn I gathered?" I stared at Rosemarie keenly for her response as this was for the most part her plan.

"The memories I collected from Luna were effortless to fasten to the ashes of the stillborn. It's dark magic that I found some time ago in one of Undine's bottle of hexes. Avery aided me along the road to deepen the curse, that way even we would believe in the ruse." It meant a lot if Rosemarie trusted the dark magic while being deceitful to friends and family, in order to protect our Luna. Therefore, I laid my trust in her hands.

Sirena looked worried as she said, "If the sea gets the impression that our Luna is alive, I'm unsure our mother would keep her distance."

Afterwards Rosemarie says, "The curse helped us market the lie appropriately even to our closest ones, we were careful and that's all we have to stay from the ocean."

Sirena and I remained in stillness for a lengthy second, when a small boat appeared with Gramps. I stared at the boat as it approached nearer, "This implies that what is left is our farewells."

Far into the night, Sirena starts packing a handbag of Luna's stuff with a journal she wrote to her since Sirena was pregnant with her. I helped my wife as I saw her tearing up unhurried to pack up the rest. Once we were finally ready, we drove off to meet up with Gramps cradling Luna at a charmed hidden destination in the middle of Carolina.

CHAPTER 32

irena and I were saying our goodbyes as we handed our Luna to Rosemarie. Sirena held her little hand and she began to speak, "The siren realm will continue watching over us, hence we must change things if we want our Luna back." I began kissing my daughter's hand, as Rosemarie swaddled her. "How could she be safe without her full family around to protect her; I don't understand why we can't all go?"

"Her aunt is the only person we can trust Luna's wellbeing with, and you know why."

After Rosemarie softly secures her niece, she stares at Luna in awe and becomes confident and protective. She smiles before assuring us that it will only be for a while, until Sirena makes sure Dionysus corrects the mess in the siren realm. Avery soon after met with us, "I finished creating a cloaking charm, the baby won't be scented by your mother or sisters. And the parents of course are acknowledged."

Sirena said once more, "No one can ever find her, if it's not her father or myself, they can't enter the house!"

Rosemarie looked at Avery then Sirena and I, "Together, we will be able to do this. Don't worry Sirena, don't worry Josh."

I grab hold of my baby once more, to get one last look before Luna leaves with Rosemarie and Avery, I whisper to her how much I will always love her and said my goodbyes. "Some realms don't understand you; they would rather see you dead or make a weapon out of you. But I will ensure you come back to a safe home. As well as each being who desires malice to you will be afflicted." Rosemarie looked alarmed, however I just felt shattered with Sirena.

Sirena held our Luna, "I pledge to you my princess, you will come back to us where you belong. And we will swim in the sea together, hand to hand." She caresses our daughter on the forehead, then her cheek, and observes Luna's little foot one further moment prior to handing Luna to her sister.

Sirena hugs Rosemarie and kisses her on the cheek, "Thank you for everything, I hope you all stay happy. I'll see you soon, I promise."

Avery smiled as Rosemarie said she would be happy for sure.

Suddenly, Avery came before us and rubbed a concoction on the baby's lips and said, "Don't worry Sirena it's just some herbs and mainly blueberry to shelter the child, keep malevolent away, and strengthen the aura before we leave."

Of course, if Luna's siren grandmother found out she was still alive, she would do anything to lock Luna up for herself. Already Luna's abilities were becoming sensitive. Her clairvoyance was becoming honed. Her foresight of being tracked through a siren song was intense, that Avery, the seer saw it and said, "We need to leave now!"

Gramps and I had a brief discussion, then I told Avery and Rosemarie, "Take Gramps with you. Drive fast and far. He practically raised me, so he'll help you with most human baby matters. Hide her."

"Indeed, we won't let my mother use my beloved newborn to consume her own aspirations." Sirena breathed anxiously.

"She *is* their grandmother," Rosemarie pointed out.

"My adoptive grandmother, she *massacred* my mother…Luna's true grandmother." Sirena shot back. "Now hurry and leave!"

We stood there as we watched them drive away.

Then we began driving away, we knew we would have to suffer and undergo a remarkable detachment that would place a void in both our heart and soul.

When Sirena and I got home she finally burst into tears, our daughter was no longer in our grasps, she was going to begin her life in a new home further away from us. Rosemarie promised that she would call us from a telephone with their designation.

"Think…Sirena," I wiped her tears from her face. "Far away from the ocean and her true nature, she will be kept safe until it's okay to open the gates of her home."

"Should any mother turn aside as of her newborn simply for the reason that she is warned to do so?" Sirena wept these words as she sniffled.

Throughout the rest of the night, we hardly spoke nor ate during dinner, it was even hard to look into each other's eyes without blaming the other. Sirena went to the nursery crying herself to sleep, I followed my melancholy wife right after her and held her as she sobbed. Falling asleep as we grasped the delightful memories of Luna for so long as we dreamed.

Along with time this came to be challenging to do…Sirena and I coping with our jobs along with secretly fighting the oceans law for Luna's safety with the new siren Queen Dianthus. Wanting the days go by, hurrying for that day of the week we would finally visit our little one, hopeful we didn't miss any important milestones as well as hoping she recalled our face.

After a long two-hour ride in search of the cabin, getting lost in the paths that lead to the hidden cabin in the Forest Acres. Sirena and I were extremely thrilled, it has only been seven days, yet it felt like we haven't seen her in forever. "Do you think the gifts we got were too much; like the mermaid lantern style globe, the starfish night-light, or my dolphin plush toy from our first date?"

I chuckled a bit, "Of course not babe, those are the most momentum gifts for any baby girl to have throughout her life…watch when she comes back home, she will still hold on to that because it kept her joyful and secure. Even better, she's going to grow up still having it! I know I sure did." Thinking about my baby blanket and my childhood books. I kept looking at the GPS which seemed confused about where we were.

Sirena smiled, "Okay, that sounds good…I like that! I wished I held onto momentum gifts from my birth…my true mother—" As her words trailed off, Sirena gazed outside the window as if she was imagining of everything she probably did have from her mother as a baby but was then damaged after the sporadic ambush. I held her hand as a tear trickled down her cheek, she attempted to slyly wipe the tear, therefore after I made a joke about us going in circles she laughed and went back to talking about the gifts. "But what about the fact we actually bought an Echo speaker to record our voices for all your favorite childhood books so she can always hear our voice, we aren't letting it truly replace us whenever we visit her, right? I still would love for us to read to Luna each time before we leave."

As we were finally getting closer to the road, I looked at Sirena, "Well, duh! Of course, we would read to her and each time that's when we're recording, just so she can hear us when we aren't. Just be warned that they probably aren't like children's stories you read when you were a little one! However, I did include a book about a red-hair mermaid."

Sirena looked outside the window a bit saddened again, "I think you forgot when I told you my siren mother never read to any of us. But my sisters loved to tell tales, legends that were passed down. They were sometimes romantic but most of all blood-lusting terrifying! I wouldn't tell those legends to our daughter…possibly if she was older, and that's still a big fat possible." She then grabs the books from the gift bag, "I do have a few questions about these books; is this even a cat because he is super tall, and fish don't have sparkly glittery scales or talk to starfish, and what mouse wears trousers when he's going to eat, and why do we need to read to our daughter everything a caterpillar eats, and this mermaid story is almost so factual as an alternative of the big octopus witch. These books sounds bizarre, she won't grow up confuse about the world, won't she?"

"No honey, children's books are good for many reasons; brain exercises, improving concentration and memory, enhancing imaginations, boosting critical thinking skills, and also developing empathy. I read in the baby books if we start super early, they'll learn the skills faster than the average age." I looked at her with a grin of hope for our future.

The sweltering temperature had become as a dramatic effect following the coolness of the air-conditioner that had chilled the vehicle over the last couple hours. Sirena thumped the door behind her, tying up her teal bohemian floral dress making it knee-length so she could feel some sort of breeze. She then took off her summer straw hat fanning herself as she stared at the cabin.

"Oh my gosh, it's lovely Josh!"

I joined her out on the meadow in front of the balcony, then gazed at the whimsicality from behind. "Wow, Gramps, and Rose really did a splendid job picking out a place fine enough for a child?"

The cabin, settled in the heart of the woodlands facing a small lake. It was something you thought came out of a fairy tale book. There was a twisting footpath that returns you back into the forests where the cabin rests. It lies on the very top of a peak raised up beyond the lot, as if it were meant to be a treehouse in the mists. Thick ivy wrapped the brick walls, and its brown slate roof with a chimney.

Rosemarie ran towards us, "Sister, Joshua! I'm so glad you were able to find us. I miss you so much, hurry your daughter is upstairs sleeping."

"Well, hello there, what do you think of our haven…I'm making pie by the way." Gramps came outside and gestured at the cabin. There was a smell of sage and rosemary placed in the bedrooms as well as the scent of homemade strawberry and cream pie. All the curtains were completely open with light beaming inside. "Avery ties the herbs around the house for protection, by the way I can tell my great grandbaby is going to grow up so smart."

Gramps showed us throughout the cabin, but most importantly he showed us the nursery. Sirena walked in slowly, as if she was nervous about the conclusion. Her face was the one and only thing Luna noticed when she opened her eyes to her pleasant thoughts. Her mother, Sirena, just as she remembered it the first time she saw her, beaming down at her, her serene periwinkle eyes, as sunlight flooded through her teal hair. It was lovely to see the bond between Luna and her mom.

That was the most amazing day throughout the week; we got to play with our daughter, hold her little hands and hear her giggle. Sirena was astonished that her newborn was clasping onto her breast and drinking her milk naturally. We ate dinner together as a family when Sirena explained to everyone that the Ruling for Luna's Protection was going to take longer than six months, simply because of Luna's staged death. Everyone was still on board, though in Sirena's eyes we can see her piercing cries for the future lost hours she would have of her daughter. After dinner, Sirena and I read to our Luna, then as she was nodding off Sirena sang to her, and once our baby eventually drifted off, we turned on the mermaid musical lantern which began playing, *Romance De Amor*. A beautiful song to fall asleep to.

Sirena began crying silently as I walked her out, "Don't worry sweetheart, we'll see her next week. For now, you just need to try to pump enough breast milk for Rose to store." Sirena agreed and went down to the kitchen to begin pumping, she had been eating healthier after learning everything that increases breastmilk. Sirena didn't have an adequate schedule like other moms, so when her breast began leaking often since her brand-new nutrition, she was able to provide as many storage bags as she could, after yesterday she had more than a two days' supply. Sirena untied her bohemian dress freeing her breast out in the open, Gramps looked at the breast pumps and decided this was a women's moment and he was too old for those recollections. As us men stood outside the porch enjoying the humid rain, Rosemarie and Avery stood with Sirena showing her their brand-new little freezer, that contained six breastmilk storages.

Avery then said, "Each storage holds up to 60 ounces, which is a days' worth of milk. So, since you gave us two days, Rose will easily put them to freeze." Sirena was looking at the milk suctioning machine, as she thought about how her nipples ache this being the most endless time she's ever pumped in a day, then she looked at Avery and Rose with a scowl. "I'm sorry my dear, I know what you're thinking and yes, I could easily duplicate it and I'm sure Rosemarie could find goatmilk, but only human breast milk present constituents that we can't replicate. I understand that the process hurts, and I understand that it takes long but right now you are pumping; millions of living cells, thousands of proteins, prebiotics, growth factors, hormones, vitamins, minerals, and so much more are flowing through that liquid gold." Avery touched Sirena's hand while she spoke to her, being able to see all the time that she was so unhappy. "Sirena, be grateful that you can create milk. You don't know how many mothers come to me asking me for help because they are dried or can't produce milk for their babies. And I know the true factor is that you feel better when your Luna is just holding onto you. I've seen your sadness, and I saw it earlier when you held onto Luna as she fed it didn't hurt. You question yourself, what is a machine compared to your baby's hands. But I promise you, it's what's going into her body that matters. I know a way I can help."

Avery began saying a few words and pressing on Sirena's breast, milk began rushing out from her breast and filling the next 240 ounces of bags. After their discussion, Sirena felt happy knowing she had finished a weeks' worth, until her weekly visit she'd see her Luna.

CHAPTER 33

Each time we went to visit Luna, Sirena felt more and more confident feeding her and to even pump her breastmilk after. We were lucky enough to visit Luna at each milestone. When Luna began teething, Gramps suggested pureeing fruits and vegetables and adding Sirena's milk as a thinner. When we all of us looked at Luna, we could tell she was paying attention to each one of our voices and trying hard to remember each of our facial expressions. I enjoyed making a bunch of baby voices and each time I played with her, she searched for my face. She happily *cooed* every time she heard our voice making goofy sounds or when she listened to Sirena singing or the Mermaid musical lantern now playing, *Beauty and The Beast*.

At six-nine months, Sirena and I were there when Luna started sitting up on her own and then when she started crawling. The one thing we missed out on, was her say the most important few words. Rosemarie recorded it on her phone, Luna was taking one of her baths when she envisioned Sirena and I again. Luna then said, "Mama," as she splashed at the water with Sirena's face and then she said, "Dada," when the vision focused on me. Every bath time she foreseen us, this vision in particular was of us speaking about Luna finally coming home. Sirena saw all of this on the phone while I was packing up Luna's stuff. Sirena was crying thinking about how she missed out on this very important milestone. Sirena didn't think about the fact that Luna's abilities were growing still at one-year-old, her only thought was missing those two sentimental words. It did give her hope that she knew who her mother and father was, that with her abilities of premonition she never forgot. But then Luna dressed in a bright yellow dress with light blue ribbons on her silver curly hair crawled to Sirena, she smiled at her as if she didn't want her to worry.

* * *

We grabbed hold of our Luna and began running into thick darkness of several streets. All of us took turns ensuring we weren't shadowed around. The minute we entered the Hanks home from the back entrance, we all felt Luna was safe as Sirena was glad, she could finally tuck her into her own bed. Aunt Rosemarie caught up to us. After grasping for breath, she described to us the undersea conversation she had with the new Queen. Rosemarie said that so far, only Carolina's siren realm are now well ordered to keep a lookout of this region of the ocean, and if as soon as Luna's feet touch the waters, they would have to keep an eye of any foreign sirens who might want to drown her, even if surrounded by people. She also mentioned that Queen Dianthus wanted to remind everybody that Dionysus and her young cutthroat twin sisters, at some point will catch the scent of Luna, especially the older she gets and would react like sharks. Rosemarie looked dismayed, "She would definitely know she's alive, if let's say…Luna learns what she truly is and uses her powers on purpose." Sirena and I wanted our darling to love everything about herself, now it seemed she had to be oblivious of all the other things that made her extraordinary.

* * *

It was the week of Luna's fourth birthday. On my way to work, I overheard a very alarming conversation between Luna and Gramps. As I snuck behind the refrigerator, my baby girl told Gramps about a magical venture she had. Through all the liveliness in her, she burst out just like her mother, "Oh my goodness, Grandpapa! I had so much excitement yesterday. I went to explore Fire Island and discovered this cove. Inside, oh my goodness, was this beautiful dormant volcano! It was so enchanting, Grandpapa! The cove for one thing was sparkling inside; for another, I noticed there were small ripples indicating another entrance…But Grandpapa, I saw the oddest thing ever. The cove had beautiful objects around. There were beautiful women clothing, lovely seashells, a gorgeous vintage-looking mirror, and objects that you can tell came from the ocean because it had so much seaweed wrapped around." Gramps stood looking bewildered since he knew this cove. "Grandpapa, why the heck would a person live in a cove?"

Gramps chuckled with his huge tummy all over the place and replied by saying, "Um, maybe because there's no rent on a small island of course, duh!"

As soon as they completed their conversation, I stood in absolute horror that I didn't know how to handle the situation. I appeared from the back of the refrigerator, and I just yelled at Luna, "I don't want you ever going there again! That was a relentless move you made, that could've been a dangerous person's shelter. You're grounded until I say so missy, go to your room!" I can't believe the way I reacted with my daughter, but as much as she swam, I never thought she would actually find her parents dating site and highly worthwhile her birthing cove. I couldn't by all means let her go there alone, what if her evil grandmother had expectations for that.

After yelling at my Luna, she ran crying to her room, leaving me in a position of guilt. Gramps looked at me with huge disappointment and yelled, "What the heck do you think you're doing shouting at that unfortunate girl? She doesn't even understand the circumstances. I know you want to protect her, but that does not give you the right to yell at Luna! She's only curious about the world just like you were at that age. And you know what, Josh, she deserves to know the truth about the ocean one of these days! The more you shout at her, champ, it just builds up more prying, and you know what they say about curiosity—"

I cut him off, "Yeah, yeah, I know. But I rather leave the curiosity to a cat than to my hybrid daughter."

Gramps looked at me disappointed, "You need to man up, and not only apologize to your daughter but figure where you're going about things…you're all over the place!" Gramps was right. Ever since we had the family together, with Luna's undiscovered fate lingering about, I always feel I have to keep an extra pair of eyes in back of my head or snatch a few of Rosemarie's defense potions. But right now, I had to speak to my wife because I just came up with a plan.

After work I had gathered everyone for a family discussion. By now, Sirena and Rose have already heard what occurred earlier. Although Sirena was furious at me, she understood what I was feeling as well. "So, we're supposed to keep Luna's secret, of what she is along with her fate. Explain to me how that is possible, if she is almost four years old and is already swimming into Fire Islands cove. We're moving." Sirena, looking distressed, said, "NO! We're not leaving. We're not going to let her win. This is our home." She looked at me as she knew what I was saying in my head. "You're correct! I'm truly remorseful. I just sought after this place to be our home always with Luna, and this place holds so much history. History that both you and your grandfather share." After discussing with everyone for about a few hours about moving with my cousin in New York, that's the day we all agreed to move in for at least a few weeks.

I knocked on her door, and she sadly let me in. I sat down on her bed as she turned away from me. "Listen, Luna darling, I'm so sorry for all that I said earlier and how I reacted as well. It's just that this family means the world to me. It only used to be Gramps and me; now we're actually a bigger family. I just want to do my best at supporting us and keeping us safe. I'm sorry. You're just my first baby, and with some things I'm still learning, can you find it in your heart to ever forgive me?" After a moment of silence, my baby girl jumped on me with a huge hug and said, "Of course." Then I said, "Oh, by the way, princess, guess what, we're moving to New York!"

* * *

Everything fell into place, I found a house on top of the hills with a huge pool that we were able to install saltwater, in addition to that I worked as a Conservation Educator at the New York Aquarium. We didn't have any close-by neighbors, so we were good if any fins were to pop out in the pool. Furthermore, I helped Sirena look for a nice shop that was on sale so she could continue her business with Rosemarie.

On my first day of work, I had to go to work extremely early to clean the Beluga whale tanks spotless. My four-year-old and her siren aunt paid me a visit. To my surprise, Rosemarie brought her to my job. Rosemarie just tossed my Luna into the tank with the three whales inside. I was so startled because my first thought was that she was going to drown. I yelled at Rosemarie who was just smirking. But as soon as I was going to dive in and rescue her, my gorgeous darling was giggling and smiling underwater. While butt naked swimming on the side of the whales, she was enjoying herself as Rosemarie said, "You see, the whales are dancing with her." As I dived in to get my baby, I scowled at Rosemarie at demanded her to take Luna home. Did she not remember that Luna was supposed to forget about that lifestyle?

* * *

During these first few years, especially in New York, it was challenging for Luna. Though Luna was our distinctively gorgeous girl, the prekindergartners didn't see her as unique. Instead, they ostracized her desire to become friends with her for the reason that Luna's appearance was extremely rare. She had beautiful long wavy white hair hiding over her elfish ears, and just like her mother she had her stunning periwinkle eyes. Because so, we had her homeschooled because of all the bullying. Routinely, during recess Luna never would get picked for games, students would later pull on her hair, children would pick on Luna by making cruel jokes calling her an 'old lady' saying she had alien eyes and calling her an elf while spitting raspberries at her. Every now and then, she would come home and weep. Every time this happened, I would call the principal and report the harassment against my daughter. On the other hand, her aunt Rosemarie or Gramps had different solutions.

Gramps always had her feeling better in no time. Telling similar tales from when I was a kid, only now he had more. Undeniably, these *fictional legends* were based only on the reality of Luna's family history.

Our family decided that for as long as we could, we'd keep Luna from knowing she was a hybrid. At some time, we knew they'd be a moment that we'd have to tell her. Many times, she almost spotted her mother's lengthy vast tangerine fin sticking out of the ocean. There were also periods when she questioned why our pool looked more like an ocean and why her mother and aunt went for late night swims almost every day.

The scariest thing living in New York was when I tried so hard for us to act like a regular family, that one time it almost put us in danger. I took all of the ladies to Glen Island beach, as long as Rosemarie and Sirena promised to stay on the sand, and that we'd come up with ridiculous reasons as to why we forgot all the bathing suits. We were all having a great time at first, playing with kites, frisbees, and building sandcastles. After we bought Luna a hot dog and some funnel cake; Sirena, Rosemarie, and I were talking about when and how we would tell Luna the truth. As we talked, Luna strolled away from us and started playing close by the shore. As soon as it felt oddly quiet, we all looked up to check on Luna, when we noticed huge tidal waves coming in stopping people from swimming. As soon as the beach alarm went off, Rosemarie yelled, "It's our mother and the twins!" Then I sprinted toward Luna and hurriedly snatched her away from the tip of the water. As for Rosemarie, she swiftly leaped into the sea where she found the twins eyeing her with a revoltingly vampiric urge. The twins looked up at the ocean feeling disappointed they failed to execute Luna and swam away following their mother's siren call.

CHAPTER 34

fter a few years, we all realized that in a month it would be Luna's thirteenth birthday, which also meant it was time to tell her. Oftentimes, we began letting Luna walk to and from school by herself. looking up from the mail I asked, "Hey, Luna darling, how was your day at school?"

Very enthusiastically as always, she said, "Father, today was wonderful, I made friends with the new student, his name is Adam! But above all things…I finally saw my best friend! I don't really see her as much, but when I do, it's always extraordinary! The way she sings is exquisite." Though I was freaked out about her having a friend who is a boy, something more stuck out in the conversation.

"So, who's this *extraordinary* friend? You never really mentioned a best friend before." If Rosemarie and Sirena were home, I bet they would've agreed.

Along with an anxious little look she said, "Well, I was told to keep our friendship a secret that's why." I began becoming uneasy. What friendship requires such secrecy? Was it because of her appearance?

I gently told her, "Sweetie, don't you think she isn't a very good friend? A friend wouldn't want to keep a friendship a secret." Luna began explaining how a few months ago she went with her friends near my job to Coney Island, unsupervised. She said that she was terrified of the amusement parks boat ride that her friends were going on.

So instead, Luna went for a walk on the boardwalk. After a while, she started walking in direction of a beautiful humming she overheard, where she met a young woman. What petrified me the most about this story, was how it sounded similar to me meeting Sirena. Then she mentioned the name of this young lady: Nerilena, the name of one of the twins! I didn't want to frighten her with my panic, so I let her continue, "Nerilena was humming before she began singing wondrously. I found it eccentric that she was resting on a massive rock looking out at the sea, however even all the more were her lyrics singing, 'Arise to me, child. I'll take you missing, hooked on a realm of enchantment,' and the rest. When she leapt into the waters, she swam towards me. She later arose out of the dark ocean and changed a bit; well to begin with she was topless. She appeared fairly pastel, in addition to her eyes and teeth seemed truly odd…"

As Luna kept telling her story; Sirena and Rosemarie finally strolled into the dialogue, I informed them to hang on and not reveal anything. Luna was worried that she was in trouble, after I told her she wasn't and that her story just sounded interesting she continued, "Well, I wasn't one to judge someone, like others used to do with me. So, as a result I kept speaking to her every single day, she'd meet me by the boardwalk almost each time, always singing the same song. Although what I thought to be extremely curious, was the moment she asked for mom and Aunt Rosemarie, after I told her I didn't want to talk about my family she brushed my hair and continued singing. Some reason I felt fatigued every time we met, but she sang delightful. Times she'd reach for my hand for some reason and ask to swim, but I snatched my hand away, which got her angry…I never understood why. I believed she loved me like a sister and wanted someone to swim with."

I was extremely shocked they found her. It didn't matter where we went or how far we left from Fire Island— they were always going to seek after our Luna. We were all speechless, but I stormed out of Luna's room and drove to Coney Island. I was in my pajamas, yelling out to the ocean, "You bitches better leave my daughter alone! She's a good girl! She's my baby girl. Leave her alone!" I remember the eyes staring at me as people believed I was drunk. They're right, though, I was absolutely wasted with my madness. Once I saw those tidal waves crashing against each other as lightning struck, I shouted out, "Shut up!" After I was done yelling at the ocean and throwing rocks at it, I went back home.

Sirena kept shoving me out the front entrance, "I needed you, here! While you just drank yourself a bottle! I can't believe you Josh! I hope that your stomach twirls around." Even after I told her why I did it all, she just stared at me with tears in her eyes. "I needed you! Not Rosemarie, YOU! Our daughter is in grave danger, and it doesn't matter where we escaped!!"

I began questioning, how the heck did a daily dose trance fail on Luna? Sirena chuckled with swelled up eyes, "Before moving here, Rosemarie and I prepared a protection oath with the Atlantic ocean's mermaids. Anytime threat might arise, Luna would sense a certain ambiance telling her to leave. It's a block, yet wretchedly only temporary." *That's just great! We had a little protection for Luna, but that still didn't stop Luna from almost getting attacked.* "I know Josh! That's why we have to tell her soon. Her birthday is in a few days, so we just have to tell her everything at that time. But for the next few days everyone's job, is keeping Luna away from Coney Island!!" Sirena said with such intense.

* * *

A few days later, it was Luna's thirteenth birthday, and she decided on a sleepover. The friends she invited consisted of only two girls and the new kid Adam. I was a bit hesitant about allowing a boy over, but the friends Luna did have were always very few, but they adored Luna just the way she was. That morning Luna was just eating her Captain Crunch cereal and checking her Facebook, just as every morning. Sirena and I walked up to her to explain the truth, with Gramps and Aunt Rosemarie also there. We started off by shouting out, "Happy Birthday!" Luna was hugged and kissed all over, then we surprised her with a big cupcake with a sparkler for her to blow out. Then we swung into action, "Luna darling, we need to explain something to you, the truth that we've been hiding from you." Luna stopped licking the icing and slowly looked concerned, therefore I just continued, "Luna, you know all those stories Gramps loves telling you about— about him saving his best-friend mermaid, about sirens being dangerous, and about a boy meeting a woman who's a mermaid and his beloved? All those stories are true."

After a gaze, Luna gave me a look of far-reaching skepticism; hence, Sirena continued. "The love birds in Gramps stories are about me and your father. I'm the mermaid and your aunt is my adoptive sister and a siren. I can imagine, this isn't going to be exactly easy to acknowledge. I remember when it wasn't very easy for your father. And yes, the stories Gramps says of the sirens are true, but history is changing instead—" Sirena was going to continue but worried about scaring her before her gathering.

Luna then snapped, "Wow! You have to be kidding me if you think that I would even consider that? I'm not that naïve. I'm turning thirteen you know! Exactly how dare you guys consider—"

I had to silence her there and we all strolled to the swimming pool in the backyard. Sirena and Rosemarie didn't wait for me to say anything; they just jumped into the water. The water began fizzing, fins started to appear, and Luna was entirely flabbergasted. "Mom, oh my gracious, you have a fin and a stunning one I might say. Wow, you guys weren't joking!"

"Why are you telling me this now? How could you keep this from me for so long?! You tell me to be honest with you about everything, that families don't keep secrets! How could you? Don't give me that- you technically didn't lie junk, because you still possessed an enormous secret from me. Don't you think knowing that my mother and aunt being actual folklore is important for me to know, and you spring it up to me on my birthday! Really?!"

I definitely related to what she was saying, I didn't even know the truth behind my own parents and ancestors. We should've told her sooner. "Luna, please understand, we wanted to tell you so many times, but we couldn't. We needed to wait for the right time. Luna, pay attention." Sirena tried to stop me, saying it was too much for me to disclose. However, I genuinely felt remorseful and needed to just uncover everything. "You're a hybrid; part human, part mermaid, and thanks to your siren grandmother, part siren and seer. Furthermore, your bitch twin bloodsucking aunts and grandmother intends to annihilate you. All of us have been trying our best to protect you, but it appears no matter what we sort out to do, they still find their ways to you." Luna started to look nervous, which was good, but I needed more. "Your *friend* Nerilena, she's one of the twins. Thanks to Gramps Luna already knew about most seafolk, eventually this was still part of her life. The one thing she wasn't prepared for, were her siren grandmother desires to destroy her.

Sirena looked at Rosemarie in astonishment, that's when Aunt Rosemarie took over. "Well, that was a bit extra frank!" Rose rolled her eyes at me and then looked back at Luna, "Nonetheless Luna…what your father says is true, and you must wonder why. First off, the twins, Nerilena and Kalidelia, are unlike me— they hunt rebelliously against all siren realm laws. Because of the sisterhood I share with your mother, I've learned to eat differently and maintain my thirst. Second of all, the former Queen, or to you Grandma Dionysus. She wanted you more than anything, you are the most powerful and deadly being, but she wanted you for the wrong reasons and because of that now she's promised the oceans to kill you." The reality was turning out to be a severe blow to Luna's soul. Learning that the ocean was convinced her destiny was treacherous to all beings. The reason why we know of so far, is because you are a hybrid of many powerful beings already, considerably more powerful than the average mermaid. You would consume all sorts of abilities that I'm not even certain of thus far... When you were a baby you showed us premonitions, especially when you felt dark auras around you."

CHAPTER 35

$\mathcal{I}$ hadn't seen my cousin Angelis since we were teenagers, hence we decided on paying her a visit. It's been ages since I've seen my trusted friend. When she decided she couldn't stand South Carolina anymore, she moved to New York. On our way driving, we decided to hold onto the family secret. Luna looked weary as she worried if Angelis would like her. I asked her why such thoughts, but I knew why. "Sweetie, don't even worry about it she'll fall in love just as you are."

Gramps helped my parents take in Angelis, after her parents gave her up. Yet, Angelis grew up as a wild child, being an absolute unrestricted spirit. She grew up doing whatever she wanted, whenever she wanted to. Angelis had immense dreams that existed beyond the settlement of South Carolina. She drew my parents' crazy, which caused Gramps and her to have a quarrel when she revealed she was leaving to New York. He said her dreams were bigger than hers, though he said it out of resentment. He didn't want anything bad to happen to his granddaughter. Therefore, he felt disgraceful to stand in front of her door.

Meanwhile, Rosemarie was off to the sea searching for answers to Luna's powers. Nobody had an inkling of what variety of powers Luna is expected to have. Thus, Rosemarie was swimming as quickly as possible to get through the merfolk borders, an area where sirens weren't allowed to pass. She was hoping to ask the king of the merfolk these vital questions; if Luna would still get a fin? When and what powers would she achieve? if Luna's expected to become malevolent? And if having a loving family can help her along the journey? Rosemarie brought a small offering of enchanted moon crystals for the king as peace offerings. We all hoped she'd be okay and would come home in one piece with an update.

Opening the door bursting with so much enthusiasm, Angelis squeezes me to death as I try to introduce her to my family, "Oh, my goodness, I'm so glad you're finally here!" Angelis didn't wince at all; she just invitingly gave them both massive hugs and said how excited she was for me. That's when she mentioned how she was quite a family person herself.

I was dumbfounded, "Angelis, really? WOW!"

She started on how she met her husband about fourteen years ago. "I sort of have a family nowadays. I met my husband, Raphael Lopez, during college for theatre after I left South Carolina. At first, we were decent friends and then became lovers. You know, best friends with benefits—then out of nowhere he just looked different to me, and I fell in love. He has handsome gorgeous brown hair, his smile is to die for, though I will admit he's not truly clever. I love him! You know, he majored in business so he can work with his father. Now he owns the company." Oh, my goodness, I looked at Sirena and said in my head I didn't remember Angelis talking this much she's such a different woman now. Then the kitchen felt like it became totally soundless when I stopped speaking to Sirena, while Angelis asked with a huge smile on her face, "So how did you guys meet?"

I was not expecting that question— though it's a familiar question a host would ask any guest. Oh fuck! We didn't prepare ourselves for this. Suddenly, I blurted out, "Similar to you, college, so um, where's that fine husband of yours? I would like to meet him. Make sure he's treating my cousin right!" I snickered while sweating bullets, Sirena rested her hand on my back to calm me.

Angelis became glum and said with a bit of tension in her tone, "Well now that he maintains the establishment, he's not around often. Consequently, he couldn't be around today just like he couldn't be around for any of the parent-teacher conferences or school plays or our sons' soccer games!"

My cousin used to be this wild being who dreamt of fame; but now she had this beautiful house, a husband, making pot roast, and even a son! But now things were making sense. Sirena then whispered to me, "Don't fail to recall how greatly your life is altered. Don't be a fool and judge your own cousin! At least she made worthy of herself." Sirena was right as always, then she asked Angelis about her son.

Angelis's eyes glistened full of delight once she started talking about her son. You could tell she loved him so much. She explained about how amazing her 13-year-old stepson, Adam had been ever since Raphael adopted him as a newborn. As much of a brainy boy he was. The description of her son Adam was very familiar. Dirty blonde hair, gray eyes, and freckles. "Let me call him. Adam honey, come down and meet your cousins!"

The minute her son came downstairs, Luna screamed out, "Adam!" and he screamed out her name. They gave each other gigantic hugs, which I ended. Though, Angelis was confused on how they knew each other she kept telling me they were cousins, and I was exaggerating. But Luna looked as if she was blushing a little and troubled understanding that Adam was her cousin. When I looked at Sirena, she didn't seem bothered since distant relations were still suitors.

* * *

During dinner I asked Sirena if she was okay, she look baffled. She said she'll tell me at home. After our goodbyes, on our way home Sirena looked so confused. Later Sirena kissed Luna goodnight, we sat on the porch, and she immediately blurted out, "I sensed a merman in that house. Evidently it wasn't the husband. It has to be Adam. Once I got closer to him, the aroma was even stronger." I was utterly astonished— Adam a merman? Hold your fire. If she sensed him, does that mean he sensed her and Luna? Sirena looked at me and said, "Perhaps! He wasn't raised by merfolk, possibly he doesn't know such senses."

By changing the topic, a little I said, "Did you notice how Luna and Adam looked at each other, almost as if they liked one another?"

Sirena grinned as she thought my overreacting was charming, "Surely, I noticed, though it would never be. She's a hybrid that the entire undersea fears, and he's a pure merman."

I thought I would be happy, but if my Luna fell in love with him...I would be a hypocrite to say it can't be!

"Never, listen we're still unsure about Luna's near future, Rose will—" Sirena was going to continue, but then we saw Rosemarie running towards us.

Rosemarie had a few gashes on her from the twins on her journey. She described the mermaid crossings being unlike what she imagined, they appeared undisturbed and picturesque, and the King had a benevolent spirit notably when he received the peace offerings. Hastily, Rose expressed the facts, "Coming-of-age Luna will gain her tail. She will rapidly gain her powers after, and as a hybrid she would have to learn from a teacher of each how to control all of these powers. She would gain a diverse of kinetic abilities. Rosemarie said that because of these many abilities she can become self-destructive, especially if she can't control her emotions."

* * *

The next day I decided taking Adam and Luna to the aquarium. I wanted to see how they would react with each other and the sea creatures. I wanted to know if he knew what he was. As they went off to watch the sharks feeding, they act like normal children.

Though when I talked to Adam at the seal tanks, he started going off with a bunch of facts. "Did you know that seals belong to the order Pinnipedian, which means *fin footed*? Also, there are three types of pinnipedian: seals, sea lions, and walrus." He was staring at the seals as if he knew what they were feeling or even saying. Then I noticed he had similar appearances to Luna.

When I asked him about his 'rare appearance,' Adam shrugged, grinning while he said, "Yeah, my eyes and ears are relatively rare like Luna's. I got them from my birth parents…I guess, much like Luna. I guess that's what started our friendship, our unique appearances. Luna doesn't make fun of me like the kids in school used to do. She said it was the same for her also." What did he mean?

"You know what I mean. Luna has her eyes and ear like her moth—" Wait, Adam just read my mind like Sirena! "Mr. Hanks, I think we can stop dancing around here. I certainly know what Sirena and Luna are, and I think you know what I am. We're seafolk."

I began to stare at him, "Who told you? does Luna know anything? and most of all, why aren't you frightened of Luna?"

He smirked and said, "As a full-blooded merman I can sense it. And no, I never opened up to Luna about this. Our friendship is very sincere, I honestly can't be scared of her if a care for her." Adam expressed to me that he received a note in a bottle on his birthday. His biological parents never abandoned him, the foster parents were fishing and accidentally captured him. Falling in love with him they kept his secret, however they found Adam a stable home with their son, Raphael. He learned how to adapt and keep his secret.

I thought it must've felt lonely living between two worlds as a child, "Well, a bit. Anyways I hear about her destiny every school day, you know from traveling from here to Carolina. Yet, I don't believe in it, she has too much of a big heart. If anything, I promise you I will help in any way possible." I started to like this kid; he didn't seem so bad after all. Adam giggled and said, "Thanks, you're not so bad yourself." I gave him the *okay* to tell Luna, because now she knew the truth and she would need a friend as well as family.

CHAPTER 36

or the next two weeks, we've noticed we were looking after Adam a lot, and that my cousin's mood seemed dismayed. Adam told me; Angelis was distraught these days after her husband forgotten about their anniversary without a reason nor apologies. The day after, my cousin invited us all to a surprise party celebrating her douchebag husband's promotion. I watched Angelis while she was getting ready. Ready for this excruciating misery she hid behind that makeup. As always, my cousin looked radiant, she actually looked like my mom wearing a stunning, sleeveless long navy gown. She wore the long beautiful three-string pearl necklace that Sirena made for her. "Angie, we need to talk! I want to ask you about something…um, something serious." I wanted to bring her into the family secret.

Angelis looked up from her vanity while placing on her blush, and while looking into the mirrors, she stared at me very peculiarly. "Well, go ahead then. If you have something to say, say it! Otherwise, please leave. I don't want to keep my husband waiting." She was so concerned about embarrassing her husband that our conversation wouldn't matter. She surprised her husband with these socials every now and then, ideally demanding his attention for her. That night though, was an evening for the husband; hence he demanded her to *smile more*. Angie turned from her vanity and scowled at me, as if I was going to pass judgement. "So, what do you have to say?" I supposed she was on the edge, so I made the clever decision and stayed voiceless before leaving her room.

* * *

It was the morning of Lunas underwater themed sweet sixteen, along with a sense of anxiety, there was an aura of irritability floating about the seafolk. Luna didn't feel entirely herself, she mentioned feeling overly skittish and an extremely unwelcoming feeling. Sirena excitedly told her, "Oh my princess, don't fret. You're carrying out through the passage soon."

Late morning, Luna took a swim to unwind. Rosemarie sat with Luna since she needed to let her tail unbend. Yet, after some laps in the pool Luna then felt some relief, and decided it was time to get ready for her birthday. Rosemarie was nevertheless enjoying herself inside the water just before a second of looking at Luna, along with a siren shriek, "Wait, Luna! Oh my gosh! Look!" Luna glanced down at her legs and noticed she had a number of teal fish scales. She looked at her aunt with pure exhilaration then called out for me and Sirena. When we reached her, the scales vanished as she was all dry. Luna ran to us, "My transformation's starting."

Surprised, after some silence all at once both Rosemarie and Luna explained. Sirena and Luna were so thrilled this was happening, yet I couldn't find myself sharing the same excitement with them. Anxiously, I sauntered away creating an excuse for the ladies, that I had to check on the caterers. Rosemarie looked at me nervously when she caught up to me, "You don't have to block your mind, I still know what you're contemplating. Trust me, I can perceive it from your utmost obvious paranoid features, we're both thinking the same…Luna's destiny." It reassured me knowing I wouldn't be the only one feeling this way, "Quite soon, we're going to need to stop celebrating and discover what our future action is. This is rather new for both Sirena and me, so even we're not sure what we're dealing with."

We were about to find out shortly. As Luna set out to take a bath all we heard was her shouting out for her Sirena. Hoping it was a small girl's problem like a broken nail or messy hair, I still ran leaving Rosemarie. As Sirena ran into the bathroom, I stood outside waiting outside the door with Adam. When Sirena finally came out, she had a huge smile. *Please tell me she just started getting her red ninja.*

After Adam read my thoughts he said, "Luna and I pretty much share everything with each other. When she was 14 years old, she started that. Don't worry Mr. Hanks, sometimes I have to help her in embarrassing situations."

Sirena looked at us with a huge smile. It was almost frightening; her smile was wide and secretive as Harley Quinn. Then she snickered. "Dear, she has encountered new mermaid scales. The hue is like the teal of my hair. Luna said she originally had a few, but now she already has nearly half her fin."

While Adam was congratulating Sirena, I was in shock. I had no words. Instead, I said, "I should recheck if the dancefloor over the pool is sturdy." The makeup artist and hairdresser were waiting on Luna for hours, she was taking an even longer bath than usual. I knocked on the bathroom door, and to my surprise Luna let me in. I covered my eyes, until she said it was okay. She had her shirt on, and her bottom half was now a full tail.

At the sight of this, I grasped that Luna's high school swimming team was going to have to replace their best captain, and her swimming scholarships might as well be shredded. Luna's lifestyle was going to change significantly.

Since Luna's fin, Sirena was so happy she already started making plans with Rosemarie. They both agreed that during Luna's winter recess, we would all go as a family with Adam and Angie to Hawaii. Their explanation was that the sirens weren't around those waters because of all the poisonous coral; therefore, Rosemarie still needed to be careful. We all just wanted one real ocean swim with Luna as an ocean family, so how could I disagree with that?

On the night of Luna's sweet sixteenth, she didn't make it to her grand entrance. We began searching for her. Something felt odd again, when we found clues from her dress and shells in her hair that had fallen. Once we discovered her, she appeared fascinated by the full moon while singing as she strolled barefooted on the sand. Adam and I ran to her, trying hard to snap her out of it, stopping her from going into the water but she was entranced. Rosemarie then said, "Luna was born during the full moon, the reason for her snowy hair. Tonight, is her first full moon, as a full-blown mermaid, well hybrid. The moon is technically baptizing her."

"What's with the siren singing?" Adam asked her.

Rosemarie looked confused as she listened in, "That kid...I'm not sure of, but it feels powerful. Like she's using echolocation, but what for?" Then Sirena pointed out to her sister what it was.

When I looked at what she was pointing at, I saw the siren twins and Dionysus, "Great, it's a fucking family reunion!" They were all waiting for Luna to act as easy prey.

These sirens appeared to have knowledge of everything about Luna. They were constantly two moves ahead of us. Luna's forthcoming fin and abilities were their highest threat. They stood together in the obscurity of the ocean, as they eerily sang, *"Arise to me child. I'll take you missing, hooked on a realm of enchantment."* Dionysus started creating tides and the louder they sang, the bigger they grew.

Rosemarie and Sirena sang a counter-song to shield Adam and myself while we attempted hard clinging onto Luna. It's like the moon had its grip literally on her. Then Adam went in front of her, "Luna, please it's me Adam." As soon as he touched her hand, she awoke from this trance, and Adam didn't waste any time. He hauled her over his shoulder and we then all ran to the car. The sirens ferociously shrieked that the weather shifted to a storm. The frenzy deserted our plans for Luna's party; she hadn't had her waltz with me on the pool dance floor, not even a possibility to show off her birthday gown.

* * *

We all thought Luna's birthday was severe, but these sirens weren't ready to quit. The day after, Luna received a package on our doorstep. As soon as Luna opened it, confetti popped out, and there was an enormous, awesome cupcake inside. When Rosemarie asked suspiciously who it was from, Luna said, "I'm not exactly sure. It just says, 'Happy birthday, Luna. Sorry I couldn't make it to your birthday, it would've been a splash!' Ewe, must be from a creepy admirer." I peeked at Adam; the poor kid looked quite jealous. He's known my Luna for a long time, and I actually admired his sweet devotion. However, I'm guessing she only saw him as family.

As soon as, Luna was ready to take a slice, Rosemarie screamed, "NO! That cake wasn't meant for you. It was meant for all of us!"

Luna looked at her aunt strangely and said, "Okayy…then you can all have your slice. I wasn't going to hog it all for myself anyways, sheesh Rose!"

As Luna was preparing to cut slices for everybody, Rosemarie looked frightened and said, "No! What I meant was that cake was made by *THEM* with poison for all of us! There's a very rare squid. The ink tortures you to your death once you've ingested it. Firstly, it dehydrates you no matter how much water you consume. Then gradually it tears your skin. Next, your bones feel as if they're breaking though really, it's not. Later you go blind and deaf. Last of all your heart stops beating, and you're gone. I know that they've poisoned that cake, not only for Luna but for all of us, as we not only lied to them about Luna's death, but with Luna still living just terrifies them especially with her phase beginning."

My mind was blown for a minute, my daily life sprang from Grimm's version of Ariel to this Grimm's version of Snow White. Only that instead of a poison apple it was a poisonous huge cupcake, that would kill all of us not just put us to a deep sleep.

Sirena finally came home from work, as she stormed in with tears running down her face and a furious face, "I know how to take care of these—" She grabbed Luna's enormous cupcake, rushed towards our backyard, and threw it off the cliff into the ocean.

Luna was crying loudly having a panic attack in Adams shirt. "That's it! I can't take it anymore! You guys aren't always going to be able to switch shifts all the time to watch over me." Luna yelled. "I just can't take it anymore, if I almost risk my own life with a cupcake what makes you think these sirens won't have anything else up their sleeve."

Gramps went to hug his great-granddaughter, "Obviously, you make a fair point. If they were able to siren a baker, in order to trance them to pour that potion in the mix and deliver it…it just makes you wonder to what greater extent will they go to next?"

"I need to start doing exactly what the king told you Aunt Rosemarie, I need to get into the ocean. I need to begin my lessons and learn from every instructor, as soon as possible. I need to be prepared to have my own back." Luna wiped her tears away from her face, as she stood tall standing up for what she meant.

Adam took Luna's hand and walked her to the balcony. He wiped her tears and gave her a huge embrace. Then he made Luna giggle when he asked her to dance to a slow song. They were talking, laughing, and making funny faces. I was happy just to know there was someone to make her laugh through everything.

Rosemarie then said, "She's right guys! She won't be able to survive in the ocean or even on land much longer if she doesn't learn how to use those powers. Dionysus and the twins have been on all of our tails since she was a baby, they won't stop until they feel that her destiny is burnt out."

215

‖‖‖‖‖‖‖‖‖‖‖‖‖‖‖‖‖‖‖‖‖‖‖‖‖‖‖‖‖‖‖‖‖

THE END